THE

Scandalous
LADIES of LONDON

The Duchess

THE
Scandalous
LADIES *of* LONDON

The Duchess

SOPHIE JORDAN

AVON

An Imprint of HarperCollinsPublishers

THE DUCHESS. Copyright © 2024 by Sharie Kohler. All rights reserved. Printed in the United States of America. No part of this book may be used or reproduced in any manner whatsoever without written permission except in the case of brief quotations embodied in critical articles and reviews. For information, address HarperCollins Publishers, 195 Broadway, New York, NY 10007.

HarperCollins books may be purchased for educational, business, or sales promotional use. For information, please email the Special Markets Department at SPsales@harpercollins.com.

FIRST EDITION

Designed by Jackie Alvarado
Chapter opener art © m2art; Alena Ohneva / Shutterstock

Library of Congress Cataloging-in-Publication Data has been applied for.

ISBN 978-0-06-327074-9

24 25 26 27 28 LBC 5 4 3 2 1

For all the survivors

THE
Scandalous
LADIES of LONDON

The Duchess

Chapter 1

The happiest two days of my life were my
wedding day . . . and my husband's funeral.
—Valencia, the Dowager Duchess of Dedham

11 April 1822
River Thames
London, England

The Duchess of Dedham's husband was dead.

The wretch had expired nearly a year ago, found with a broken neck at the bottom of the stairs. No one was surprised given how poorly his health and how dependent he was upon whiskey and laudanum to get through each day. No secret, that. Perhaps the only surprise was that he had survived as long as he had before plummeting to his death in the midst of a country house party.

Now, as the *Dowager* Duchess of Dedham, Valencia was free and ready for revelry. Truth be told, she had been ready upon the discovery that she was a widow, but there were rules. So *many* rules. Rules that she had followed all her life. Not that they had ever served her well. Rules, she found, rarely served women well. And yet those rules had changed now that she was no longer Dedham's wife. At long last.

She was done with mourning. Done with her widow's weeds. Done with hiding away in her Mayfair house.

She had made it a year. Eleven months to be precise, but that was time enough not to raise eyebrows. Time enough devoted to starched bombazine and the denial of all Society, to eschewing drawing rooms and teas and soirées and balls and nobles with their false smiles.

At first, she was fine with that. Preferred it, even. After her husband expired in so dramatic a fashion, she needed her solitude. She had cloaked herself in isolation, taking comfort in her own company, growing stronger with each and every day, until she felt ready to emerge and rejoin the Living.

She was now ready.

Today was her birthday, and her husband was gone from her life forever. That was perhaps the greatest present of all. Terrible as the thought was, it was the truth of how she felt. The Dedham she had once loved died years ago when he was thrown from a horse. Another man took his place. Not her true husband. A ghost. A stranger. That stranger had died nearly a year ago, and she could feel no remorse for the loss.

She no longer had to suffer Dedham's glowering, controlling presence anymore. No more hugging the shadows. No more making herself as small as possible. She was celebrating life—the rest of *her* life—and she had long years of marital misery to make up for.

More than a dozen revelers, all her closest friends (and foes), occupied the less-than-steady vessel as it departed the docks and glided slowly down the dark waters of the Thames to the South Bank as dusk descended. Destination: Vauxhall. Objective: a carousing good time.

And who knew? Perhaps she would find a handsome gentleman to take her down one of the infamous dark walks. She would like that very much indeed. It had been far too long since she had been touched. Since a handsome gentleman had made her heart race. Since she had been held. Kissed.

Oh, she liked kissing. She had been good at it. There were many things at the start of her time with Dedham that seemed a hazy dream now, but that bit was true. Her pleasure in kissing had been real.

The yacht's weight limit had perhaps been exceeded, but that did not concern the guests. They laughed. They drank. They applauded the opera singer who performed for them on a small dais. They hooted at neighboring boats—calling to people they knew across the water . . . and people they would like to know.

Ladies in gowns of every color lounged among the cushions, laughing and sipping champagne distributed by liveried servants managing the deck with acrobatic dexterity. Torches blazed along the perimeter of the conveyance, popping and crackling and doing wondrous things for the glittering silks, satins, and brocades. Not to mention the jewels. Extraordinary gems winked from deep décolletages and coiffed hair.

The marchioness's improbable red wig flashed like flame on the night air as she laughed gaily. Valencia narrowed her gaze at her stepmother. *Witch.* If the woman was not married to Valencia's papa, she would not have been invited, to be sure. Societal expectations and all that rubbish. Valencia rolled her eyes and sighed before sipping her champagne.

"Do not let the sight of her ruin your night," Tru advised, very correctly guessing the reason for Valencia's sigh.

"I cannot believe I must tolerate her. Especially tonight." It was a celebration, after all, in *her* honor, and yet she must endure her father's ridiculous wife.

She eyed Papa in distaste. His gnarled, paper-thin-skinned hands clutched the gold-knobbed and gem-studded cane as the conveyance rocked its way toward the entrance of Vauxhall. His equilibrium was poor, and yet somehow, with great assistance, he had managed to climb up the ramp of the yacht. She had not thought he would brave a party to Vauxhall, and yet here he was.

A nearby barge of gentlemen noticed their yacht. It was hard to miss. They waved and hooted across the waters at them. One young man stepped dangerously close to the edge and pressed both hands over his heart as he called to them, "Beautiful ladies, please accept my escort throughout the Gardens!"

Valencia gripped the railing and waved gaily back with a laugh. She glanced again to Tru. "Look at all those randy young bucks."

And then in a lowered voice, "Could Hazel not have chosen one of them? Why did she have to pick my father?"

Maeve, ever rational, shrugged from beside Tru. "Why not your father? He is wealthy and titled and dotes upon her."

Valencia shook her head. "All these years later, and I still cannot believe Papa married her." *His mistress.* He had married his mistress. It shamed her mother's memory.

"Of course you can," Maeve returned. "Like so many men, your father is a vain man, and it feeds his ego to have a young and beautiful wife. He's not extraordinary in that respect."

"Could he not have chosen someone who was *not* a paramour to half the gentlemen in our set?" she grumbled.

"Oh, you exaggerate," Tru chided.

"Exaggerate she does not," Lady Ashbourne inserted, stepping close and sliding into their conversation, nodding in the direction of the marchioness and lifting her glass in mocking salute. "I just know *my* dear Ashbourne dipped his quill in *that* inkpot." The lady deliberately lifted her voice, making certain to attract Hazel's notice with these inflammatory words.

Hazel frowned and inched closer toward them. "Are you speaking of me, Lady Ashbourne?"

The lady looked Hazel up and down with a flare of her nostrils, clearly ready for battle. "In truth, I was speaking of your . . . *inkpot.*"

Hot color splashed Hazel's cheeks, and Valencia almost—but not quite—felt sorry for her. Valencia could not deny it. She enjoyed watching her stepmother's discomfort. Until Hazel reacted.

The marchioness lifted her hands and shoved Lady Ashbourne hard, pushing her squarely in the chest. The action sent the lady colliding into Valencia, the force of which propelled her directly over the railing of the yacht.

Valencia plunged into the dark waters of the Thames with a scream. Brackish water rushed into her lungs. The weight of her beautiful gown pulled her down, down, down.

She fought, clawing water, kicking at the tangle of skirts, fighting to rise to the surface. It was impossible. She writhed and twisted. Suddenly she was no longer certain which way was up or down. The fight seeped out of her. Her lungs burned like fire, and her limbs turned to lead, powerless to move . . . to save her.

She was drowning, dying . . . dead.

On her birthday, no less.

Bloody hell.

Without warning a hard band looped around her waist, and she was yanked, soaring, breaking free through the surface. She gasped and coughed, sucking in sweet, reviving air.

The band around her waist was an arm. An arm that belonged to a man. A man who was rescuing her, pulling her aboard a boat.

Grateful for the solid surface beneath her, she rolled onto her side, coughing and spitting up ghastly river water. A large shadow fell over her, blotting out the torchlight. She came up on an elbow and glanced wildly around. This was not her yacht.

She was on a barge.

The barge full of randy young men.

Her gaze shot to the soaking wet man crouched over her, his

impossibly broad chest rising and falling from his exertions. *From jumping in and saving her.*

His mouth lifted in a crooked, much-too-handsome grin. The kind of grin that said he knew just how handsome he was. "You did not need to jump in the river if you wanted to get my attention, sweetheart."

She opened her mouth to speak to the man who was quite prettier than she but only managed to cough and sputter up more river water. It could not have been an attractive sight. *She* could not have been an attractive sight. Not as she had been when she started the evening, powdered and primped and so carefully arranged.

Another man spoke, this one with a deep guttural accent full of deliciously rolling *rrr*s. "Leave off the flirting, Dewey. Can you not see she's trying *not* to choke to death?"

Hands pressed flat to the deck floor, Valencia's gaze shot up to the gentleman speaking as she struggled to steady her breathing. He was a handsome devil. There was nothing pretty about *him*.

He was ruggedly attractive. Midnight-dark hair. Deep brown eyes. The dusting of stubble against his square jaw. He was unerringly the manner of man she would like to cavort with on a dark walk. A handsome stranger. Not too young. Not too old. Just right for her tastes.

He was no pasty-skinned dandy unused to the rigors of the out-of-doors. His skin was sun-kissed. A quick scan of his person revealed that his body was not that of a dandy either. His shoulders were wide. Arms strong. Biceps thick within his jacket. And tall. Taller than her own husband had been, and he'd loomed a few inches over her. An altogether virile package. Her mouth dried, and she swallowed. A few faint lines of experience webbed his eyes, evidence of laughter or smiling. Perhaps both. Not that he was doing either of those things now as he glowered at her.

Scowled was the apt word. He was scowling at her. Insensibly. Unjustly. *Rudely.*

That scowl almost blinded her to the fact that this man was exactly what she had determined to find for herself tonight. *Almost.* Minus the scowl, of course. A scowl had never been a component of her fantasy.

It was impossible not to appreciate him though, scowl or no.

She flushed warmly beneath the droplets of river water on her face. It was wild that *these* were her thoughts when mere moments ago she had nearly drowned. Nearly perished. Perhaps that was the way of it though. The way *through* things. After narrowly escaping death, one observed things very clearly—perhaps with more clarity and precision than ever before.

Perhaps that was why she could look upon this man with an appreciative eye, how she could consider him as a huntress might consider prey. Contemplative and thoughtful . . . assessing. She was reminded of what tonight was all about.

She had waited a lifetime, it seemed.

A good deal of time had been lost to her marriage, to Dedham. And then following his death at that most inauspicious (or auspicious?) of house parties, she had sacrificed nearly a year to mourning the man. Now she was free. Free to do whatever she wanted.

The stern set of the stranger's expression did nothing to detract from his looks. Perhaps, in fact, it enhanced his handsomeness, highlighting the angle of his jaw, the strong line of his nose, the slashing, thick eyebrows over his deeply set eyes. Mesmerizing eyes. Her fingers curled into the wet deck, digging into the hard surface until the pressure threatened to bend her nails.

Her rescuer, Dewey—clearly the charming one with proper manners and an easy smile—gently took her by the arms and helped her to her feet. "There now, madam."

She looked down at her soaking dress and gave a miserable moan. "My gown," she got out.

"Gowns can be replaced. 'Tis lucky you are alive," the stern devil muttered.

She harrumphed and sent a glare across the water to the distant yacht holding her friends. She was indeed fortunate to be alive. The weight of her gown could have pulled her under, lost forever to the depths of the Thames. *No thanks to Hazel.* Her stepmother was probably reveling in Valencia's misfortune. No doubt she wished Valencia had drowned.

Oh, she had not pushed her overboard directly, but the young woman would not regret Valencia's mishap. There was no love between them. There was not even *like* between them. From the very start there had only ever been tension, and it had only worsened over the years.

"Perhaps the lady will think again before overimbibing," the handsome devil added, giving her a condemning look.

She stiffened at his rudeness. "I beg your pardon?"

He waved his long, elegant fingers at her person. "Clearly you cannot manage your drink, madam."

"Coz," interjected the young charmer with disapproval as he clasped her elbow. "Be kind. She's been through an ordeal."

Indeed, she had. Not that Dewey's *coz* appeared to be the least bit sympathetic. He looked her over with a faintly curling lip that was decidedly *unkind*. Apparently he did not think her deserving of kindness.

It was all too much.

It was *her* thirty-second birthday, *her* celebration as her year of mourning came to an end, and here she stood a drowned rat—being insulted by this man from . . . Well, she could not place his accent. It reminded her of a Scottish brogue but not quite. No doubt he was from some place far from here. Some remote corner of this country that did not instill good manners and breeding among its male denizens.

He was dressed as a gentleman, but that did not signify. Clothing did not make a man good or decent. Her heart clenched a little, the memories close, nipping sharply at the edges of her fraying composure.

She knew that better than anyone.

Dedham had always been impeccably outfitted, the most handsome, well-dressed man in any room, and her young heart had fallen for him so blindly, so completely.

She'd fallen for him and it had cost her so much. Years of her life. Never again would she be lulled into thinking herself in love . . . that a man might be constant and never change. That if he professed himself in love he forever meant it.

Forever was not as enduring as she had thought it to be.

Indignation swept over her. "I had one glass of champagne," she muttered, even though she owed this man no explanation. Still the words emerged.

"One glass too many, apparently."

Oh, the arrogance!

"Not that it is any of your affair, but I am not foxed, *sir*." She flung *sir* at him as though it were the foulest epithet, a barbed arrow launched. How dare he! It had been a year since she was subject to any man's . . . criticism. She would not suffer this stranger's censure. She did not have to suffer such nonsense from any man ever again.

She reminded herself that she was a duchess—correction: a *dowager* duchess. And more than that. She was a woman who had endured. She was someone who had struggled. She had gone through *it* and made it to the other side, and still she stood here, a survivor. Alive. Strong. Reborn with another chance. She would not squander it.

Lifting her chin, she swept her gaze over all the men surrounding her. She managed an air of haughty regard. She pretended that she did not appear a drowned rat, that she was still the fashionable lady of moments ago and not the unfortunate soul who had been shoved into the Thames.

The gentlemen looked her over appraisingly . . . admiringly, and that made her feel hopeful, stronger. The years, and Dedham, it seemed, had not taken everything from her. She had not lost all. If these men could admire her looking as she did now . . . Well. There was hope. Life left in her yet, and was that not what this day, this celebration was all about?

But she also felt a little uneasy beneath their avid attention. She was a lone woman on this barge full of men. The latter emotion she suppressed. She would not reveal her unease and reveal herself a target, a potential victim. She swallowed. She would never be that again. Never afraid. Never small. Never trapped.

She brought her chin up a fraction. Her life, moving forward, would be only about being strong. She was free, and there was strength in that. Power. Control.

The charming cousin, Dewey, who had fished her out of the Thames, gestured toward Vauxhall. "We are almost there, madam."

She glanced toward the not-too-distant dock they were approaching and willed them there faster. Willed herself off this barge full of strange men.

Water lapped at the sides of the barge. Her gaze crept back to Dewey, but it did not remain there. Truthfully, she scarcely gave him a glance. Her gaze went to *him* again. The beautiful devil was the one who drew her attention, and she really had to question her good sense.

The barge bumped against the dock. A cheer went up among the men. She heard the rope hit the wood planks and a grappling sound as their vessel was tied off. She heard, but she did not look. She still stared at *him*. The hard-eyed villain who, unlike his companions, did not appear jovial and eager for revelry.

The grump returned her stare, appearing as though he might like to push her off the barge and back into the river. And yet for all his severity, he was the one to snare her notice. That frightened her. What did it say about her? The handsome and charming Dewey should be the one to attract her. Not his ill-tempered cousin. It was as though she had learned nothing. Nothing at all.

The ramp dropped with a thud, stretching between the barge and the dock. At last, she looked away. The courteous Dewey assisted her across. She moved forward with her head held high, not looking behind her. Even as much as she wanted to.

Chapter 2

A lady does not lower herself to fights of a physical nature. Her battles are waged on the higher plane of social influence and innuendo.
—Valencia, the Dowager Duchess of Dedham

Valencia woke to a raucous invasion the following morning. She lay in the comfort of her bed for a long moment, her hand flung limply above her head, fingers coiled lightly in her loose mane of hair, absorbing the jarring, discordant sounds, knowing she needed to rouse and see what was afoot, but she could not be motivated just yet.

Her birthday had *not* gone according to plan.

Upon reaching Vauxhall last night, she had reunited with her friends. They had been eagerly awaiting her when she disembarked from the barge. Together, they descended upon one of the assembly halls in Vauxhall, where they acquired a dress for her from one of the ladies employed there—but the damage had been done. The gown they procured fit her poorly, fashioned for a woman several inches shorter and with far fewer curves than Valencia. The frock ended inches above her ankles, and she felt squeezed into it like a sausage packed into casing.

Valencia's hair had been repaired as best as possible, but a dunk in the Thames had not done it any favors. The sour aroma of river water still clung to her person, and she felt wretched, craving only a bath and her own clothes—her own chamber and bed, for that matter.

Over the protests of her friends, she had called it quits on the celebration, leaving her party to revel without her, and returned home to a hot bath and the enticement of her bed.

Despite the disappointment of her party—or rather the disappointment at her *lack* of a party—she had fallen asleep still hopeful. Her future beckoned brightly. Her life belonged to her for the first time in too many years to count. The night might not have gone the way she planned—there had been no heated kisses shared with a handsome stranger on a dark walk, but there would be other chances, other nights and opportunities for that.

For some reason, that churlish boor on the barge flashed across her mind now. Too bad he had not been of better temperament. A temperament that better matched his face. The memory of which made her stomach fill with butterflies. Deep-set brown eyes. Thick eyebrows. A jaw covered in unfashionable scruff that begged for a razor. Hair too long. Thick and wavy on top, fighting the wind. The image of him was as fresh as the night before, and it kept her captive in her bed, dreamily contemplative, delicious and cozy and warm.

A loud crash reminded her that she had pressing matters to investigate. Something was amiss. Her staff was well trained. They were quiet as church mice as they went about their tasks. They'd learned from years of tiptoeing around Dedham.

With a groan, she shoved her dreamy thoughts aside and rolled over.

Sitting up, she rubbed at her eyes and dragged a hand through her loose hair as loud voices and banging continued to shake her house.

"What in heavens," she muttered, easing out from under the covers and reaching for her robe, discarded at the foot of the bed. She was sliding an arm through it when her door opened and her maid slipped inside with what could only be described as a panicked expression, the color high on her cheeks.

Valencia stilled in alarm. "Tildie, what is it?"

"Your Grace," she murmured, holding out a hand. "Calm yourself . . ."

"Calm myself?" she echoed.

Did that ever work? Did telling a person to remain calm *actually* keep them calm? Apprehension bubbled up inside her, and she demanded, more insistently, "What is it, Tildie?"

"The new duke—"

"The *new* duke?" she cut in, having difficulty understanding those words.

"Yes, Your Grace." Tildie was now holding out both of her

hands, bouncing them on the air as though the motion might steady Valencia—as though she were a wild stallion needing to be calmed. "The Duke of Dedham has arrived—"

"He's been found?"

The agents of the estate had been searching for him the past year. She knew that much. That very little they had bothered to inform her. *Fret not, Your Grace. We shall locate him with all haste.* As though she were fretting over such a thing. That was to say, she had not fretted over their *inability* to locate him, but rather their inevitable success.

The rumors had always been there. Fanciful and plentiful. She'd grown accustomed to them. *The Duke of Dedham is residing off the Cape of Good Hope in Africa. He's with pirates in the Seychelles. In a house made of bamboo in Japan. Painting the pyramids in Giza.*

She'd lived with the myriad false reports for the better part of a year, but she had no idea that the agents had actually, *finally*, located him. Not that they were overly concerned with keeping her apprised of such things. What was she to them but a woman?

Noblewoman or not, she possessed breasts, and that seemed to rob her of intelligence or consequence as far as they were concerned. That had certainly been their protocol whilst her husband lived, and they had not changed their custom since his death. She was not significant enough to warrant a by-your-leave on any matter.

True, a week ago she had heard that they'd located the heir and that his arrival was imminent. This information had come from Maeve. Her husband was well positioned in the Home Office—

not to mention the third son of a prominent viscount. He moved in high circles and always had his ear on the pulse of Society, but it was the first time Maeve had passed along information that yielded little or no results. Valencia had chalked it up to merely another rumor. A possibility, to be sure, but unlikely.

She supposed she had wanted to believe it untrue. Valencia had begun to dream that the heir might never surface. Although she knew that would present its own host of problems. Would the Crown bestow the title on someone else? Or would they retire the title and revoke all its entitlements? Where would that leave her?

Change was coming. It was inevitable. She knew that. And yet she had been living as an ostrich with its head in the sand. Today, it seemed, she would pull her head out. There was no longer any other choice.

"Yes. He's been found. And he has arrived . . . with his family in tow."

"With his family?" Her voice lifted an octave. She had not even considered that, but of course. What were the odds that he would be alone? He would likely have a wife. Children, perhaps. Parents. Siblings. An entire retinue. She swallowed against the panicked knot forming in her throat. The vociferous commotion now made perfect sense. Dreadful sense.

Her house was typically quiet. Peaceful after the era of Dedham, when everyone tiptoed about the place. In those days, they all walked on eggshells, in fear of eliciting Dedham's wrath.

Her late husband had been known to have the occasional

outburst—especially on his bad days when the laudanum and opium and spirits had waned and his need for them became particularly acute. Everyone felt his displeasure. Everyone suffered if he suffered. That was the way of things.

Presently, it sounded like a herd of elephants was tromping up the stairs. Several sudden thuds and crashes overlapped the tromping, and then a woman screamed. Valencia jerked. Tildie flinched.

This was her house. Her responsibility. She was still the mistress here. That had not changed. Her lips firmed into a mutinous line. *Not yet.* Casting aside her modesty, Valencia hastened from her bedchamber and burst out into the corridor.

And into chaos.

There were people everywhere. Servants—and not her own. She did not recognize any of their faces, but from the matching livery they wore, she knew them to be in service. Just not in *her* service.

Her head whipped to and fro, trying to determine what was happening and whom she might approach to get to the bottom of matters.

A bespectacled, fashionably turned-out young lady stood at the top of the stairs, waving her arms and screeching as she looked down the steps, "My darling! My Poppet!"

Alarmed that a child may have fallen down the stairs, and not a little reminded of the time her husband had tumbled to his death down a set of stairs—a memory that still woke her up in the middle of the night in a cold sweat—Valencia hurried forward with her heart lodged in her throat, certain she was about to come face-to-face with a calamity. Again.

She reached a comforting hand for the young woman's arm. A stranger in her home. Later she would learn her identity, hers and everyone else's who happened to be currently invading her life.

"Are you—" Valencia's gentle question died swiftly in her throat as she spotted "Poppet" at the bottom of the stairs. Not a child. Not a baby. Not anything with a pulse.

It was a stuffed dog.

A rusty-brown schnauzer to be exact. The white fur dusting its nose and muzzle attested to the fact that he or she had lived a long life.

"That is . . . Poppet?"

The bespectacled young lady nodded. "Yes." She clapped her hands together and called down sternly to one of the many liveried servants. "You there! Fetch her and bring her to me. Have a care, please!" She glanced back at Valencia as though seeing her for the first time. "Oh." She looked her up and down, taking in her flowing hair and state of undress with a lifted eyebrow.

Normally Valencia would have been horrified to be caught in such dishabille. But this was a most unusual situation.

Who are all these people? Who let them inside my house?

"Oh," Valencia echoed, and then, following a moistening of her lips: "Who are you?"

This young woman was standing inside her home, after all. There was no way in which to ask that question rather than baldly.

"I am Isolde," she responded, evidently thinking that served as explanation enough.

"Isolde," Valencia repeated. That sparked no recognition. She did not know this girl. Not by sight or name. She knew of no Isolde among the *ton*. Whoever had inherited the dukedom— and this girl was obviously attached to him in some capacity—he was not a well-known figure of Society.

Countless servants rushed past them with frantic energy, bearing all manner of luggage and items. Isolde, who could not be a day over twenty, smiled brightly and nodded, her lovely red hair a thing to be admired. She again eyed Valencia's state of undress curiously, pushing her spectacles up the bridge of her nose. "And who might you be?"

She spoke in a rolling, lyrical accent Valencia could not quite place. Pressing a hand to her chest, she declared, "I am the mistress of this house you find yourself standing in." She said the words as much for herself as for the benefit of this interloper. If the duke had indeed arrived, then she was suddenly superfluous. She felt the overwhelming need to insert herself here, to put her stamp of ownership on the place, as though that might make a difference. She stifled a grimace.

Isolde blinked. "You . . . live here?"

"I do."

"Are you a servant?"

Valencia blinked and glanced down at herself. Even attired in her dressing robe, the fine lawn was clearly a costly fabric. She gathered up her hair with one hand and draped it over her shoulder with as much dignity as she could manage.

Before Valencia could answer, Isolde continued. "Hmm. No. I do not think you are a servant. You would already be awake and seeing to your daily tasks, would you not? Instead of lounging about like a slug. So then. Who are you?"

A . . . *slug*?

Was there no end to the insults and indignities?

Valencia bristled and lifted her chin, calling forth her dignity. Some days that was all she felt she had left.

She was the daughter of a Spanish noblewoman, her grandfather a *grandee*. Valencia was a descendant of the first Prince of Asturias. She possessed royal blood. As a girl, her mother had reminded her of that many times. Mama had wanted to make certain she knew this, that she never forgot her origins. However little that mattered in her life.

Still, she would not stand here begging for recognition or consideration. Her lineage could be traced back to fourteenth-century royalty. She would not beg anything of others.

"I am the mistress of this house. The Duchess of Dedham."

The *dowager* duchess to be exact, but she did not feel the need to add that. Dowagers were old women. She did not yet consider herself to be that.

"Oh." The announcement surprised the girl. She blinked several times. "I did not realize . . ."

"Do you not mean the *Dowager* Duchess of Dedham?"

Apparently someone did see fit to consider her that.

At the arrival of this new voice, Valencia turned to observe another young woman advancing up the stairs. This one every bit as lovely as young Isolde. Her hair was a deep shade of auburn. The two were obviously related, and yet this newcomer was the elder by at least a few years, though without spectacles. She possessed an air of maturity—both in manner and appearance.

She arched an eyebrow and added, "Unless you have married my brother unbeknownst to me, that is." Her smirk let Valencia know she knew that was not the situation.

Valencia assessed her, taking in her words carefully. "Your brother is the Duke of Dedham?"

Of course he is. Valencia swallowed thickly, something akin to panic rising up in her. Desperation *and* panic.

Of course. I am the last to know.

Her days here were coming to an end. If the right and proper duke was taking up residence on this very inauspicious of days, then that meant she was no longer welcome. She was as good as gone already. Her departure to the dower house in the remote wilds of Yorkshire was imminent. Expected, even. Required.

Well. That would *not* happen. She would not be summarily exiled.

She had much living left to do in London, and if she left now that would not happen.

Isolde nodded in affirmation at her question. A quite cheerful nod at that. Annoyingly cheerful. "Yes. Yes. He is. Is that not marvelous? Our dear brother is a duke!"

Marvelous?

No. No, it was decidedly not, but Valencia bit back that rude reply as she faced the duke's sisters. Rudeness would get her no-where. She needed to be her most charming.

The older sister of the two watched Valencia with a cheerless

expression, her eyes narrowed. She angled her head thoughtfully. "Should you be here? Still? I thought the late duke expired
a year ago."

Isolde released a small gasp at her sister's rudeness. "Del!"

"I've resided here for well over a decade." Valencia pulled back
her shoulders proudly. "You mean to imply I should *not* be here?"

"Well. It is not your home anymore, is it?" The sister known
as Del lifted one shoulder in a shrug. "Is that not the way the law
works among you English? Are you not supposed to vacate the
house and make way for the new duke?"

Valencia and Del stared at each other in silence. She could
not summon a response because Del was completely correct,
of course. That was the way the laws of primogeniture worked.
The male was the heir. The heir inherited. Always. Valencia had
been granted a modest widow's jointure and a dower house in the
country. She was entitled to nothing more than that. If she had
given Dedham a son, she could have remained here, but successful procreation had never been her forte.

Her heart pinched, distracted at that heartache, but she veered
away from such painful thinking. She'd wept enough tears and
devoted enough sorrow to that loss—two losses to be specific.
Two babies she could have had, but they were gone. Lost. Never
drew a breath. No sense going over it again.

Isolde's head whipped back and forth, gawking at the two of
them. "Del," she murmured, still clearly affronted at her sister's
lack of courtesy. Isolde cast an apologetic look at Valencia. She

was a sweet girl for all her . . . oddness. The girl was in possession of a taxidermied dog, after all.

At that moment *another* well-dressed young woman advanced up the stairs, reaching the second floor. Unlike the other two women, her hair was a deep chestnut, but there was a similarity they all shared in the eyes—the wide-set brown eyes beneath dark eyebrows. In her arms, she carried the stuffed Poppet.

"Isolde," she scolded. "The staff is busy enough without managing your"—she sent the stuffed creature a repulsed look and passed it into Isolde's ready arms—"belongings."

Isolde sighed and accepted her prized possession, cradling the long-dead dog in her arms lovingly. "All of you are heartless," she accused. "You know what Poppet means to me—"

"Poppet is no more, Isolde. She died years ago. That is an inanimate dog in your arms." This sister was younger than Del, but every bit as matter-of-fact in manner. Hopefully she was friendlier and did not treat Valencia with similar rudeness.

"Heartless. Just heartless," Isolde continued to grumble.

Del continued in the same vein, "Were I to die, would you insist on stuffing and mounting me? And carting me around everywhere with you?"

Young Isolde snorted, tossing her fiery red hair as she pushed her spectacles up the bridge of her nose yet again. "Of course not. I love Poppet. I do not even like you. Why would I want to keep you around?"

Del glowered.

Valencia resisted the urge to laugh. She must have made a sound. The newest sister to arrive looked Valencia up and down, catching sight of her standing in the corridor in her dressing robe.

"Oh," she murmured.

Isolde took it upon herself to introduce them. "Elin, this is the Duchess of Dedham."

"*Dowager* Duchess of Dedham," Del smoothly corrected. Of course. Del had already demonstrated just how much the distinction mattered to her.

Elin executed a graceless and overexaggerated curtsey.

"Oh, for goodness' sake, Elin. That is hardly necessary," Del snapped.

"She *is* a duchess," Elin pointed out evenly.

"Dowager," Isolde cheerfully added.

"Precisely," Del agreed. "She is the dowager, and our brother is now the duke." Del sent Valencia a proud, censorious look. "That puts us on rather equal footing, I believe. We do not need to curtsey to her like she's the queen."

"Do we not?" Elin considered this as though Valencia were not listening. "She is a dowager duchess whilst we are merely the sisters of a duke. I am fairly certain she outranks us. A month ago I was in trousers and fishing at the local pond with lads from the village. Now I'm rubbing elbows with blue-blooded prigs and standing next to paintings that belong in a museum." She waved at a sixteenth-century painting of one of the Dedham dukes, bewigged and sporting a jutting white ruff about his neck.

Del sniffed, clearly unwilling to let her sister's words change her mind.

Her sister. *Sisters.* Valencia let that penetrate. *Three* sisters. And none of them timid or reticent from what Valencia could determine.

The duke had three sisters all beneath her roof. Well. Not *her* roof anymore. Del had made that clear, and she was correct, of course. She would soon be expelled from her home.

Several grooms ascended the stairs, carrying a chest between them, a heavy burden if their red, panting faces were any indication.

"Ah." Del clapped her hands together and stepped closer to examine the chest. "This one belongs in Nesta's room. Her chamber is the fourth down on the right."

They'd already designated rooms? It was incredible. Valencia had gone to bed last night alone in this house with the exception of her staff. Now she woke to a house full of noisy, ill-mannered inhabitants, all of whom had claimed rooms for themselves.

And who is this Nesta?

If Nesta was yet another sister . . .

She counted in her head. Four sisters. *Four!* Good God. A veritable army.

Were any married? That would mean husbands. Perhaps even children. More guests staying over.

Guests.

She supposed they were not guests at all. Indeed not. These people were more permanent than that. Perhaps *she* was now the guest. That was a jarring thought. A dismal thought. And yet no less her reality.

The fourth door down on the right belonged to the blue room. Valencia often placed guests in that chamber, because, aside from being a lovely room, it was far removed from her late husband's room, and, given his unpredictability, a lack of proximity to him had seemed wise. She had never wanted any guests to be alerted to his foul moods.

The town house boasted more than a dozen rooms. Plenty accommodation for the largest of families, which the new duke seemed to possess.

Suddenly, Valencia knew.

The chaos that wrenched her from sleep would not be fleeting. Four sisters . . . and that could not be the all of it. These girls . . . *women* . . . could not be unaccompanied. Was there even more family than just them? They could not be alone. Their staff would be crowding in with the existing staff. All moving in. All taking over.

And there was still the duke. Ah. Yes. He was the reason they were even here. He was at the heart of all this. The duke, of course, would be here, nearby, reveling in his new good fortune.

A wife? Was the duke married?

Was Valencia already replaced as the Duchess of Dedham? She swallowed thickly.

From the pitying way these young women were looking at Valencia, even the singularly sweet Isolde, it became clear that as big as this house was with its bounty of chambers . . . none would be for her.

There was no room for Valencia.

She had to go.

Chapter 3

There is nothing worse than marriage-hungry debutantes.
Except for six marriage-hungry debutantes.
—Valencia, the Dowager Duchess of Dedham

Rhain arrived at the Dedham town house cursing his bad luck.

His mother and sisters were already on the premises, no doubt merging the staff they'd brought with them with the current staff of the house. The front doors were thrown open, allowing easy access for his staff coming in and out of the house carrying an infinite amount of luggage. He nodded in greeting at the familiar faces. His mother and sisters could not be content to leave them at home. No, they'd practically transported every servant, from the highest butler and lady's maid to Cook and her retinue of kitchen maids.

He did not know any of his new staff yet, but he felt sorry for them. Poor unsuspecting souls. They had no notion of what was descending upon them. They were lambs in the field. And his mother and sisters were the invading wolves.

But he knew.

He knew his mother and sisters only too well. They were a handful.

He knew, and he should have been here to intervene and cut them off. It should have been Rhain who properly introduced himself and his family to his new staff. It should have been Rhain through the door first.

Of course, he had no one to blame except himself. He had not been enthused about this. About *any* of this. Coming to London. Laying claim to a title, to lands and the responsibilities of all the tenants therein. Taking ownership of all the Dedham properties. He wanted none of it. He had his own life. His own business back home. He did not need this.

Standing in the foyer, he glanced around, taking it all in. The marble floors. The vaulted ceilings. The crystal chandelier, glinting with thousands of diamonds, was the size of a carriage. All of this was his now, and he was going to have to figure out what to do with it. Like it or not. He winced. And he did not like it.

Expelling a heavy breath, he gave his head a slight shake.

Rhain had never even met the late duke, and yet in a vagary of fate he was the man's heir. They shared a great-grandfather. At least that was what the agents of the Dedham estate had relayed to him when they tracked him down in Wales.

His great-grandfather had been the youngest son of the Duke of Dedham. Even more horrifying was the discovery that Rhain was a fraction English. He'd been ignorant of this transgression of birth.

His forefather was a bit of a legend in family lore. Everyone knew he had left home at the tender age of eighteen, when his family insisted he marry a lady of excellent breeding whom he had no interest in wedding. Except no one knew *home* had been *England*. It had been omitted from all mentions of his great-grandfather.

Rhain's family had passed down the story of his great-grandfather's glorious escape, depicting him in such a proud, intrepid light. His great-grandfather had been pressed into marrying a woman twenty years his senior. A lady deeply afflicted with the pox, given to her by her late husband. No matter how much he pleaded with his father, he had not relented. His father had insisted. The marriage would go forward.

These facts had been part of his family's history ever since he was a lad. Only, it had never been shared that his great-grandfather had been the son of an *Englishman*. A *duke*. That sour little tidbit had been either unknown or a well-guarded secret. Bad enough he was English, but a duke? There was nothing the Welsh liked less than English aristocracy, after all.

His great-grandfather had cut all ties to his early life. Perhaps it had not been such a challenge. He'd walked away from that grandiose existence. It likely finished him in his family's eyes, effectively disinheriting him. He was undoubtedly a disgrace. Not that he ever attempted to return and reclaim his former life—at least not as far as Rhain knew.

From all accounts, his great-grandfather had been a congenial man, happily married and a contented father to three. A dukedom had served as no lure. No enticement. Rhain could understand that. He felt the same way. Unfortunately, his family did not agree.

All ties to Rhain's forefather must not have been completely cut. The estate agents had tracked him down. It took some time evidently. Nigh on a year had passed since Dedham perished, but eventually they had located Rhain in Bryn Bychan. A pair of agents from the Dedham estate had knocked on his door—or rather his mother's and sisters' door. He did not reside under the same roof with them anymore. Not since he'd entered manhood had he shared a house with them.

He kept rooms above his office, beside the quarry. The very quarry he had toiled in alongside his father and grandfather for years. They had scrimped to build it, so that they could have something of their own, so that they could be in control and live under their own authority—so that they could offer their fellow Welshmen, laborers like themselves, a livable wage and a worthwhile life.

They'd started with that single ore mine. Rhain had since expanded it to four mines, keeping it outfitted solely by Welsh workers, all incentivized by a percentage of the revenues.

Unfortunately, his father and grandfather were no longer with him to see how much their enterprise had grown, but he felt their spirits in every venture, in his every decision and every reward.

Living, sleeping where he worked was partly a measure in convenience and partly to live separately from his mother and sisters and maintain his own sanity.

He built them a big house with plenty of chambers. Spacious, well-appointed rooms. One even for him that he never bothered to occupy. He needed his own space. Carpeted floors that did not reverberate with the pounding of slippered feet. Walls that did not vibrate with shrill cries and laughter and squabbling.

He adored his sisters, but there was only so much he could take of the bickering. And, oh, did they love to bicker. It was their everyday language—squalling and shrieking over a stolen hair ribbon, a real or imagined slight, a particularly salacious bit of gossip.

The Dedham agents had appeared at his family's house. Naturally the gentlemen assumed he lived in the grand mausoleum he'd built for his mother rather than in the modest rooms he'd outfitted to his specifications above his quarry office.

He came and went and did as he pleased in those comfortable rooms, a single manservant keeping house for him in his bachelor lodgings.

He entertained there at his leisure without his mother's prying—or disapproval. Card games. Dinners of the food he preferred, whiskey to go along with his rack of lamb. And women. Bedmates he could enjoy as often—and as loudly—as he wanted. There he was his own person as a man of five and thirty ought to be.

His mother had invited the gentlemen inside and served them tea. Over biscuits and refreshments, the agents had informed Al-wena of his sudden change of status—*their* change of status. His sisters' shrieks of delight practically carried all the way to the mine.

There had been no possibility of refusal. No rejection. No chance of that. He could not very well deny his sisters and mother. When they set their minds upon something, it was impossible to dissuade them. Even his married sisters insisted on accepting this sudden "good fortune"—that it could only help the unwed ones find eligible gentlemen, as was their mission. It would take a far stronger man than he to resist the pleas and urgings and arguments of twelve sisters and a formidable mother.

There had been no escape. No denying this windfall. No refusing it. Not with six unwed sisters all longing for husbands.

Eligible husbands in Bryn Bychan were in short supply. His other sisters, the married ones, had snatched every likely candidate up for themselves. A point of fact often bemoaned by the remaining six. He could understand their eagerness at the prospect of fresh ground to source for potential husbands. Ultimately, that was the only reason he had obliged—the only reason he was here at all, leaving the comfort of his life—his home and business—for this ghastly city. He did this for them.

A duke he was not, and yet here he was. Living as a fraud. Living as the Duke of Dedham, at least until he found husbands for his unattached sisters.

Hopefully he would not have to stay here long. Just long enough to see his sisters settled—perhaps one of them betrothed.

If they made quick work of it, he could return to Wales to resume his life and business in Bryn Bychan.

He would not abandon his dukedom entirely. He was not that indifferent. He'd keep up with Dewey via correspondence to make certain he appropriately managed the estate.

A rather harried-looking gentleman approached. The butler, presumably, doubtlessly wondering at this man who had not even bothered knocking before entering the house—but perhaps it was just another element of what had to be a most peculiar day. Rhain did not need to know all the details to *know* that it had been a peculiar day. How many times, in the course of one butler's life, did his employer die and an army of women arrive with a houseful of servants in tow, all insisting they were relations of the new duke?

The butler smoothed a hand over his pomaded silver hair as though seeking his composure. The man was dressed impeccably and smartly, almost certainly in the Dedham livery. "May I help you, sir?"

The older gentleman spoke in the crustiest of upper-class English accents. Most of Rhain's staff did not even speak English. They'd been born and bred in Wales and spoke only their mother tongue.

Rhain opened his mouth to respond, to inform this man that he was, regrettably, the Duke of Dedham, but the words never escaped.

"Rhain!" His mother burst into the foyer from the nearby drawing room, her arms stretched wide as she held open the double doors. "There you are, my dear! Finally!" She shot a glance over her shoulder, and then stepped forward, closing the doors behind her with an air that could be described only as cautious, and that was . . . *different* for his mother.

She was a decidedly incautious person. Just as his sisters were. They *all* were an incautious bunch. They had the freedom to be so. The freedom to do and speak as they wanted. His father— and now he himself—had worked hard so that they could have such independence. He'd seen what came of women without resources, without men in their lives who were decent enough to step aside so that they could live and function with autonomy.

It was an unfortunate testament to this world that a woman's liberty was so often left in the hands of men, but that was the reality. A reality he was acutely aware of as a son and as a brother to a pack of sisters. He had taken measures to protect all of them should something befall him. He would not leave them stranded and without means, depending on the generosity, or lack of generosity, of his fellow man.

The butler spoke. "You are . . ." He looked Rhain over, eyeing the considerable length of him. His father and grandfather had been tall men, and he had followed suit. Idly, he wondered if that was another thing he had inherited from his English bloodline. "The Duke of Dedham, I presume?"

Rhain nodded once, curtly, finding it difficult to make even that acknowledgment. Would there ever come a day when it felt natural?

The butler executed a bow. "I am Mr. Wilkes, Your Grace, the butler."

"Wilkes," he returned. "I hope you're adequately managing under the day's . . . challenges."

At this, the butler offered a tight smile. "Just so, Your Grace. All is well. I am doing my best to see that your mother and sisters are settling in comfortably." From his pinched look, all was *not* well, but he dared not utter that. "Would you like me to call the staff for your inspect—"

Rhain's mother waved a hand hastily. "Not now. There is time enough for that later, after everyone is settled in."

Her brown eyes shimmered with concern. It was not an expression Rhain had seen on her since the news of his inheritance. She had been in a state of perpetual joy ever since then. Something had her distressed. He hoped his sisters were not giving her any difficulty. As he said to Wilkes, the day had been full of challenges. His sisters were naturally vexing creatures. That's what they did. Vexed their mother.

Hopefully it was not too much though. No hair pulling or stealing personal items. They loved to hide Poppet from Isolde and drive her mad.

The butler tried not to look offended at his clear dismissal, but it was there on his face. Rhain saw it cross his strained features in a flash before it was gone, replaced with the stoic deference due a duke's mother. Inclining his head, Wilkes stepped back, allowing Rhain his own space with his mother.

Alone in the foyer, she stepped close. "We sent servants to find you. I am so glad they did."

He was not *found*. He'd left Dedham's solicitor's office hours ago and then taken a long walk through the park, ignoring the ominous storm clouds, alone with his thoughts, before inevitably turning in the direction of Dedham House and the dreaded role awaiting him there.

"Where have you been?" she whispered loudly. "We have not seen you since yesterday. Did you stay out all night with Dewey?" She shook her head in disapproval.

He had taken breakfast with his mother and sisters at the hotel yesterday, advising them to wait for him before descending upon Dedham House. Clearly they had ignored the request. More than likely they'd viewed it as a suggestion. A suggestion they chose to disregard.

Oh, they had likely waited as long as they could before their sizable retinue departed the hotel. Restraint was not their forte. He should have known. He knew them, after all.

Indeed, no one had found him because he had stayed the night at Dewey's house; comfortable lodgings but nothing like the Mayfair house he now stood in—the duke's residence. *His* residence.

Although he preferred Dewey's place. He would take a humble and modest abode over this monstrosity of a house. His cousin had said the duke's town house was one of the grandest in Mayfair. He had not been exaggerating.

Dewey was a cousin on his mother's side. He had moved to London with his family as a lad—no one understood why. Dewey's mother had been different from her family, from her sister, Rhain's mother. She dreamed of a life outside their small Welsh hamlet for some bewildering reason. Dewey appeared more English now than Welsh, but family was family, and Rhain had fond memories of racing over green hills with Dewey, avoiding their sisters (Dewey had three of his own) and wreaking general childhood havoc, coming home filthy, with breeches shredded at the knees.

His cousin made a modest but respectable living as a bookkeeper. He appeared to have a solid mind for numbers. Rhain had been subtly evaluating him and approved of the way he comported himself. Even if he was gregarious, a flirt, and nauseatingly charming, he was a decent man. And family was family.

Dewey seemed an ideal choice to appoint as his man of affairs to oversee the Dedham estate. Rhain was confident he would be up to the task, and who was more trustworthy than family? Than blood?

Rhain could rest easy when he left London and returned to his life in Wales—for there was no question about it. He would be returning to Wales. If any of his sisters chose to marry some Englishman and remain, so be it. He would be leaving, easy in the knowledge that Dewey was in London to look after any sisters he left behind—*and* the Dedham dukedom.

They had gotten in late from Vauxhall, but Rhain had roused early after a restless night's sleep and made his way to his meeting after downing copious cups of coffee, prepared for him by Dewey's cook.

He had wanted to enjoy himself last night. If only for Dewey. His cousin wanted him to enjoy himself. London was his home, and he wanted Rhain to love it as he did. He'd coordinated the entire evening, inviting his closest friends. Dewey insisted Vauxhall Gardens was a spectacular sight to behold and anyone new to the city must experience the pleasure gardens firsthand.

Unfortunately, Vauxhall had failed to dazzle Rhain, and yet he could understand the appeal for some—for many. It was one great revelry for adults. A buffet of delights. Vice and sin at the ready for all. He grasped that at once. From the moment they boarded the barge, floating down the calm waters of the Thames alongside other vessels—all on the same course, heading directly into temptation, sailing toward a modern-day Sodom—he understood what it was all about.

Incidentally, temptation, as it turned out, had appeared *before* reaching the dock. Indeed, he did not have long to wait. The pleasure gardens did not offer that particular enticement. The river itself produced it. *Her.* A woman. And she arrived in the most unorthodox manner.

She had fallen into the river, and they fished her out as though she were the prize catch of the day—and she was indeed a prize. Even at her worst. At least he assumed that was her worst. Soaking wet in foul-smelling river water, once-coiffed hair a snarled mess, her dress a soggy disaster on her frame. It would be any woman's worst. She should not have looked so appealing, and yet she had. He saw at once she was a treasure, a siren among women. Mess or not, her midnight hair and inky eyes sucked him in like quicksand.

He'd been in London for days now seeing to this unfortunate inheritance business. As much as he eschewed this city, it was not his first visit to London. He had even visited before, once, years ago, when he wanted to investigate a piece of machinery to potentially use in his mines.

Never had an Englishwoman turned his head—not years ago and not in the past week. Not a single woman on the street or in a shop or the hotel. He'd found them all rather colorless. The crisp English words they murmured did nothing for him. He assumed they were simply not to his tastes, that his preference ran to Welsh women with quick tongues and lively eyes and dark curls. He was biased, to be certain. He was a Welshman with no love or admiration for the English.

Except the disheveled woman dripping all over the barge last night had proven him wrong. A bitter discovery. He did not want to be here in this city . . . and he certainly did not want to find attractive some silly Englishwoman who could not handle her cups and remain aboard her boat. And yet, even spitting up river water on the deck, she had transfixed him. He had been stirred to his very core.

"Where have you been?" his mother repeated, displeasure evident in her voice. "I thought you would fetch us from the hotel this morning. Your sisters were convinced you were abducted by ruffians. You must take care. Now that you are a duke, you're much more valuable."

He scowled. "So when I did not arrive this morning your conclusion was . . . abduction? A bit dramatic, do you not think?"

His mother's eyes widened. "Dramatic?" she scoffed. "I think not. You are a very important man now, Rhain. There could be any number of scoundrels looking to hold you for ransom." He liked to think he was important before . . . and that his mother thought so, too. She was his *mother*, after all. Before he could respond, she went on. "Enough of this." She took hold of his arm by the elbow. "We have a calamitous situation here that needs your immediate attention." She waved toward the drawing room.

Calamitous?

For having raised thirteen children, Alwena was excitable and easily given to histrionics. She did not cope well with stress. Never had. His father could always soothe her with a word or touch or pretty bauble. Rhain lacked that particular skill. In any case, he doubted what she deemed a "calamitous situation" was anything to truly discompose anyone.

With a firm grip on him, she dragged him toward the drawing room, as though he were a lad of five and not a man full-grown. "I will show you, and then you can tell me whether I am being overly dramatic or not." Now it almost sounded as though she hoped for calamity to validate her words.

He had been brought up in a household of women, and one or more of them was in a state of indignation at all times. It was simply the law of averages when dealing with so many. He knew better than to react to every display of emotion or temper.

Individually, his sisters and mother were very sane, rational, reasonable people, but taken as a whole, as a collective, they were quite hyperbolic and capable of destruction. There was no other apt description. Devastation had trailed them like smoke all their lives.

In this instance, he did not react to his mother's indignation. Idly, he wondered which sister had misbehaved now. They could ruffle their mother's feathers like no one else.

His mother pushed in one of the double doors and waved him forward with a wide flourish.

He stepped inside the room and froze.

The sight of his sisters was expected. Six faces turned to gaze at him with varying degrees of anticipation. But not for the reasons they anticipated. Like his mother, they knew he would have thoughts—a decided reaction to the lady sitting in their midst. A woman who was not a kinswoman.

A woman who did not belong here.

He swallowed, fighting against the sudden lump in his throat.

This lady was the same one from last night. His one and only very nearly drowned damsel.

Chapter 4

*The weightiness of multiple unwed daughters is a
mighty burden for a mother. There is no measure
too drastic to alleviate that condition.*
—Mrs. Alwena Lloyd

His one and only very nearly drowned damsel. *His.*

Rhain winced at the gross inaccuracy of that. She was
not *his* anything.

She was, to be sure, the very same woman Dewey had fished
out from the Thames and flopped down on the deck of their
barge like the day's catch, her red dress soaking wet, so heavy it
hung low on her chest, exposing the delicious swells of her breasts.
The bodice had dipped dangerously low, the shadowy edge of one
areola winking out at him—at the other men on the barge, too.

The sight had shocked him. And stirred him. He was flesh and blood, after all. The image of her was burned upon him like a brand.

The men had stared down at her with hunger. A palpable, crackling hunger that she seemed naively and wholly unaware of, and that only inflamed his ire at her. At *them*.

Daft chit. Damnable men. He did not know those men on the barge. Only Dewey. He had wanted to toss a blanket over her and shield her from their ravenous eyes.

He had not liked it. Not then. Not even reflecting upon it now.

He trusted none of those men with the woman leaving an ever-expanding puddle on the deck. For that reason, he had been curt with her. Perhaps, unjustly, he had directed his spleen at *her* when it was really his leering companions who deserved his wrath.

Rhain was grateful when they reached the dock and she departed their company, rejoining her waiting friends. He had assumed that would be the last he ever saw of her.

Except now here she sat in his drawing room—for it was *his* drawing room.

His drawing room. His house. His title. His life. And she was not supposed to be here.

His sisters called out warmly in greeting. As vexing as they were, he loved them and they loved him.

"Brother!" Isolde exclaimed. "You are home."

A rather unnecessary comment, but he fixed his smile and tried not to flinch at the notion of this house being their home, reminding himself not to take his suddenly foul mood out on his sisters. It was not their fault that he had inherited this blasted life—or that he had already come face-to-face in a somewhat sordid encounter with the woman poised so elegantly upon the sofa across from him.

She did not resemble the chaotic mess of yesterday, but it was undeniably her. Still so attractive he felt a deep ache looking at her.

Truth be told, those men on the barge and this woman hadn't been the only targets of his ire last night. A heavy dose had been directed at himself, for he had *understood* the hunger in their eyes. He had understood, because he'd felt it, too.

He felt it still.

He felt it now, standing in his drawing room, gawking at this person who should not be here.

Why was she here?

It was astonishing and inappropriate. Unwanted, to say the least.

"You," he breathed.

"You," she said in turn, the color bleeding from her face, giving her olive complexion a sickly pallor—as though the sight of him made her ill.

His mother did not miss the exchange. Her head whipped back and forth as she looked between them in bewilderment. "You two know each other?"

Neither of them answered, only continued to gawk at each other. At least, *she* gawked. He hoped he looked more dignified than that.

"We have . . . met," he managed.

"You have met?" His mother frowned. "You only just arrived in Town. How? How could you have possibly met? This is your first time here in this house."

He could scarcely digest his mother's words, let alone produce a response.

Why is she here?

The lady angled her head, and the motion sent a dark ringlet sliding over her shoulder as she answered in a soft, lyrical voice, "We met last night. At Vauxhall."

The drawing room erupted.

"Oh! Boo! You went to Vauxhall!" one of his sisters called out in complaint. "Without us, brother? How could you?"

He did not bother to look and see which one voiced the protest. Several others shared the sentiment. Vocally. Shrilly. Rhain could focus only on that one voice so different from the others presently congesting the drawing room. The soft, crisp accent was appealing in a way he could not account for. It belied everything he thought about himself and what manner of people—*women*—intrigued him.

This woman. She intrigued him as she looked around her in wide-eyed wonder, doubtlessly overwhelmed by her sisters. They were indeed overwhelming.

"Who are you?" he demanded, not caring at his abrupt tone, at the audience surrounding them. He could see only her sitting in the center of the room she ought not to be in, as though a beam of light from the heavens shone down on her.

His mother made a sound beside him. "Rhain."

"She is the duchess," Isolde cheerfully volunteered.

"Dowager duchess," Del, always the one to insert her opinions, corrected.

Isolde shrugged as though the distinction were of no consequence.

And yet it was of consequence. It meant she was a widow. His late kinsman's widow, to be exact. And this was her house. Or rather it had been. It had been the place she had lived with her late husband for . . . *Hellfire*. He did not even know how long. Several years, he would surmise.

Although younger than himself, he would place her over thirty. Lovely as she was, her skin flawless and unlined and luminous, she was not in the first blush of youth.

Those infernal solicitors had made no indication that she was so very . . . mouthwatering. Mention of her had been cursory. A dismissive flick of the hand as they assured Rhain that she would not be underfoot for long. The dower house awaited her as it had all Dedham widows. A long line of women who had found themselves alone. With no husband claiming them. No man in their beds. No man in *her* bed. No man to keep *her* from him. He flinched at that thought. Somehow he had gone from considering past Dedham widows to thinking only of her. It was wrong.

So very wrong.

He shook his head, appalled at the baseness of his thoughts. It was not like him. He was not a man ruled by his cock. His life was purposeful. He had his work. Family. Friends. When he chose, he fit in women around all of that. A welcome diversion from time to time.

"Yes," his mother said. "It appears the dowager is *living* here." His mother's tone was rife with accusation, her gaze sharp and demanding on him.

He angled his head. "Yes. The estate agents mentioned that."

Her tight smile conveyed her displeasure with him for failing to pass that information along to her. What could he say? He had assumed the dowager was some wizened old lady and not the delectable woman sitting in their midst.

She could not stay here. Not beneath the same roof with him. That would be far too distracting. He was not here to find himself a woman. Not even this one. None of this venture, this trip, was for him. All of this was for his sisters.

He blinked long and hard as though that would erase her from the drawing room. No good. She was still there. The Dowager Duchess of Dedham. How? *How?* She could not be that woman. Never once had he considered the possibility that she might be close to his own age. Dowagers were old. Not this ripe female before him, her lush body too much for her gown. Too much for him.

Almost as though she were reading his thoughts, she spoke again in that voice that affected Rhain as it should not. Damned inconvenient attraction . . . rearing its head and settling its attention on someone totally unsuitable.

"I *am* the Dowager Duchess of Dedham."

He took a breath. Turned that over in his mind.

"Then you should be in the dower house, should you not, and not living here?"

He paused, acknowledging how his words could be interpreted as rude. And yet he would not retract them—or regret them. They felt very necessary. She could not think she was welcome to remain here.

The room went silent at the bluntness of his words. His sisters glanced from him to one another, doubtlessly astonished by his lack of courtesy.

The late duke's widow had naught to do with him. She had her own place to live somewhere in the country. Her own home. Her own stipend. She was not his responsibility. *She cannot stay here.* Not in this house. Not in London. Most definitely not soaking wet on a barge en route to Vauxhall, turning every man whose gaze feasted on her—including himself—cock-hard. And yet that had already happened.

Blast it all.

She gulped, and he was mesmerized by the way her lovely throat worked. He had the mad, wild impulse to press his mouth there, to taste that skin, run his tongue along the delicious slope of her neck. *Damn. Damn. Damn.*

She had to go. Out of this house he would share for the indefinite future with his mother and sisters. Immediately. Away. Far from here. Far from him and his lurid ideas about her. She did things to him—was doing things. To him. *Hellfire.* He could only think in fragments. Not even a complete thought.

"Rhain," murmured Isolde, by far the sweetest of his six sisters in the drawing room.

He ignored the chiding look she sent him.

The dowager cleared her throat and spoke. "I was just packing to leave for the dower house now."

"Were you?" He cocked his head.

"I was . . . *am*. I am." She rose to her feet with a whisper of silk, her chin notched high in a dignified manner. He skimmed her figure once before wrenching his gaze back to her face.

Best not look there. Her body was sin. All curves. Flesh that would spill over in his hands. She was built to take and cushion a man. He grimaced at that, the notion spiking lust into his veins—a reaction he should not be experiencing for a woman he hardly knew. In front of his family, no less.

"My maid is no doubt waiting for my instructions. Never fear"—she motioned around them with a sweep of her hand, encompassing the room—"all household items are safe from me. I will take no more than the clothes on my back," she finished in a voice that cut as sharp as a flaying whip. Her gaze held his. There was only the faintest quivering of her lips to indicate that she was affected in any way. He hoped tenderhearted Isolde had not noticed that quiver. He would hear about it later if so.

He nodded once in approval, decisive and curt. *Yes. Please, go.*

She floated past him, and he was struck by an enticing whiff of vanilla and bergamot. He did not turn. He did not look. It was a struggle, but he forced himself not to watch her leave the room.

"Goodness," Del murmured once she disappeared from sight. "That was uncomfortable."

He stifled a snort. Uncomfortable for Del? She had no notion. What of the dowager? What of himself?

"Did that really just happen?" Isolde asked accusingly, glaring at him. "Did you toss a duchess out of her home?"

"It's not her home anymore," reminded Del tartly, with a single arched brow.

"Oh, of course it is," Isolde argued. "Her husband died a year ago, and she's been living here ever since. And goodness knows how long before that." She tossed Rhain a reproachful glare. "How could you be so uncharitable, brother?"

The stab of remorse was instantaneous. He was not without pity for a woman displaced by the inconvenient death of her husband. And yet he could not have her here in such close proximity.

His mother cleared her throat and reached for a cup of tea. "I never thought I would see the like of it."

"What?" Isolde asked for clarification, the disapproval still lingering in her voice. "Your son behaving so very rudely?"

"No. My son behaving like a duke."

The House Party

Valencia's life consisted of nightmares. For a long time now that had been her existence. Awake and asleep, they plagued her.

She floated in a space, a hellish landscape populated by two. Herself and Dedham. Woman and man. Wife and husband. Prey and predator. It was all the same. No difference. No distinction.

She knew he was unhappy with her. That was always the case, but tonight especially.

She had felt his glares, cutting like knives, amid the parlor games. But then, that was her existence. An unhappy husband perpetually glaring at her. Unhappy with her. Unhappy with life. His life. Her life. All life.

Since the day of his accident, the day he transformed, the day Dedham became another individual, a man unrecognizable to her, there had been only glares. Heated looks and heated words, and sometimes the heated sting of a palm. The rough shove of a hand. The hard floor rising to meet her. If she angered him, if she stood too close, if she was not quick enough and he could reach her. If she was not what he wanted her to be, which really was all the time. In those days and still now.

She could never be what he wanted. There was no way she could be the woman he wanted, because he could not be the man he wanted to be—the man he had been before. She knew that. Understood that. Far better than he, because he was past understanding anything. He was past logic. His life was pain, and that was everything. Everything he could absorb. Everything he could inflict.

It was incredible, really. The man who had once sweetly courted her, whom she had enjoyed at the beginning of her marriage, was not the same man as the one she now called husband. She thought of them as two individuals. Before Dedham and After Dedham. There was a definitive line of demarcation between the two.

Before the accident, he was young, with laughing eyes and sweet kisses and a teasing manner. A man who lived and took pleasure in life and those around him.

After the accident, he turned old overnight, afflicted with pain and rancor. A man who hated himself and those around him.

Before Dedham was gone.

After Dedham might wish to be dead, but he was not.

She had to stay one step ahead of After Dedham at all times. It was exhausting. She felt unfairly aged. Far older than her years.

Tonight, she had gone to bed ill at ease, wondering if he would make his way to her chamber, materialize in her room to vent his spleen upon her. He had not liked her dancing with Lord Burton.

She had seen that in his face. He had looked especially enraged when they played Kiss the Candlestick and Burton boldly landed his mouth on her lips.

If they had been at home, Dedham would have wasted no time meting out what he deemed a proper punishment. She could only hope that she was spared his wrath as they were now miles away at Chatham's country house. Hopefully that would spare her. Hopefully once they were back home he would have forgotten all about tonight.

She had not wanted Burton's attentions. She never did. She was not interested in a lover. Even one as handsome as Burton. She had made her disinterest known on multiple occasions, and yet he was always so assertive. He was not even hindered by her husband's presence. Tonight, she supposed, that was partly because Burton was so deep in his cups. He clearly did not care that she was married. Or that he was married. Or that her husband was in residence, watching darkly as Burton flirted with her.

She was simply glad to be alone in her chamber, free to breathe. Free of Dedham's glares. Free of everything that constantly had her shoulders clenching and tightening and her stomach knotting.

Except even alone she was never truly free.

The worry found her. The dread. The constant need to look over her shoulder.

Her sleep was restless, fraught with dark images, with the coppery taste of fear coating her mouth. Her bedchamber was unlit, the damask drapes parted, permitting the barest sliver of moonlight to flood the space.

That was when she saw it. When she saw him.

The dark shape of a man. Coming toward her in the gloom. Dedham. He would deliver his punishment after all, it seemed. She had not been spared.

She released a small cry and sprang from the bed. She was quick. She had learned how to be. Even restricted by a corset or gown, she had learned to maneuver with haste, to dive and dodge. Presently, she was in her nightgown, which was even better. She was fleet of foot. He did not catch her. With distance between them, he rarely did. He lacked the physicality, the vigor he once possessed.

She was almost to the door of her bedchamber, almost out into the corridor. Almost free. She could taste it. Envision it. Escape. She imagined herself fleeing toward the stairs, intent on bursting out of the house if need be. Away from him. Away. Away. Away. As she always longed to be.

Later, she would face the reality that she would have to return. Later, she would remember that she was married and could never fully break away. That there was nowhere to go.

Except she did not reach the door. He *did* catch her. He was quick. And strong. Quicker and stronger than he ought to be. And that was when she realized.

He was not her husband.

The man who wrapped his hands around her was not Dedham. She gulped back a sob.

Perhaps there were even worse things than her husband.

Chapter 5

I like children. Especially when they belong to someone else.
—The Right Honorable Lady Rosalind Shawley

Valencia married at nineteen and spent twelve years with Dedham. That, combined with her year without him, brought the total amount of time at Dedham House to thirteen. *Thirteen.* Thirteen years of her life in this house.

She had redecorated the Dedham residence shortly after her wedding and made it her own. It was *her* wallpaper that covered the drawing room walls where the new duke and his sisters and mother presently sat after having expelled her from this house. *She* had been the one to choose, with great care, the violet and cream stripes with little bouquets of poppies dotting the vertical panels.

She seethed at the injustice of it all. For everything that had transpired here, the good and bad and in between, it was her home. It was all she knew.

She nodded to Wilkes as she passed him in the foyer. He paused and executed a polite bow, his gaze full of pity. She knew what he saw when he looked at her. A woman kicked out from her home, displaced and unwanted. She inhaled thinly at that. Her pride smarted.

It was pride that had motivated her to keep her secrets all these years . . . why she had not even confided to her dearest friends the manner of man she had married. They assumed much, she knew, but she had made no confessions. Pride had prevented her. She had endured in silence. She did not want their pity. She did not want anyone's pity, and she mightily resented that the arrival of the duke had brought about such a look in her butler's eyes.

Pride, she acknowledged, was a curious thing. It made one do things. Hide things. Hide yourself. Hide the truth. Lie.

Just as she had now been lying, of course.

She had been lying to the new duke and his sisters and his mother. She had not been in the midst of packing. *Ha.* Indeed not. In no way had she been in the process of preparing to leave her home.

She'd had a year to prepare for such a fate, but instead she had been living as though the day would never come . . . because that had been her futile hope. Now she could admit it had been foolish. The day was always coming.

Just as she had not planned to leave, she had not planned on flinging out those bold words of deceit. And yet seeing him, the stony-faced cad from the barge last night, the words had emerged in a desperate bid for her dignity.

He was the Duke of Dedham. Everything was his, and she would not lower herself to beg for anything from that wretched man. She would not ask to remain here. Even if that meant her fate was destined for a remote dower cottage in Yorkshire.

She took hard, biting steps as she left that drawing room behind, thinking only of him—of his handsome, dreadful face. Why must the foulest things come in pretty packages? It had been the same with her husband. He had been attractive. Charming.

A lie.

She inhaled deeply, filling her lungs as she approached the stairs. Although beyond his handsome mien, he had thus far presented himself as he truly was. Unfriendly. Cold. Calculating.

She was smarter now. Experienced. Gone was the green girl of years before. Her naivete had vanished alongside her youth. Now she was a mature woman. Now she could recognize him for precisely what he was.

He had, after all, wasted little time in letting her know she did not belong here. That she was unwelcome. Once that rude, awful man clapped eyes on her sitting between his sisters, he had practically demanded her departure. Perhaps that was how things were done where he was from. Bluntly and without courtesy.

One of his sisters had informed Valencia that they were Welsh. Who could have imagined Dedham had relatives in some tiny hamlet in Wales? Dedham had certainly never known. Or at least he had never thought to make mention of that to her. In fact, he had never mentioned who his heir might be. He had always assumed they would have children. That *his* son would be the heir. She swallowed painfully as she took the stairs. She had assumed it, too.

Upon her marriage, she had thought it would be only a matter of time before she gave the duke his heir. And, perhaps most importantly, her own child to love, as her dear mama loved her. The kind of unconditional love found between a mother and child. She had yearned for that. Especially as it became clear with every passing year that her marriage would not yield any sentiment as substantial as that.

Of course it had not been so simple. Life, she learned, rarely was.

After losing two babes, the family physician assured her that she could still bring a child into the world. She had wanted to believe him. He was a man of medicine who knew such things, after all. Desperately she wished for him to be correct. She was able to conceive, it seemed. It was keeping the baby that proved difficult.

She could not pass a pram without looking inside. Could not see another lady increasing, her belly swelling against the folds of her gown without feeling the sting of tears in her eyes. She practically avoided Maeve during her confinement, always finding excuses not to accept her invitations to tea.

She had prayed and hoped. Hoped and prayed.

Until she had not.

Until one day she stopped wanting and stopped praying and stopped hoping. At least for a babe. Her prayers then turned to other things. Things like surviving each day with her husband.

She smiled tightly at a pair of maids who bobbed curtsies as she passed them in the corridor en route to her bedchamber. She did not know them. They wore unfamiliar livery, and she knew they belonged to *him*. Another reminder of their usurpation.

Her door came into sight, and she burst inside her chamber, her solace for so many years. Falling back against the closed door, she inhaled and exhaled as though she had run a great race.

It was the end of an era. Her life here was finally done.

She blinked suddenly burning eyes, thinking of her friends. They could visit, of course, as could she, but it would not be the same. Yorkshire might as well be the other side of the earth. As remote as the moon.

She rubbed a hand against her forehead, feeling the stirrings of an ache in her head. She must pack, and she did not even know where to begin. How did one decide what to take? Her clothes, certainly, but what else was permitted? What was not entailed? What belonged to the house? The dukedom? She might have said she would only take her clothes, but really . . . was she not entitled to more than that?

Was her jewelry her own? And her books? And her favorite pashmina blanket? What about the painting she had commissioned in the parlor where she liked to read and pen her correspondence whilst seated at her favorite escritoire? Oh . . . but that cherrywood escritoire had been another purchase she'd made a year after her marriage. With a sigh, she sank down onto the bed and smoothed a hand over the rich silken counterpane. She had chosen it last spring and adored the texture.

It would all stay, she assumed, along with most of everything she valued. Valencia chided herself. They were all merely things. Possessions. She should not care.

She glanced around her bedchamber with a sniff. She doubted she would ever sleep in here again. She would not be returning. They would not be inviting her for Christmases. Indeed not. Her time here was over.

A knot formed in her throat. She had never even visited the dower cottage in Yorkshire. She only knew of it. Knew it was far away. Her own mother-in-law had not resided there after Valencia and Dedham had married. It had not been good enough for her. She had spent her final years at a house in Town. Dedham had granted her that, caring enough for his mother that he had not sent her away. She had lived out the last years of her life in grand style among her friends. Valencia would not receive the same kindness.

A knock sounded at her door and she bade entrance to Tildie.

It seemed her maid had an idea of what was happening, for she immediately pulled out Valencia's valises from the bottom of her armoire.

"You heard I must leave?" Had the staff been listening at the drawing room door?

Tildie nodded as she buzzed and flitted about the room. "I've already requested a trunk be sent up." She moved with her usual efficiency, pulling garments from the armoire . . . except her movements were perhaps too brisk, too jerky. There was a stiffness, a rigidity to her spine that was not usually there. Valencia peered closer at her. Red splotches marred her face.

"Tildie?" she queried softly, seizing Tildie's hand, halting her from her work. "Come sit for a moment." Tildie obliged stiffly, sinking down beside her on the bed. "Are you . . . well?"

Tildie nodded, her mouth drawn tightly in a way that indicated she was *not* well.

"Come now. Tell me," Valencia coaxed.

Only a few years younger than Valencia, Tildie had been with her for almost a decade, and she had seemed happy with her life, with her role as Valencia's lady's maid. She'd always followed Valencia's cue, never daring to speak of the late duke, but always there to attend Valencia when she needed her.

"I shall miss . . . London," the maid admitted.

"Of course." Valencia nodded in commiseration. "I know."

"And my family and friends." Tildie's friends and family lived in Town. Just as Valencia's did. Except she knew Tildie to be close to her family. Closer than Valencia was to hers.

"Tildie," she said slowly, moistening her lips. "Do you . . . wish to stay here?"

There had never been any doubt in her mind that Tildie would accompany her. They had been together for years, after all. Tildie would not simply walk away from this life. The position of lady's maid was a coveted one. There were few positions higher. Situations of the sort were finite in number, and many a domestic spent years trying to land such an exalted station. But perhaps Valencia should not have assumed Tildie would automatically go with her.

Tildie shook her head vigorously. "Oh, I cannot do that. I will go with you, of course—"

"Because I understand if you wish to remain in Town rather than move to some far-off corner of Yorkshire with me." She winced, just thinking of it.

Tildie chewed her lip, looking so small and forlorn in that moment. "I must go."

"Your life is here. Your friends. Family. I understand that."

"It is because of my family that I must go. My grandmother and my sister rely on me and my wages. There is no guarantee I could find myself another lady to serve. Such positions do not become available often." She took a breath before continuing. "Pardon my candor, but if I stay here, I would likely have to return to the life of a housemaid, and that wage will not be enough to support me and my family."

Valencia nodded once, feeling a flicker of discomfort. She should have before considered that she was not the only one with limited choices. It was humbling. She could be more grateful for her lot in life, she supposed. It could always be worse. It *had* been worse.

Despite her many trials, she never had to worry about such things . . . never had to contemplate whether she possessed funds enough for food or clothes or a roof over her head. Even now, expelled as she was from this house, she had a place to go. Another house. Smaller, to be sure. More modest than anywhere she had called home before, far away in remote Yorkshire, but a roof over her head nonetheless. Food on the table. A home with a staff, small though it was. It all awaited her.

"Of course," she murmured, then moistened her lips, feeling somehow to blame for doing this to Tildie. For not providing better so that they did not have to leave Town. Unreasonable, she knew. She had no choice in this matter.

When had she ever been prepared for independence? She was the daughter of a marquess who then became the wife of a duke. The only way she could have achieved control over her life was in providing an heir. Then she would have had her son to hold up to the world. That would have been her security—her power. She frowned, feeling a stab of anger that it should be this way. That a woman's power rested on her womb.

Shaking her head, she said, "I am sorry that I could not keep us both in London."

"You have nothing to apologize for." Tildie covered her hand with her own. "You've endured enough, Your Grace." Of course she meant Dedham.

She forced a smile, not wishing to appear ill-tempered with Tildie. Sliding her hand free from the maid's, she stood. "Come. We have much to do. I do not see us leaving today, but with luck, we can be on our way tomorrow. Tonight, you shall go see your grandmother and sister so that you may say your farewells."

For a moment, Tildie's face looked ready to crumple. Then she collected herself. Composure regained, she smoothed a hand down her skirts. "I will try, but we have much to pack—"

"Tildie, I insist. Have dinner with them."

Nodding, she resumed packing, saying with forced cheer, "Thank you. And you must see your friends, too."

The thought of her friends created a sharp pang in her chest. It would be a difficult good-bye, but she could not simply disappear without seeing them. A rueful smile teased her lips at the notion of that. They would hunt her down.

"You are correct. I'll call on them this afternoon," she agreed. It had to be done.

AS IT TURNED out, Valencia did not need to go to them. Her friends came to her.

Word traveled fast in the *ton*. Gossip flowed quicker than salmon moving upstream. There was not an abundance of dukes to be found in the *ton*, and when a new one was minted, all of London knew.

They flocked to her side. Wilkes—still bestowing that bloody pitying look upon her—brought them directly to her bedchamber, and for that she was grateful. It was the only space that still felt like hers in this house. Everything else belonged to the new duke and the women in his family now. Especially the drawing room. That was no longer her domain but theirs. She could not entertain her friends there with any level of privacy.

Tru, Maeve, and Rosalind exclaimed loudly as they entered her chamber, their hands aflutter.

Her room was spacious. As the bedchamber of the Duchess of Dedham it was the second-largest chamber in the house.

The largest chamber was next door. The duke's bedchamber, of course. Where her husband had slept for so many years, alone in his great bed. And yet, spacious or not, her chamber felt cramped, crowded with the large personalities of her friends in their silk and velvet day gowns.

"Valencia!" Tru clucked, tossing her reticule down upon the bed. "Whatever is happening?"

"Is it true?" Maeve asked pragmatically. "The new duke and his family have arrived?"

Ros collapsed back on Valencia's bed in dramatic flourish, plucking her ribbon-trimmed capote from her head and tossing it aside. "First last night and now this? You are not having a good week, my friend." Propping herself up on her elbows, she looked at Valencia expectedly.

Tru sent her sister a withering look. "Try to be more supportive."

Ros shrugged and flipped her hand vaguely in the direction of Valencia. "I only speak the truth. You do not think she knows the bad turn her life has taken?"

"Rosalind," Tru reprimanded sharply, clearly vexed with her plainspoken sister. Nothing unusual there. Sisters or not, they were highly dissimilar.

Tru was newly widowed, a mother of two children: one a fully grown daughter on the cusp of her second season on the Marriage Mart and the other a son finishing his last year at Eton. Rosalind was a spinster and very contented in that fact. She still lived with her parents and felt no inclination to give up her independence to marry and have children. All this whilst

Tru was *already* planning to remarry—this time (the *first* time) for love.

Maeve peered at Valencia in concern. "Is the man . . . unkind?"

"Let us get to the point, shall we? Is he tossing you out?" Ros demanded, sweeping a glance around the room at the many valises and the trunk Tildie had been in the process of packing.

"It is time for me to retire to the dower house," she said, leaving it at that.

"Retire to the dower house?" Ros scoffed. "You're not some white-haired dowager of eighty."

Valencia exhaled, refusing to let Ros incite her. "I knew this was coming. We all did. I'm fortunate to have had the house to myself for this long."

"The cad!" Ros shook her head, a vigilant light entering her eyes. "I say we march up to him and explain to him just who you are and that he cannot treat you this way."

"Oh, he can." *He is.* She had a flash of his handsome face then. His brown eyes resolute, the hard slash of his eyebrows as he banished her from her house.

Not my house. Never has it been mine.

Ros continued as though Valencia had not spoken. "Who does he think he is?"

"A duke," she murmured. "The Duke of Dedham."

Ros harrumphed in a way that made her sound like an old dowager herself. She carried herself as a woman of the world. At times it was difficult to recall that she was younger than Valencia. "That is no excuse."

"Oh, but you cannot go. Perhaps a conversation with him isn't such a terrible idea," Tru suggested, sinking down onto the edge of the bed, her hands neatly folded on her knees in a manner much more decorous than her sister's. "He must be a reasonable man."

Must he be?

He had not appeared very reasonable when he found her in the drawing room with his sisters. He had been rude and visibly relieved when she announced she would be leaving.

Tru went on, her manner more sedate than Ros's, but then when was she not more sedate than her sister? "Certainly he can see that a house *here* in Town will better suit you than Yorkshire. Even the late Dedham provided a town house over on Fletcher Street for his mother."

Maeve nodded sagely. "A lovely house."

"That is a splendid notion. As the new duke, he is quite ignorant. He should be enlightened on what it is he ought to be doing." Ros clapped her hands theatrically as though she had arrived at the solution. "*I* will go to him. *I* will explain how things are to be. If your husband could put up his old dragon of a mother in a house in Town, then this fellow can outfit you in a manner—"

Tru cast her a shushing look and wagged a finger at her. "Not you, Rosalind. *You* will not speak to him."

Ros scowled. "Why not me?"

"Because you frighten men," Tru snapped. "*I* will talk with him." She gave Valencia a tender look full of warmth. "Alongside you, of course, Valencia. We will do it together." She squinted her eyes and looked Valencia over critically. "Do you have that marigold dress? You're a vision in marigold."

"It will do no good." Valencia shook her head solemnly. "He wants me gone, as is his right. You all know that." She leveled a stern look at each one of her friends. She appreciated what they were trying to do, but the duke had all the power. And she had none.

"It may be his right . . . but it is not *right*," Maeve said meaningfully. "Any decent gentleman can be made to see that."

"And yet I will not be the one to make him see that. Nor will any of you."

She winced at the notion of appealing to him, this man, this stranger, for more than she was lawfully due. He did not owe her anything. The agents of the estate had been very clear on that point. She had her stipend and the dower house. Anything else would be charity. Pity. And a debt she could never repay.

She would have none of that.

Ros made a disgusted sound from where she lounged on the bed that Valencia interpreted as aggrieved acceptance.

Tru nodded once firmly. "Very well. Then you can live with me."

Valencia started. "Oh, no, I could not—"

"I would offer, but I doubt you want to live with my parents. My mother's parrot has a seat of honor at the dinner table." Ros grimaced.

"That does not sound very sanitary," Maeve contributed.

Ros shrugged.

Tru continued. "I have plenty of room, and Cordelia and I would love to have you."

"Oh, no, I cannot do that." Valencia shook her head resolutely. She wanted to remain in London but not at such a cost. "You and Jasper will soon be married, and it would not be the thing at all for me to impose on you both as you begin your new life together. I will be quite content in Yorkshire," she lied. "I will have a home of my own with a staff to attend to me. I am quite fortunate."

Tru opened her mouth to argue further, but a loud commotion drew everyone's attention to the door of the bedchamber just as a herd of young women burst inside. No warning. No knocking. And certainly no invitation.

Chapter 6

*There is little more dangerous a thing than
an ill-mannered debutante. Except perhaps
numerous ill-mannered debutantes.*
—Gertrude, the Dowager Countess of Chatham

The duke's sisters tumbled into the room like a pack of frisky puppies.

Valencia's friends turned to her almost in unison, the question clear in their eyes.

"Who are you?" one of the young women demanded rudely. Valencia was not certain, but she thought it was Del voicing the question.

Tru blinked, clearly shocked at such a poor display of manners.

Maeve's mouth hung in a small O of wonder as young Isolde pushed to the front, holding her stuffed dog in her arms. *Poppet.* Did that girl never leave it behind? Did it go everywhere with her?

"Goodness, you are all very pretty and dressed so smartly," the sweet girl exclaimed, reaching to finger the richly embroidered sleeve of Maeve's walking dress. Maeve did not react, merely continued to blink her eyes in astonishment at the sisters.

All six of them were here. Valencia quickly counted to be certain. Yes. Six. Not one was silent. They chattered with each other as well as pelted questions at Valencia and her guests.

Her friends took them all in with wide-eyed wonder.

"Who . . . are . . . they?" Maeve asked in a low, halting whisper.

"What is that thing?" Ros pointed, her eyes fixed scornfully on Poppet.

"Ladies," Valencia said in a voice loud enough, she hoped, to be heard over the sisters' not insignificant chatter. "May I introduce you to the duke's sisters?"

"Six?" Ros's voice rang with incredulity. "There are six of them?"

One of the sisters cheerfully announced, "We are the six he brought with him." She gave a wink. "The *unmarried* six."

The unmarried six.

That dropped and settled like a rock into their midst.

Tru leaned back on her heels and expelled a breath as though understanding. She then shared a meaningful look with her friends. They *all* understood.

Their presence here was no coincidence. The new duke had brought his *unmarried* sisters to London to marry them off. That was what men did, after all, Valencia thought with a decided lack of charity. Use and manipulate and arrange the lives of the females in their charge.

These provincial young women were about to enter the cut-throat jungle of the Marriage Mart. It would not be easy. It would not be pretty. They would be fodder for the sharks.

One of the girls coarsely elbowed another one. "The *better* six."

The sisters laughed as though this were a long-enjoyed jest.

"Oh my. How many more are there . . . of you?" Maeve murmured.

"Thirteen of us altogether. Twelve girls and our brother. Six are married. My brother and the six of us *here* are not."

He was the lone brother amid so many women. That had to be . . . something. Quite the experience growing up. Quite the experience even now.

"Oh my. Thirteen," Tru breathed, assessing them. "So many of you."

"I cannot place your accents." Ros managed to look politely curious and not her usual critical self, which was a feat for her.

"Bryn Bychan, Wales."

"Wales." Tru nodded as though that signified something.

Ros angled her head and murmured for their ears alone, "Apparently they do not have children in Wales, they have litters."

Tru cast her a disapproving glare. Maeve quietly hushed her.

Stifling a laugh, Valencia waved to each of her friends, recalling her manners and properly introducing them to the duke's sisters, whose names she had not yet committed to memory. There were so many of them . . . Would she *ever*?

"Allow me to present Mrs. Bernard-Hill, the Dowager Countess of Chatham, and Lady Shawley."

The girls exchanged looks and one by one executed awkward, overexaggerated curtsies that were wince inducing and would only elicit scorn and ridicule in the ballrooms of the *ton*. Sisters of the newly minted Duke of Dedham or no, the grand dames of the *ton* would devour them. Newcomers were always treated to withering scrutiny and rarely found approval. She read this knowledge in her friends' eyes. They, too, recognized that these young women would not fare well in Good Society. Not without a thorough polishing first.

At that moment a shadow filled the doorway, large and looming, and she knew whom it belonged to before her gaze even landed on his face. Her friends had not noticed him yet. They were too preoccupied with the awkward tableau of his sisters. And yet she noticed him. Her every pore seemed to contract and vibrate in awareness of him.

Isolde, the one sister whose name she could, in fact, easily remember, spoke first. "I am Isolde." She looked suddenly to her sisters as though needing confirmation. "Er. Rather, I am Miss Lloyd." She mouthed to them: *Is that how I am to be addressed?* Her very ignorance on such matters would be laughable if it were not so appalling. Fodder for the sharks, indeed. "It's such a delight to meet bona fide blue-blooded ladies."

"Isolde, *our* brother is a duke now."

"So," she said rather defensively. "He's been a duke for what? A week? Two days? These are clearly veterans of the *ton*."

Ros snorted and muttered something under her breath that sounded like: "Save me from green girls."

Isolde lifted her taxidermied dog higher in her arms, adding, "And this is Poppet."

Maeve blanched, smoothing a hand nervously over her impeccably coiffed dark hair. "Is that thing . . . real?"

"Meaning, as in once alive? Yes," one of the sisters volunteered with a chuckle. "Do not worry. You'll become accustomed to the sight of him. She only takes him everywhere with her."

Everywhere?

Valencia glanced again to where the duke glowered in the doorway, his presence still unknown—somehow—to everyone else in the chamber, a miracle of miracles. How could anyone be unaware of this man's presence? He radiated vitality. The air practically hummed with a crackling energy that she could taste on her skin.

He closed his eyes in one long-suffering blink as though pained at his sisters' behavior and searching for composure. A muscle feathered in his taut cheek, indicating that he was not without feeling in this moment, however implacable his expression.

"You take that . . . dog . . . everywhere?" Tru echoed, no doubt imagining the stuffed animal accompanying the young woman to dinner parties.

Another one of the sisters affirmed, "You will grow accustomed to the sight."

Ros cringed, conveying that she would clearly never become accustomed to it.

And Valencia would not grow accustomed to it either, because she was leaving. The dower house and rustic wallowing awaited her. Contrary to Tru's kind invitation to stay and live with her, she would be moving on. That was her fate.

Certainly it would be no worse than anything she had already endured. Her aloneness following Mama's death. The slow stretch of years married to Dedham. The long days. The lingering hours. The heavy moments.

That summed up so very much. Encapsulated the forlorn nature of her existence.

And yet she still wished. Still longed. Foolishly.

She should know better than to hope.

She would be leaving the new duke and his sisters to their lives here.

In with the new. Out with the old.

In this scenario, she was the old. A sobering thought.

A small, humorless smile tickled her lips as she thought of these six young women, shiny and new and guileless, entering the Marriage Mart. They had no notion of what they were in for—no notion of how to navigate the complex social hierarchy of the *ton*. It would be quite the spectacle.

Young debutantes spent their entire lives studying Debrett's and training in the art of dance and courtship and pianoforte and needlework and the management of a household, preparing for their entrée into Good Society. Their curtsies at Almack's would merely be the induction, the threshold they would pass through into greater glory . . . or hell.

Valencia fought back a laugh as she imagined Isolde taking her bow with Poppet in her arms. These girls were headed for disaster, and she was rather sad for them—but selfishly regretful to not be here to witness it. It would be pure entertainment.

The duke cleared his throat, announcing his presence at last to the room at large. "Girls. I hope you are not disturbing these ladies."

Yes. They must not disturb me and keep me from doing what needs to be done for me to take my leave.

Her friends swung their gazes to the man looming in the doorway. Their swift intakes of breath were audible.

"Who is *that*?" Ros whispered indiscreetly. For a proudly self-proclaimed spinster, she was not above admiring admirable gentlemen.

He inclined his head slightly, and that, perhaps not so surprisingly, was somehow both dignified and appropriate. Regal, even. "Ladies."

Of course he would be suited to the role of noble duke. He gave her such a look then. One that seemed to say a great deal. *Should you be entertaining when you are preparing to depart?* As though it were his place to manage her.

Arrogant arse.

Valencia lifted her chin a notch and then performed her due diligence, introducing her friends to the new Dedham. She flinched at that. *The new Dedham.* Staring at him, she felt a shiver of distaste applying her late husband's name to him. It did not sit well. It never would.

Her Dedham was dead. Gone. This man was not him.

As far as she was concerned, there would never be another one again, and that was as it ought to be.

Her friends all executed flawless, well-practiced curtsies, intoning with dulcet, genteel deference, "Your Grace, it is such a pleasure. Welcome to London."

His sisters gawked. A few giggled. The one fond of using her elbows sent a bony point into the sister nearest her, nearly knocking her over.

Isolde, whilst stroking Poppet with curling fingers, said in an awe-filled voice, "Wow. You all do that so much better than we do." Grinning, she looked to her sisters for agreement. They scowled back at her, not responding. "Perhaps we should take lessons from them, hm?"

The words were uttered teasingly, but Valencia could only think: *Yes. Yes. Yes. Yes.* They indeed needed lessons before entering Society. Lessons. Training. Schooling.

Those things happened in the normal course of life for young ladies of the *ton*. Their brother would not know about any of that though. He was new to being a duke. New to London Society. Valencia did not know anything about him, really, but she knew that much.

She did not know who he was or what he did before inheriting, but she grasped enough to know that this world was not something he understood. He was a man who did not have an inkling of how life functioned in the *ton*. He would be educated in the hard realities of it soon enough, though. Sadly, at his sisters' expense.

Ros blinked at the girl stroking her stuffed schnauzer as though it were a living, breathing pet. Her eyes glittered. She was enjoying this far too much.

Tru sent her sister a quelling look.

The duke himself did not miss any of the byplay. He was perfectly alert with his watchful eyes. His mouth pressed into a hard line—the lips still attractively full, but she wasn't giving any notice to that.

He was decidedly aware of the fact that his sisters were less than poised. He looked them over with an exasperated air, confirming that he was not as oblivious to nuance and subtext as his sisters appeared to be. Good for him. Not so good for the girls, but perhaps he would seek help for them. Perhaps he would not toss them directly into the melee of the Marriage Mart.

Even though they were displacing her, Valencia did not wish the girls ill. Good Society could be a hard, cruel mistress. She would not wish such cruelty on anyone.

"Sisters," he said, "why do you not leave the ladies alone so that they might visit?"

One of the girls groaned. Another muttered something in protest. A third actually gave a tiny stamp of her foot. Clearly these young ladies were unfamiliar with denial and rejection. Their first season in London should prove quite the rude awakening for them, as denial and rejection were as common as iced biscuits at teatime.

The girls filed out in an undignified line, Isolde walking especially slowly, sending longing looks back at Valencia and her friends.

The duke lingered in the doorway after she departed, inclining his head slightly. "Ladies."

His hand closed around the latch, and he started to pull the door shut, but not before catching Valencia's gaze and pausing, holding her stare for what felt like an eternity, until he finally closed the door behind him.

"So *that* is the new Dedham," Maeve murmured on an exhalation, notably impressed.

Valencia tried not to scowl. She did not want Maeve or any of her friends to be *impressed* with the man. She wanted them to dislike him as much as she did. And she did dislike him—this man who had been so very ill-mannered to her from their very first encounter. This man who was uprooting her from her life, wrenching her away from the sudden freedom she had found before she could even properly enjoy it.

Logically, she knew he was not personally responsible for her change in living. If not him, it would be some other man. And yet he was the boorish scoundrel who seemed not the least bit sorry about it.

So what if he was young and strong and handsome and in possession of a delicious voice if he was wretched to her? So what if he displayed an admirable dedication to his sisters?

How different her life would have been if she had a brother like him to look out for her . . . or at least to accept her with such kind forbearance. It was as though he was a better version of the late Dedham, and *that* made her feel many uncomfortable and unhappy things. Thoughts she did not care to examine. She would not admire him. She would *not* feel this . . . attraction.

"As handsome as the last one," Ros added matter-of-factly.

"Rosalind," Tru chastised, shooting an uneasy glance at Valencia.

"What did I say?" Ros shrugged. "Both are attractive men. Er, *was. Is.*" She looked perplexed for a moment, and then she shrugged yet again as though it was of no matter.

It was all maddening. The old Dedham was dead, but as soon as he expired a new one sprouted to take his place. Like a bloody starfish.

The Dedham library boasted a wide array of books, many on the topics of nature and anatomy and biology. One of the previous dukes had a great affinity for such subjects. Valencia had read that starfish had the ability to regenerate. They could lose a limb and later grow a new one. Such was the way with dukes. When one was lost, another sprouted in its place.

"They do *not* look alike," Valencia could not help insisting. The two men were not the same, but more importantly . . . *she* was not the same. She was not that dewy-eyed girl taken in by a handsome countenance and a silken tongue. Not anymore. Not again.

She refused to see her late husband in the new Dedham. Outwardly, her husband had been charming, his fair locks quite captivating—at least at the beginning, when he was in a proper state of body and mind. She had been thoroughly taken with him. Enough to have melted into a puddle when he baldly announced upon their first waltz, which happened to be only the *second* time they had met, that his search for a bride had ended and he would take her as a wife.

"Should you not properly ask me, Your Grace? And my papa?" she had queried breathlessly as he whirled her around in his arms.

"A formality," he had mused with a self-assured grin. "I want you. You shall be mine."

Her young and foolish heart had drummed wildly in her chest, finding his bold confidence terribly romantic. Now she could perceive just how arrogant he had been . . . how very selfish. It had only ever been about him. His whims. His pleasures. His claim on her.

"Of course they do not look alike," Tru agreed in what was almost a consoling manner—as though Valencia needed consoling. It was pity, that very dreaded and loathed thing, and she was well sick of it. "They are nothing alike." She shot her sister a meaningful glance.

Ros blinked, as though recalling something. She looked at Valencia and said quite unconvincingly, "Of course. Nothing alike at all. Other than good looks and wealth and a title that grants him the finest of everything in life whether deserved or not."

Tru shook her head with an exasperated breath. "Is that not every nobleman?"

They stayed for another hour, her friends forcedly cheerful and trying to make the most of their fleeting time together. They made promises. All of them. To come together in Yorkshire. To never lose contact. For Valencia to visit them in Town or at their country estates. No one could say when yet. Only that they would make it happen. Somehow. And perhaps they would.

Valencia's throat thickened, a lump forming as she thought about them. As she thought about all they had been through these many years. The good times. The not-good times when she had especially needed them and they had been there for her, supporting her and loving her and making her laugh when there had been so little to laugh about. Would she laugh in Yorkshire without them?

She hid the worst from them. They knew of her lost babes, but not her deepest shame. That she kept from them. She knew, logically, it was not her fault, but she never revealed the full scope of her husband's ill treatment. She never put it into words, but they were no fools. They had eyes and ears. They knew enough, and she would not have survived all these years without them. She would not have made it through. There was the family you were born into and the friends with whom you surrounded yourself, your chosen family.

The country house party rose in her memory . . . Dedham twisted and broken at the bottom of the stairs whilst screams filled her ears. *Her* screams. Her stomach quivered with familiar nausea at the reminder of that night. Indeed, how would she have survived without her ladies?

She escorted her chosen family downstairs to the front door, where they exchanged copious hugs and tearful farewells. Ros and Maeve especially. They clung to her harder. Longer. Their hands rhythmically smoothing up and down her back as though they were loath to let go of her. Their gazes full of words unspoken, words that did not need to be said because they were very much heard.

Tru had had her hands full in the last year with her own life's foibles. Like Valencia, Tru had been married to a wretched man, and wretched husbands took their toll. It was a full-time occupation contending with them. *Surviving* them.

Valencia did not blame her friend for being less than cognizant of her troubles whilst their husbands lived. One could only bear so much.

Chatham died shortly after Dedham. Another tragic accident. Funny how accidents befell wretched men. It was almost providential. Like some greater force, a guiding hand, had a play in it for both her and Tru. She winced and hastily veered her thoughts in another direction safer for her sanity.

The indignities endured at the hand of her husband had understandably occupied Tru. Then his death had occupied her. Then Jasper Thorne. That particular man *more* than occupied Tru. He consumed her—and she him. In the best of ways. They were madly in love—a true and deep, abiding love—as their upcoming nuptials attested.

As though thoughts of that impending wedding had summoned the mention of it, Tru called out as she took her leave, descending the front steps, "You will come for the wedding. You must. Promise me you will be here."

"I will," Valencia promised, meaning it.

She would figure out later how she would manage that . . . where she would stay. Likely with Maeve. Ros had not exaggerated. Her parents were a bit much. Ros's mother had a bird who liked to insult guests over tea. It was as natural as breathing to the infernal creature.

And yet even Ros and her parents would be better than Valencia's staying with her father and stepmother. She could not stomach that—could not abide staying with her stepmother and father. The father who had not been there for her all these years. Papa, who had not questioned it when the Duke of Dedham offered for her hand after only a few encounters. Papa, who had not noticed—or cared—when she lost her voice in her husband's presence. When she faded to shadow.

Her friends had cared at the change in her. Even as she'd kept her secrets, never divulging the things that happened inside the walls of her house, they'd surrounded her with love.

Closing the door behind them, she pressed her forehead to the cool wood for a long moment, screwing her eyes tightly shut in a long blink, staving off the heartache, the longing, the solid lump forming in her throat that threatened to burst into a sob.

She would miss them.

She had been telling herself she wanted to remain in London to experience life, to have an adventure, to taste independence . . . perhaps even to take a lover as she was now free to do so. While all of that was not untrue, there was perhaps more to it. There was *them*.

Her friends were here—the family of her heart. There was nothing and no one waiting for her in Yorkshire. Just wind and moors and silence. Very few people, and those few were strangers all. While she might be venturing to the remote dower house, her heart would be staying behind in London.

Sighing, she exhaled and turned, ready to escape to her bedchamber and finish packing so that first thing on the morrow she could start her journey north.

There was a slight sound. A scuffing bootheel.

Her gaze darted around, searching and then landing on the duke, standing on the opposite side of the foyer. He leaned against the doorjamb to the drawing room with an idleness that she did not feel. She felt only tension, only jaw-tight strain as she assessed him assessing her.

His arms were crossed over his broad chest as he studied her . . . and she knew he had been watching her for a while. Watching her with those deep-set brown eyes that looked like they were lit from within. Watching her through all her good-byes, in the long beat she took for herself afterward, grappling for composure, leaning her forehead against the door in what she thought was a private moment. He had been watching her.

He still was.

She lifted her chin indignantly, telling herself that his opinion of her did not matter in the slightest.

He continued to stare. She stared back, holding her breath, unblinking, her eyes threatening to tear up from holding them open for so long.

Then he spoke, his gravelly burr rubbing her skin to gooseflesh. "Dinner is in an hour." A pause fell in the thick air. "Join us."

He did not wait for her reply.

Turning, he disappeared back down the corridor toward the study—his study now—leaving her alone to wonder why he wanted her to sit down to dine with him and his family. It seemed uncharacteristic of the man who had dismissed her so coldly, so casually, so *finally* from her house. She grimaced. *His* house.

Join us.

She bristled. Not so much a request as a demand. Already behaving as a duke. Or perhaps he had always been authoritative. He was a man, after all. Experience had taught her that men were bred to be domineering, as though it were their God-given right.

He wanted her gone. So why should he invite her to dinner with them?

Her nape tingled with warning, and her stomach fluttered. It was more than a dinner. She felt that truth in her bones. She did not know his reasons, but she would. Before it was all over, she would know.

She would accept his invitation. She would *join* him and his family for dinner or whatever it really was in the guise of a dinner.

The Dowager Duchess of Dedham would arrive at the dining table in all her splendor, with all the dignity and aplomb and hauteur she had been spoon-fed since she had been in leading strings, since the day she'd performed her first curtsey.

He would marvel. He would gape.

And then he would know just *whom* he was casting from this house.

Chapter 7

The largest thing in any room is a lord's ego.
—Valencia, the Dowager Duchess of Dedham

They were gathered in the drawing room before dinner, waiting for the dowager duchess to join them. Rhain was seated near the softly crackling fire, sipping his brandy, trying not to reveal his eagerness. His sisters made no such effort.

"What is keeping her?" Isolde asked anxiously to no one in particular. She had been most excited to learn the former lady of the house would be dining with them tonight. The rest of his sisters' reactions ran from mild interest to annoyance.

"Does she not know we are hungry?" Del grumbled, smoothing a hand over her auburn hair, her fingers busily running along one of the small plaits woven into the knot at the back of her head as though she were playing the flute.

"How would she *know* that?" Isolde asked, stroking the blank-eyed Poppet, who sat in her lap.

He was past reacting to the sight of his sister with her taxidermied dog, but he could see it now only as those fine ladies had seen it earlier. He'd read the distaste in their eyes. They thought it strange. They thought *Isolde* strange, and that did not sit well with him. Isolde was a sweet girl, and he wanted only the best for her. That was what she deserved.

He could well imagine how the rest of the *ton* would react to her, however. He expelled a breath. He could not let that happen. For Isolde's sake. Somehow . . . Poppet had to go.

His mother and sisters envisioned only the good things that would result from this inheritance. The parties and the glittering galas and dancing until midnight. Eligible suitors lining up at the door with bouquets of flowers and boxes of candy.

They thought this dukedom meant only beautiful things. They considered no other possibility. They did not foresee the challenges.

He'd agreed to bring them along because it made them happy, and, ultimately, that was all he wanted—their happiness. Except he did not think happiness was in store for them here. He predicted heartache. Humiliation. There was no guarantee they would receive politeness from others. These fucking blue bloods were going to chew them up and delight in every moment of it. Whilst the ladies this afternoon had been polite enough, his sisters' awkwardness was at once evident.

He wished he could protect them from all ugliness, but this

world was beyond his control. It wasn't Bryn Bychan. He knew a great many things and considered himself an accomplished man, but he was able to recognize his shortcomings. He could not help them in this, and they needed help in the most vital way.

Those ladies had known. *She* had known. The dowager duchess. Valencia, he had heard her friends call her. *Valencia.* The name suited her. It was lovely and unique just like her.

Rhain suspected her tardiness was deliberate. He supposed it made her feel powerful. As though she were still in control. As though this remained her domain, her realm where she had the upper hand. As a man of business, he recognized the tactic. It was a worthy maneuver, but in vain. He was in control here. He did not make the rules, but the rules existed. They were what they were, and they had stripped her of her power here.

She could be as late to dinner as she wished, but she was no longer in control.

A footman stepped inside the drawing room, holding the door open.

Rhain lifted his brandy to his lips for another sip as he waited for her to appear, his expression carefully neutral, impassive.

She glided into the space, and he sucked in a breath, all hope of appearing impassive gone in an instant. Suddenly he did not feel so in control.

She was a vision to behold.

His sisters and mother immediately ceased their chatter to gawk. For good reason.

He already knew she was beautiful. Even when she was soaking wet on the deck of the barge, stinking of the Thames, he had been struck by her beauty. He had experienced that inconvenient, unwelcome attraction to her from the start. Damnable attraction. There was no controlling it. He could, however, refuse to act on it.

He *would* refuse.

He stood, careful not to ogle her as she swept into the room. He did not want to be that man. The predatory kind who looked at women and slavered over them like they were meat.

"Your Grace," he said in greeting, fixing his attention on her face and the dark waves lifted off her shoulders, the pile of tresses so glorious, so magnificent that his hands ached to touch, to gather up the strands and bring them to his face.

He was aware of her lush body encased in that golden gown—as though she were the sun bursting upon a dark horizon. Even without dipping his eyes downward again, he was indeed aware. He would always be able to see that—*her*. Forever. The vision of her was imprinted on him. It would be one of those images he stored away in a room in his mind, for him to visit from time to time. He cursed himself for the fanciful thought.

She executed a quick, flawless curtsey. "Your Grace. Ladies. I hope I have not kept you waiting." Despite her words and seeming graciousness, *that* did not feel true. He would wager that she had fully intended to keep them waiting.

A couple of his sisters mumbled something indecipherable. He did not glance their way as he assured the dazzling lady who stood before him, "Not at all."

He offered an arm each to his mother and the dowager duchess. They accepted and he escorted them both into the dining room, his sisters following like dutiful ducklings.

The rest of the evening passed with a steady stream of conversation. Even the taciturn Del and Elin relaxed and participated, inquiring about London and all the things they wished to see and do that they had read about in books and newspapers.

Isolde and Bronwen were more interested in the social aspects, the parties and balls and, obviously, the gentlemen.

The duchess was easy to admire, sitting at the table, resplendent in her gold gown, with her luminous skin and elegant manners, her movements like that of a bird gliding on air.

"When do you think we can attend our first ball?" Bronwen stared hopefully at him, distracting Rhain from his fascination with the young widow.

The question was out of his purview. He hesitated, glancing questioningly first at his mother and then at the dowager. The lady stared back at him without comment. And why *should* she comment? This had nothing to do with her. She was leaving.

He wished he had not looked to her. That he did so felt . . . telling. It revealed too much, confirming how little he knew of this world, the world he wished for his sisters to successfully infiltrate—because that was *their* wish. Indeed, he knew nothing of it, but she did. The Dowager Duchess of Dedham. This was her world.

His mother rattled off some reply. The dowager duchess merely watched. Listened. Smiled politely, likely thinking that they were all hopelessly ignorant. He shifted in his seat, disliking the notion and the way it made him feel so ineffectual when he prided himself on being a man of competence.

The rest of the dinner progressed. They ate a delicious meal of rack of lamb with mint jelly, sole with dill and lemon, buttered turnips, and a lovely cucumber salad.

After dinner they moved to the parlor, where his mother pressed the duchess into playing the pianoforte, which she did. Beautifully. He enjoyed the performance, clapping alongside his awestruck sisters. It could not be denied. She was beautiful and talented, too.

It was not very late when she stood to excuse herself, citing her long journey tomorrow as a reason for needing to retire early.

He rose to his feet circumspectly, watching with a tightness in his chest as she slipped from the room. He sank back down onto the sofa after she departed, listening with half an ear as his family chatted around him.

He found himself staring at the door through which she had disappeared, envisioning her upstairs in that room, packing the last of her things and readying for bed. Her last night in her bed, in her chamber, in what was once her house. His fingers tapped the arm of his chair anxiously. For some reason, the notion did not sit well with him.

And why should it? She was the only person in this house who understood anything about life in the *ton*. And he was sending her away. He grimaced. Because he was a hasty fool who had opened his mouth the moment he discovered her in his drawing room, before he had the time to properly assess her usefulness.

He had behaved as a sullen bastard, and now he was left with the consequences of her imminent departure.

"Rhain? Rhain? Did you hear me?"

He snapped his attention to his mother. Alwena stared at him expectantly, and he felt the full burden of that expectation in her look. "Do you know how we might begin to attend events in Town now that we are all moved in and settled? The girls are eager to socialize."

A valid question and one he did not know how to answer. Obviously they needed to be invited places, and so far he was unaware of the arrival of any invitations. None had crossed his desk. Should they have? How should he go about procuring invitations?

He shrugged one shoulder with a casual lightness he did not feel, words eluding him. He had not thought that far ahead when he decided to venture here with half of his family in tow. He supposed he thought it would simply . . . happen. They would arrive in London. His sisters would meet and have their pick of eligible gentlemen. He had not considered at all how the girls would be introduced to these blue-blooded swains.

His mother and sisters stared at him expectantly, hopefully.

They wanted him to provide, to deliver. As he had always done. As he always would.

He released a breath. "I will see what can be done."

They all smiled and nodded, settling back into their seats with sighs of relief, confident that he would do as he promised, that he would take care of everything.

Chapter 8

*The marriage bed and giving birth . . . two grim consequences
of wifehood. Is it any wonder widowhood is a covetous state?*
—Gertrude, the Dowager Countess of Chatham

Valencia did not linger long after dinner. This was her last
night in her bedchamber. In her house. She resented playing hostess to the very people who were uprooting her and taking
over her life for themselves.

She prepared herself for bed, undressing and carefully packing the gold gown into one of her waiting trunks so that Tildie
wouldn't have to do it for her in the morning. She ran a caressing hand over the rich fabric. She wondered if she would ever
have cause to wear the gown in the wilds of Yorkshire. Would
she even find a community there? Friends? Friends like the ones
she had here? Certainly that would be no easy feat. Perhaps
even impossible.

Shaking her head, she banished these morose thoughts, reminding herself that she would be back for visits. Tru's wedding. And she could host a house party, assuming the dower house was large enough for that. She rather suspected it was not.

A house party. She winced at the notion. She had not attended one since the previous year, since she had lost her husband, and she was still suffering nightmares from that.

She settled down on the bench before her dressing table and removed the pins from her hair. One by one she dropped them into the small dish on the table, *clink* after *clink*. The heavy mass fell down her back, and she sighed in relief, propping her elbows on the table and rubbing her scalp. She held herself like that for a long moment before moving again, picking up her pearl-handled hairbrush.

She brushed her hair until it crackled, as she had done countless times in this very spot, wondering where she would be doing this tomorrow night. Likely in some inn along the North Road, with raucous sounds drifting up to her from the taproom below. And the night after that . . . a bedchamber where countless Dedham widows had been long relegated, assigned and forgotten until they expired without note, dying alone in their beds.

She froze, her brush midstroke as a single knock reverberated in the air. The rap shook the adjoining door. The door that led to Dedham's chamber.

A shudder racked her body. No one ever knocked on that door. The chamber had been empty for over a year . . . and before that Dedham had long ceased to cross its threshold.

The chamber was occupied now though.

She stared at the long panel of wood with its unmoving latch as though she could see through the barrier, as though it were a living, breathing thing that might jump out and bite her.

She shook her head. The newly minted duke would never be so bold, never so audacious as to knock on the door as though they were intimates . . . as though she would open it to him. Perhaps, for some reason, it was one of the staff members who had traveled here with the Lloyd family. She did not know. It did not make a great deal of sense, she knew, but neither did the new duke knocking at the adjoining door between their chambers.

Staring at the closed door reminded her of times long ago. Better times. When she had been so young and hopeful and enamored of the man she married, believing she had found a storybook love. Better times indeed. When her husband was still interested in things like bedplay and would rap once out of courtesy before entering through that door—removing his robe, then her robe, and laying them down in her bed for what always felt like a much-too-brief tryst. She'd enjoyed those scant minutes even if she was always left vaguely unsatisfied, longing for more.

Her lips worked, but words did not emerge. She did not know what to call out. She was still struggling with the realization that he was on the other side of her chamber—for it must be him. She could admit that to herself now.

It was *him* and he wanted inside.

The latch turned down. Time slowed as the door began opening. Then he was stepping through. Stopping just inside her chamber.

She glared at him through her dressing table mirror.

He had been inside her chamber earlier, but that had been different. His sisters and her friends had been in here with her. Now it was just the two of them.

"I beg your pardon," she said in a tone full of indignation, swiveling slowly on the cushioned bench to face him.

He glanced around her chamber with an idleness that she did not feel. He took it all in as though it were not bold or unexpected of him to enter her chamber without invitation. "It's very different from my chamber."

She knew that. She'd styled her room and decorated the space years ago when she first moved in here. In the years since, she had updated it several times, keeping it always her own space. Currently it was all pale creams and soft lavender with splashes of gold. It had been that way for the last few years. She had been contemplating changing it again, but now, ousted from her home, that would never happen.

"It is your chamber now." She nodded stiffly in the direction of the duke's rooms. "You can make it look however you wish." She somehow managed to say this without any inflection in her voice. A challenge, for certain, as she was feeling all manner of things.

Still, there was the indignation . . . and also resentment humming just beneath her skin. Strong, biting resentment at the unfairness of it all flushed warmly through her.

Of course he could barge into her room. It was his now. His room. His house. Everything was his.

He nodded slowly. "I suppose so."

Except me. I am not his.

He had no right to behave as though she were subject to him.

Emboldened, she flung out, "Just because you are lord and master here now does not mean you have the right to stride into my room uninvited. Your authority does not extend to me. *You* are not lord and master of *me*."

He stared at her for a long silent moment, his deep brown eyes unreadable however much they perceived of her, and that gnawed at her, filling her with doubts as she wondered what he was thinking.

Finally, he spoke, his voice infuriatingly calm. "I needed to speak with you, and as you are planning to depart in the morning..." His voice faded as he shrugged.

"You thought that gave you the right to use our adjoining door," she finished.

He glanced back at the door. "Convenient, that."

She squared her shoulders in affront. "It *is* . . . but a convenience for the Duke and Duchess of Dedham."

His mouth lifted in a wicked half smile. "Are we not that though? The Duke and Duchess of Dedham?"

Oh! Heat slapped her cheeks. *Not even remotely close.* "You know what I mean."

He nodded, still with that infuriating half grin. "Yes. I do."

He was jesting with her, then? She blinked, a little astonished. She had not observed even a glimpse of humor in him since they met.

He glanced back at the door again, as though considering it. "As convenient as an adjoining door is . . . there is nothing quite as convenient as sharing the same bed. Nothing like a warm and pliant body within arm's reach at all times. One of the few perks of marriage, I wager. Why would married couples, lovers, need separate rooms? Separate beds? Or an adjoining door, for that matter? That strikes me as all rather . . . *in*convenient. Not convenient. Don't you agree?"

Her face burned even hotter. He was outrageous . . . and yet his words filled her mind with lurid images that sent tingles through her body and made her press her thighs closer together in an attempt to quell the sudden throb between her legs.

She forged ahead, finding her voice. "Things are different here . . . in London, in Good Society. Husbands and wives keep separate bedchambers."

"That is life in the *ton*, eh?"

"It is." She nodded.

"A bunch of frigid prigs," he surmised.

She stopped nodding and frowned. "Er. No."

He grunted and shrugged. "Were I wedded, I would find it vastly inconvenient."

She demanded sharply, "Do you even want to be here, Your Grace?" Nothing in his manner reflected any enthusiasm about becoming a duke or being in London or in this house. Contempt fairly seeped from him.

He grinned then. A devastating, belly-flipping grin.

"No," he said simply. "Not at all."

She blinked, not expecting that answer. She had thought he would insist that he wanted to be here, that he belonged here.

"You do not want . . . this?" She waved around them. "You do not want the dukedom?"

What sane man would not want the wealth and prestige and instant repute that came with a dukedom?

He tossed back his head and gave a rough laugh. The rumble of his voice emerged. "Fuck, no."

She jerked, startled at his use of profanity.

She somehow knew the word, but no gentleman had ever spoken it in her presence before. Not even her husband. *No, he had just tormented and hurt me.* Actions far worse than flinging out a little coarse language.

"But you," he added, "*you* want to be here."

She squared her shoulders. Was she so very transparent, then? If he knew her desires, that meant he knew her disappointment, too. He knew that leaving her home was tearing her up, and that made her feel far too vulnerable. Vulnerability only led to pain.

Was he reveling in this? Did he enjoy seeing her crushed as she packed for the dower house?

She wasn't going to argue or deny it . . . but she wasn't going to beg or plead either.

She lifted her chin. "I know my place."

He made a noncommittal sound, angling his head thoughtfully. "And what if your place is here?"

She jerked slightly, certain that she misunderstood. "I do not . . ."

"What if you remained *here*?"

Was he toying with her? She paused, wondering what game he

was playing at. "And why would I do that?" What reason could there possibly be for her to stay here? She was a relic. She served no purpose. She belonged where all the other dowagers before her had gone.

"You could be useful to me . . . to my family."

She digested that for a moment. *Useful.* Meaning . . . he wanted to use her. *Ah.* So that was it. Of course. He was not motivated by altruism.

"Your sisters," she said matter-of-factly.

He nodded grimly. "They could use your . . . er, guidance."

She crossed her arms over her chest, thinking that his sisters could indeed use help in a few areas.

"No arguing with that, I see," he added.

"They can use . . . help," she allowed, lifting one shoulder in a weak shrug.

"Who better than you, a grand dowager . . . to help navigate them through Society."

It was not a plan without merit. Stay here. Help his sisters. Except . . .

"What about when you are finished with me? When you no longer need my *guidance*? What then? What happens to me then? Will I be back here"—she gestured around her—"in this moment, packing to leave for the dower house?" Back in this terrible moment she had no wish to live through again.

"Do this and you can name your price."

"My price?"

"Yes. You wish to remain here in London. We can arrange

that. I can provide you with your own house . . . and increase your stipend." She sent him a sharp look, at which he blinked innocently and shrugged. "I met with the estate agents, remember? I know how little was provided for you. Presently your stipend would not carry you through a London season. I'll see that you have enough to last you through the remainder of your life." He nodded once, holding her gaze.

She maintained outward calm, keeping her composure, even though everything inside her was quaking with excitement at what he was offering. Excitement *and* resentment.

I know how little was provided for you. Well. That was mortifying. Fiery shame crept over her face, and that was not right. The shame was not hers, and still she felt it.

She did not want to need anything from him. She did not want his help.

And yet she desperately wanted to stay here.

Was it help if she was offering a service in return?

"I will put it in writing for you," he added, enticing her, tempting her.

"That's not necessary—"

"It is." His mouth sealed into that hard, determined line she'd seen him wear before. "I will see it done. You should have that."

She opened her mouth and then closed it with an inaudible snap. *Why not?* It was *right* that she have it in writing. She deserved that kind of reassurance. The kind of protection no man had ever given her in this life. Not her father. Not her husband. She'd never had a sense of security, but he was offering that to her now.

She swallowed thickly. For a price. For services rendered, and that was fair. It even made her feel better somehow—that she was not getting something for nothing. She would not be taking charity. This was not something he was bestowing on her out of pity. She would not be indebted to him.

She would earn this.

She had a skill, to be certain. She could do what he was asking. She knew this life, this world. She was a grand dame of the *ton*. She knew Society and all the runs and dips of it. She could navigate it blindfolded.

She rose from the bench before her dressing table and strolled forward, feigning confidence, pretending not to feel vulnerable in her nightgown. However she looked now, it was better than how she had appeared on their first meeting.

She stopped before him. "Very well. We have an agreement, Your Grace." Shoulders squared, she held out her hand, determined to treat this as any deal struck between two reasonable individuals.

He looked down at her outstretched hand for a long moment before taking it, folding it into his larger one. His warm fingers wrapped around hers as his hot-eyed gaze ensnared her. She sucked in a breath.

The contact sent a sizzle of shock through her. Perhaps it was his attractiveness. Perhaps it was those eyes of his, a melting brown so mesmerizing and compelling that she felt herself drowning in them. She took another deep breath.

Or perhaps it was their aloneness . . . the night pulsing

around them, soft sounds bleeding in from the outside world, the muted glow of lamplight bathing them both in a light that felt unearthly.

His pulse found her, penetrating from his palm into hers. Her heart throbbed a little faster, thumped a little harder, and she wondered whether he felt it, too, in their connected hands. A dull thump started in her ears, a heartbeat.

She fought to swallow.

She wanted to look away but could not. Could not pull herself free of his gaze.

She was suddenly acutely conscious that they were alone together in her chamber at night with her bed just a few feet away.

She swallowed against her impossibly thick throat. God. She really was hungry for intimacy. Starved, if she could feel this way about him of all men. The new Dedham. The replacement. The irony was not lost on her.

It had been too long.

He was too handsome and her body too long neglected. It served to remind her of her status as a widow and that there was nothing preventing her from feeling amorous toward another man. Even this wretch of a man.

For years she had relied on herself for satisfaction, relied on her own hands in the darkness of her bedchamber, sliding, roaming over her body and finding the places where she ached the most, working to achieve her own release, the climax she had never quite managed to accomplish with her husband. She got herself there through her own efforts, and that had been adequate, if not completely thrilling. She always felt there was more to it though, more pleasure to be had with a proper partner.

And she wanted a *proper* partner. Oh, not love. Never would she make that mistake again—thinking she was after that elusive, ephemeral thing. No, no. That's not what she was looking for. That led to foolish notions of happily ever after and marriage. Not another husband for her. Never that.

She meant *proper* in the respect that he could properly shag her. She wanted her eyes to roll back in her head and not because of her own ministrations, but because he possessed a body he knew how to use and manipulate and toil over hers in the engagement of sex.

Before this man's arrival she had been intent on a quest for adventure of the amorous variety. If she was staying in London, there was no reason she could not continue with that quest. She could still usher the duke's sisters through Society and get what she wanted, what she needed, for herself.

With her connections and their sudden rank as sisters of a duke, she should have no trouble helping them secure satisfactory matches. They needed only a little polishing. She could manage that task. And experience a little fun with a *proper* bed partner in the process.

The House Party

There were gentlemen among the *ton* thrilled to pursue married ladies. For many, it was their sole occupation, the thing they did more than any other hobby. More than gambling or hunting or racing about Town in their curricles. For them, women were the game. The quarry. The sum total of those gentlemen only increased in Valencia's sphere after Dedham's accident.

She had not been prepared for it—for them.

Like vultures they circled, dark blots, apparitions moving about her life. It had been galling. A mere week after Dedham's accident and they had surfaced. She and he were both still reeling from the shock, the trauma, not yet fully knowing the grim outcome, and she'd had to fend off the advances of rogues and libertines. As soon as it made the rounds that Dedham might not walk again, she had been pelted with lewd invitations from men who thought she must be suffering in her cold bed. As though she were ruled only by her desires.

Lord Burton had been one such man. He had been so bold, so

shameful, to appear in her drawing room in the guise of checking on Dedham, but really to let Valencia know he was there for her . . . in any and every capacity.

Since then the wretched man was always there. Always hovering. At every ball, musicale, and opera. Every gathering or fete or house party. It mattered not that he was a married man or she a married lady. She was always dodging his advances.

Whilst Dedham still lived, she honored her vows. Never stepped outside her marriage for diversion as so many other ladies did. Society would scarcely blame her—as long as she was discreet.

It had been years since his accident, after all. A long time to go without a man in her bed, and yet she dared not. If Dedham ever learned, she would not see the remainder of her days. He could only tolerate so much—so very little, really—and she knew that was one thing he would not endure.

She had not invited Lord Burton, but he was here just the same, in her chamber, in her space with his hands on her now.

"Unhand me," she choked out.

His fingers tightened on her arms, and she was certain there would be marks there the following day. Tildie would see them and dip her head, looking away as she always did, but not before Valencia read the pity in her eyes. As before. It was a shame she had borne before.

"Cease your games." His breath fell hot and wet on her face. "You've been toying with me long enough, nigh on a decade now. I should have had you long ago. The moment Dedham went lame you should have been mine. God knows he's not giving you his cock now." He pulled her flush against him, and she felt the insistent bulge of his manhood bump against her stomach. "How you must be aching for it after all this time, my dear."

She swallowed back a sob, wondering what she had done to give him any notion she was receptive to his advances—and what made everyone assume her husband was not up to performing his conjugal duties? It was true, but why must everyone think that? Was it so very obvious? Was there a sign proclaiming her abstinence hanging around her neck when she went about Town?

His hand inched up to her neckline, and she heard the sharp tear of fabric. "Now cease your struggles, Your Grace. It really has become quite tedious."

It was strange, hearing him respectfully address her with her honorific whilst assaulting her.

And yet she knew that rank and title did not offer a lady protection. At the end of the day, in the dark of night, a woman could always find herself a victim.

Cool air wafted over her skin, and it launched her into action. Her arm stretched out, hand reaching, fingers searching and fumbling and finding a small brass clock upon the nearby side table. Her fingers circled it and lifted the heavy object. Sucking in a breath, she brought it crashing against his head.

He may have chosen her as his victim, but she would be her own rescuer. She would survive.

He grunted and dropped her.

She fell back, staggered a pace, and stood there a moment, panicking, heart hammering in her throat as she stared down at his motionless form. Her hand flew up to cover her mouth.

Lord. I've killed him. I. Killed. Him.

No one would believe it was an accident. And was it? She had meant to strike him.

Shaking her head, she sprang into motion, lunging for the door. He had closed it behind him—of course—when he'd crept in like a thief intent on his nefarious purpose. She opened it now, clutching the torn, gaping flap of her nightgown in place.

She hastened down the corridor, determined to fetch Tru. She would know what to do. It was her house and her house party, after all. And Tru was always so level-headed, so calm and self-possessed. A born mother, a nurturer. She never panicked in any situation.

Valencia stopped in front of the double doors of the chamber she knew Tru occupied. Lifting her hand to knock, she hesitated, pausing with a cringe, stopping herself from bringing her knuckles down. A panicked thought flitted through her mind: What if Tru's husband was with her? The Earl of Chatham— who also happened to be Burton's friend. What if he was in her bedchamber?

It had to have been a decade since the earl and the countess had hosted anything together. Since they'd slept under one roof or shared a bedchamber. It was unlikely Chatham would be in there now, but then, this house party had also been an unlikely gathering. And yet they were here together.

Chatham had looked at his wife tonight with hot interest

gleaming in his gaze. Valencia had not missed that. What if he had decided to visit his wife's bed? She could not intrude and risk Chatham learning about her mishap. He counted Burton a friend. She could not admit that she might have killed him. He would not believe it an accident.

She gulped against the sudden thickness in her throat. That would not go well for her. Dedham would be alerted. And he only thought the worst of her. He would not believe her either.

She lowered her hand to her side listlessly and turned from the door, thoughts spinning. She quite possibly had a dead man in her chamber. At the very least she had knocked him senseless. He could be dying at this very moment. In *her* room. It was too much. She gnashed her teeth until her jaw ached.

Heart still lodged in the vicinity of her throat, she turned for her chamber, resolving to find out Burton's status so that she would know what she faced. Her steps were reluctant, dragging slowly over the plush runner.

She stopped on the threshold of her chamber, gripping the doorframe tightly, fingers clenching into bloodless appendages. She stared into the hushed gloom of her chamber, looking down at the carpet.

Gone.

He was not there. She looked around wildly. No Burton anywhere.

Feeling very much like a stalked animal, she backed out into the corridor, glancing about frantically, straining, peering into the interior of her room as though he lurked in some dark corner and might pounce on her at any moment. Where had he gone? Was he—

"Thought you bested me, did you?"

She whirled around at the sound of his voice, but she did not have time to react. No time to speak. No time to move.

His hand lashed out, wrapped around her neck, and pushed her back against the wall of the corridor. He leaned close, his cheek aligning with hers, his lips moving against the whorls of her ear. "It could have been so pleasant for the both of us. Now it will not go easy for you."

There was no mistaking him. He wanted to hurt her.

With his hand at her throat, he reached down, indifferent that they were out in the corridor for anyone to happen upon them. He did not care. He was wildly furious, fumbling for the hem of her nightgown whilst she struggled between him and the wall.

"Cease your moving, you stupid cow. You're no untried maid. 'Tis just a house party. It's what is done at these things."

"Sorry to interrupt, my good man, but kindly find yourself another whore for the night. Perhaps your wife will suffice? I believe that is her room yon."

Valencia gave a single miserable blink, her head falling back on the wall with a thud.

At the words, Burton gasped and hastily stepped back from her.

Valencia reacted slower, well familiar with her husband's voice . . . and equally familiar with his moods. This was not a rescue. She would trade one evil for another.

The barely concealed fury in Dedham's voice was not reserved for Burton. No, she would not be spared her husband's wrath. His voice trembled with ire for her. Always his disappointment was directed at her. Irrationally. Unreasonably. Unfairly. She bore the blame for all his life's disappointments.

"Dedham." Burton cleared his throat and smoothed a hand over his hair as he stepped free of her. "Forgive me. I did not mean to offend . . ."

Did he not? It was remarkable, really. Was that an apology? The very notion of it astounded her. Burton did not think to offend a man by accosting his wife?

"Remove yourself from my sight, Burton."

Dedham leaned heavily on his cane. Whilst he did not present much of a threat physically, he was the very image of intimidation. Even broken-bodied, his eyes sparking and a bit wild from the pain that chronically plagued him, he was still the Duke of Dedham. Still a man of power and influence. All the more frightening for his very unpredictability and his penchant for unleashing his wrath upon Valencia.

Burton ducked his head obligingly. "Of course, Your Grace." He sent Valencia one last glance loaded with an emotion she could not even begin to unravel in that moment. She had too much else to contend with—too much else to fear.

Then he was gone, scurrying down the corridor.

And she was alone with her hard-eyed husband.

The flatness of his gaze fell squarely on her. This was not a rescue. It would be a punishment. A sentencing. Perhaps even an execution.

"Wife . . ." he began, and then, as though he thought a correction necessary, "Whore . . . what have you to say for yourself?"

Nothing, she realized.

There was nothing to be said that would not condemn her more in his mind and sink her lower into that abyss. Years had passed since her initial descent. The only things she had, her only salvation, were her friends, her ladies. She had no papa to intervene. No mother in whom to confide. No children of her own to give her comfort.

Not that she confided in her friends. Not about this. She could not. She knew it was not right for her to feel such shame over her husband's poor treatment of her—God knew Tru was married to an arse. She would empathize. And yet Valencia held silent, keeping her secrets.

Dedham thought only of his loss. His pain. Never hers. Never the possibility that anything could have been lost to her, too, the day of his accident. That a part of her had also died.

They were alone in the corridor of a sleeping house. Dreadfully alone. She stood much too close to him. Within reach. She took a sliding step back, seeking only self-preservation, as she always did in these scenarios, but he was quick to anticipate and seized her arm, twisting it, the skin bruising beneath the unforgiving pinch of his fingers.

Anger flared in her chest, a burning flush that spread throughout her. "Nothing. I have nothing to say for myself, because there is nothing I need say. I haven't done anything. I have never done anything, but you will never accept that."

His nostrils flared. "I am to believe that you have stood by me so faithfully through the years when I have not served you as a husband ought—"

"Yes! Yes," she snapped. "Precisely that."

"Because you love me so," he sneered.

"Oh, no," she tossed back, feeling dangerously bold. And reckless, perhaps, but what did it matter any longer? She was the one accosted this night, and now she faced her husband's wrath for doing nothing more than suffering Burton's mistreatment. She went on. "Not anymore. Any love I felt for you long ago died."

"Of course!" His eyes flashed as though delighted, as though vindicated by this confession. "The moment I was injured you—"

"No," she cut in. "It had naught to do with your accident. It was you. All you. You killed my love for you, and I did love you." She paused for a choked breath, pressing a hand to the center of her chest. "But you could never accept that. You destroyed every shred of softness that existed between us."

He shook his head. "No."

"Oh, yes." Still she went on, saying the words she had never dared to say before. "You killed us. You killed what we had—"

"You think I wanted this?" He motioned to himself, his face contorting with pain that went beyond the emotional. It was physical. She knew that. She pitied him that. Truly. He lived in pain. As much as he had hurt her, she knew he suffered, too, but that did not mean she forgave him for all he inflicted on her. There was no excusing that.

"No." She shook her head sadly. "You did not. But you made certain that your suffering became mine."

"Your suffering," he spat, and spittle dribbled from his lip. "Do you hear yourself, you selfish bitch? What is your suffering compared to mine?" His grip on her intensified, becoming excruciating.

Nothing, she realized grimly. Just as she was nothing to him, too. Only his pain mattered. And inversely she wondered if it had been only his joy and pleasure that mattered in their early years together, too. Had she not seen that? Had she not ever recognized the real Dedham, the man beneath the veneer? It had always been about him. About his love. His happiness.

She did not reflect long on that though, for his fingers were visiting far too much pain upon her tender skin. "Ow," she protested, trying to pull her arm free.

"You know nothing of true pain, wife," he charged, and his eyes flashed with that dangerous temper again, and she knew what was coming. "I shall have to educate you on that."

She knew before she ever felt the fall of his hand on her face that it was coming. He would see to it that she felt pain. He was very good at that. Very good at furthering her education.

Chapter 9

One must never underestimate the preparation involved in readying for the season. The strategic planning that went into Waterloo was less complex.

—Valencia, the Dowager Duchess of Dedham

The following week was a whirlwind of activity in the Dedham House, the likes of which had never been seen during Valencia's tenure as duchess.

The sudden influx of people, both residents and staff alike, only added to the chaos. The noise, din, and activity were overwhelming. She never thought the grand Dedham town house could actually feel small, but with all these people the place felt full, tight and suffocating . . . no longer so empty.

She imagined this was what families felt like. *Big* families. Boisterous and crowded. The bickering did not hide the fact that they loved each other. The squabbling did not conceal that closeness.

There was a time when she'd had that in her life. When she'd felt such closeness. When her mother was alive, Valencia had that sense of kinship and belonging.

She might not have had the lively, plentiful family surrounding her, but she'd had the security, the absolute conviction that she was loved and treasured.

Then Mama died, taking that sense of security with her and leaving Valencia with her wastrel father. Papa, who never cared for her or even dear Mama quite as much as for himself and the pursuit of his own pleasures: namely his women.

And there had been many, *many* women.

He had not been a vision of health and vigor for a goodly number of years, but he'd always had young ladies about him. Lovers and mistresses. Other wives after Mama. Somehow Papa had outlived two wives. Strange, that. They were younger, but unlucky to have died before him. Mama from a fever that raged for days before taking her. The other from an overdose of the laudanum she was overly fond of consuming.

His marriage to Hazel, who had been his mistress at the time, was a bold move. Shameless. Outrageous even for him. But the Marquess of Sutton always did as he liked. At least Valencia had been out of the house by then, married to Dedham and living her own particular hell. She did not have to suffer the sight of Hazel in her mother's chair across the dining table every day, or Hazel sitting at her mother's writing desk, or Hazel wearing her mother's jewels.

Dedham House was a different place now with the arrival of

the Lloyd clan. For years the place had been quiet, menacingly silent, tense and pulsing like a heartbeat just under the skin.

Now it was bursting with life and vitality. Everything was out, on the surface, nothing hidden, nothing repressed. The place felt . . . lighter.

Valencia enjoyed the change, the bustle, the frenetic energy.

The girls were wild and unconventional, true . . . but there was the ring of laughter in the air. The absence of tension, the absence of . . . threat.

Tildie was also delighted with it all. "I am so glad we are staying. I just knew the new duke was a proper gentleman."

Valencia suppressed the urge to debate that point.

Their pact may have been an easy decision for her to reach, but she was unconvinced of his inherent decency. Like her, he was motivated by selfish reasons. He needed her services, and she needed his pocketbook. A fair exchange and certainly *not* altruistic.

Still . . . in the ensuing days, she was plagued with doubts about their arrangement. In the light of day, it gave her pause. It would not be an easy task. She was not certain the Lloyd sisters even wanted her advice on Society. Or on any matter. The ill-tempered Del, particularly, did not appreciate Valencia's interference in their lives.

Valencia felt as though she were herding fractious toddlers and not a group of young women. There were times amid the melee that Valencia found herself standing at the top of the stairs staring around her in wonder, turning in a small circle as the six girls rushed to and fro. They did not walk or stroll in elegant fashion either. They did not speak in dulcet tones. Sometimes they even tossed things at each other. Oh, nothing harmful. Pillows mostly. And yet it was all very undignified.

Clearly the little corner of Wales they called home was not High Society. From what Valencia had gathered, their village was small, their way of life small, too. Provincial. Everything revolved around the quarry. *Their* quarry. Or rather his. The duke's quarry. *His.*

The village of Bryn Bychan was apparently a safe place, where the Lloyd girls could *be* anything, *do* anything, and toss as many pillows as they liked.

The duke's sisters had free rein to go about as they pleased without impunity, without judgment. Valencia had to wonder why they would not stay there and enjoy that freedom and delight in a life where they could be whom they wanted to be without censure.

She would have reveled in that freedom as a young woman. She winced. She would revel in that *now*. She supposed their reasons could be the same as her not wishing to retire to Yorkshire. There was not a great deal to do there. A definite lack of Society. A life of boredom. Day after day of the sameness.

She began slowly with her charges, determined not to startle or overwhelm them. The first few days she made a study of the young women—each of them. One would not send a soldier off to war without proper training. And the Marriage Mart was war, in a manner. A battlefield to be braved, for certain.

They possessed different weaknesses, different strengths.

Valencia jotted down her notes in a journal. At the top of her list was Isolde, and beside her name: *Lose Poppet*. This she underlined twice. It was perhaps her most important goal.

She tapped her chin thoughtfully at that. Somehow she would have to come up with a way to part the stuffed dog from the girl.

She made other lists, too—of all the tradespeople they would need.

And then she sent for them.

All her favored dressmakers and corsetieres and milliners and cordwainers and glovers and jewelers ventured in and out of the house at all hours. And those were just the tradespeople. There were the necessary instructors, too. It was a coordinated effort with many fronts of attack.

A few of the sisters grumbled, primarily Del and Glynnis, but they all generally fell into line like dutiful soldiers. Ultimately, they wanted a successful entrée into Society. They were here for that very reason, after all. It united them with one another and even with Valencia.

And who did not love beautiful things? They were in awe of the quality of garments and accessories paraded before them. They petted the velvets and brocades and silks with rapturous sighs. Donned every sample with rounded eyes.

Valencia sent for Mrs. Cohen, her favorite coiffeur. Everyone's favorite coiffeur. The woman was an artist. She worked marvels on hair. The girls, however, did not yet realize or appreciate the coup of scoring an afternoon with London's renowned Mrs. Cohen. Their screeches carried through the house, and Valencia followed the din, entering one of the upstairs bedchambers to investigate, only to find Isolde sitting on a seat before a dressing table, shrill sounds escaping her as she stared down at seven inches of her fiery hair strewn about the floor.

The other sisters watched in wide-eyed horror, surrounding her, waiting their turns in trepidation. Except for Elin. She was the one sister who appeared ready and willing to get her hair cut.

"Come now, Isolde, you're being dramatic. No one needs hair hanging past the waist. If I could chop off all mine and wear it as a man, I would." Elin fingered a strand of her hair wistfully. "No more tangles to work through. The lightness of it would be heavenly."

Mrs. Cohen pointed her scissors at Elin approvingly. "You," she pronounced in a heavy accent. "We shall do something properly adventurous and stunning with you."

Elin beamed.

Isolde continued to snivel into her hands. Mrs. Cohen appeared exasperated. Pausing, she waited for Isolde to regain her composure so that she could continue her work.

Valencia patted Isolde's shoulder. "Trust me, Isolde. Mrs. Cohen is very good at what she does. You will be thrilled with the results."

Isolde gave a watery sniff and stared straight ahead with a nod. "I will be brave."

"That's a girl." Valencia patted her shoulder encouragingly, and departed the room with a rueful smile. They were in good hands with Mrs. Cohen. Shaking her head, she left the steady chatter of the sisters behind. After only a few days, she was well familiar with the sound.

She wore a smile as she rounded the corridor, stopping suddenly, the smile slipping from her lips as she came face-to-face with the duke. His strides slowed as his gaze landed on her. He looked as handsome as ever, his hair a little windblown as though he had just come in from outdoors.

He had been busy, too. His mother kept her apprised of his activities. She adored her son in that way mothers adore their sons. According to her, he was much like his father. Pride glowed in her eyes when she spoke of him—which was a frequent occurrence. Valencia did not have to pry any information out of her. Mrs. Lloyd gladly shared everything. Details small and large. All was revealed, gushing forth as she relayed his deeds.

Not that Valencia required his mother's comprehensive reports. She had her own eyes and ears, and what she could not herself glean, her staff was only too happy to divulge. Tildie naturally kept her informed.

THE DUKE WAS closeted in his study most days, meeting with various people, including the agents of the estate—the very gentlemen who explained her new situation to her following Dedham's death, specifically the particulars relating to her stipend and the dower house. These same men called upon the duke multiple times.

At dinner her view of the duke lasted longer than these glimpses throughout the day.

The Lloyd family would all gather at the large dining table, the young women volleying to speak, to outdo the others and be heard.

Except for him. He was ever composed. A taciturn figure at the head of the table. He was always very proper, very cordial, if a little stilted in manner. He offered no hint of the man who had let himself into her chamber as though it were his right. He behaved as a distant and polite stranger. She almost suspected she had invented that encounter.

At night she would find herself hovering before the adjoining door, listening to the subtle sounds of him on the other side, trying to imagine him in there. She knew the room well enough. She could see him in that space, envision him among the dark woods and heavy damask drapes, undressing and readying for the night, climbing aboard that great big frigate of a bed.

Now she recovered her smile and greeted him circumspectly. "Your Grace."

A cry went up from within the room where Mrs. Cohen was working on his sisters.

His gaze flicked over her shoulders. "Is anything . . . amiss in there?"

"Everything is in order, Your Grace. Just a little . . . hair maintenance."

"Ah." His attention lowered back to her. "I was actually looking for you."

She blinked. "You were?"

"Yes. I told Wilkes I would fetch you. Your father is downstairs, waiting in the drawing room."

Her light mood vanished, and her stomach sank. "Oh."

If her father was here, she would assume her stepmother was, too. He could not get about with ease these days, and she accompanied him on every outing. He preferred Hazel at his side rather than a servant attending to him. There was more dignity in that for him. She supposed any man would prefer a young and beautiful wife on his arm rather than a servant or nurse helping him up from his chair, in and out of the carriage, holding on to his arm as he ambled through every room.

As though the duke read her mind, he confirmed, "Your stepmother is with him, too. She seems very kind."

Kind?

She shifted her weight on her slippered feet, ill at ease with that notion of Hazel.

He was studying her closely, and she struggled to reveal nothing. He didn't need to know all the sordid details of her past. She curled her hands into fists at her sides. Opened and closed them. Opened and closed.

"Thank you. I . . . ah, shall join them."

She strolled past him, her steps quick.

Hopefully he would not follow.

Hopefully no one would intrude on their visit.

Hopefully it would be brief and Papa and Hazel would be on their way soon, and she could go back to forgetting about them and resuming her new duties shepherding the Duke of Dedham's sisters through the Marriage Mart, bringing herself one step closer to creating the life she wanted for herself.

Chapter 10

Be it a prison or salvation, marriage can take many forms. The trick is in predicting which before one walks down the aisle.
—Hazel, the Marchioness of Sutton

Hazel, the Marchioness of Sutton, did not believe this day's business was a good idea, but once her husband made up his mind on a matter, there was no dissuading him.

She supposed she should be grateful for this character trait. It was the very thing that prompted him to take her to wife, after all. Marrying her had been contrary to the opinions of everyone around him and yet he had done it anyway.

She would still be living by her wits and bodily wares if not for her husband's stubborn ways and his inability to be swayed from his cause once his mind was made up. For no other reason would she be a marchioness, rather than still sharing a seedy third-story tenement in Seven Dials with three other working girls.

However, in this instance, as they were ushered into the drawing room of her daughter-in-law, his stubbornness was decidedly a character flaw and did not work in her favor.

"This is a very bad idea," she repeated, for the little good it would do. They were already here.

Hazel stood before the window and faced the courtyard. Beyond that was the bustling street. How she longed to be free of this house and out there, anywhere else. Valencia did not like her. She would not want her here.

Sutton sat enthroned in an oversized wingback chair, his frail, blue-veined hands gripping the head of his cane.

"The new Duke of Dedham has arrived and taken residence, my dear. It is all the scuttlebutt, and I had to learn of the news from Tobias as he helped me from my bath," he complained yet again. "Can you imagine that? Me learning such information from my valet rather than my own daughter? Can you imagine?"

He had a strong penchant for repeating himself these days, and she did not know if he simply did not recall having already said certain things or if he was so aggrieved that he felt compelled to repeat himself.

"I should have been the first person my daughter informed," he added in a huff, reminding her of a petulant child.

Hazel marveled at his obtuseness. It had been a long time, if ever, that her husband came *first* in his daughter's life.

He thumped his cane upon the floor with a dull thud and continued. "I cannot understand how Valencia has not sent for me. I should have been notified at once."

Hazel suppressed an eye roll. Little did he know how far down on the list he was among the people Valencia considered worthy of her trust and confidence. The only one lower than him was Hazel. Father or no, he was not someone Valencia ran to when she had news—be the news of the good or the ill variety.

Sutton had marked himself as no longer worthy of his daughter's trust long before he married Hazel, his mistress, a woman of dubious morals who happened to be younger than Valencia—but that had not helped matters. Valencia tolerated her father. Hazel she would not even pretend to like.

Hazel was astute enough to have realized all of this long ago. Her husband was either blind to his daughter's feelings or indifferent. Perhaps it was a bit of both.

Hazel recognized Valencia's frosty treatment for what it was. Dislike. Resentment. Animosity. Plain and simple. Animosity that often manifested in public. Much to the pleasure of the *ton*.

The *ton* had a salacious hunger for the ugly. Good Society really was not *good* at all. It required constant feeding. It enjoyed drama. Gossip. Spectacle of the juiciest variety. Members of the *ton* were sharks. When there was blood in the water they came to feast. On more than one occasion, Valencia and Hazel had offered them a veritable banquet.

Hazel winced. That day on the barge en route to Vauxhall was a perfect example. She had not meant to send her stepdaughter overboard, but she had done that very thing. Sent her plunging into the brown waters of the Thames. No wonder they could never reconcile. She had not seen Valencia since that particular indignity.

Hazel glanced back at the still-closed double doors. She was not certain, but she suspected Valencia was keeping them waiting deliberately. Perhaps she would send her excuses, plead illness.

Sutton occupied himself with the generous fare of food spread out on the tea service before him. He was all bones, but the man still possessed a hearty appetite. Hazel continued to gaze out at the courtyard.

She had thought this would have happened a year ago. With Dedham dead, typically the new heir would have arrived to displace his widow. That was customary. That was the thing done, wretched as it was. She had not been brought up in the *ton*, but she knew that much about heirs and primogeniture.

The doors opened then. This time it was not Wilkes or even the handsome new duke who had introduced himself to them. It was Valencia. At last.

Hazel's stomach filled with familiar rocks as her stepdaughter's dark eyes fell on her, cold as night.

"Daughter." Sutton greeted her, holding out an arm widely for her. "Come give us a kiss."

She dutifully moved forward to give her father a kiss. For Hazel, she treated her to a nod of acknowledgment. It was the most one could expect of her.

Sinking down onto the sofa across from them, she motioned to the tea service. "I see you've been provided refreshments."

"Yes, your Wilkes is ever attentive," Hazel said.

Valencia smiled humorlessly. "He is not my Wilkes anymore though. Is he?"

Her father thumped his cane on the floor. "To that point. Why did you not send for me when the duke arrived?"

Valencia shrugged and smoothed a hand over her skirts. "Would it have made any difference, Papa? He is the duke. He is here. I am the dowager. It is as simple as that. We have all known this was coming since the day my husband expired."

Hazel studied her stepdaughter. Always so cool and self-possessed. Nothing ever seemed to discompose her. She was very good at sporting her masks.

"Is he sending you packing?" Sutton demanded, color flooding his sallow face.

"Not yet."

"Yet?" Hazel could not help echoing.

Valencia looked at her frostily before returning her attention to her father. "I have agreed to help usher his sisters through the season."

A beat of silence fell before Sutton erupted, leaning over his cane. "You mean he will *use* you and then send you packing when he's done with you? Unacceptable!"

"Why should that strike you as so objectionable? Is that not something you have done with ladies over the years, Papa?" Angling her head, Valencia considered her father for a moment. "Use them and then discard them?"

A smile played about Hazel's lips. The woman was correct.

Sutton had taken his second wife months after his first wife expired, eschewing the rules of mourning, and even in that time, at all times, he kept a mistress whilst still cavorting with women all about Town.

He scoffed and waved a hand. "That is different, my girl."

"Why? How? Because *I* am not *them*?"

"Indeed you are nothing like them. You are better. You are *my* daughter. You are a duchess, dowager or no. And you're much too young and lovely to be cast aside and left to rot in the country."

Her lips compressed, and Hazel knew that Sutton's outrage did not work to endear him to her.

"So you are *permitted* to stay here . . . like a hired servant?" he sneered. "Essentially, a domestic."

"I do not mind, Papa." She folded her hands in her lap. Her gaze flicked to Hazel disdainfully. "It's a fair exchange. My expertise for room and board. Do you not agree, Hazel? You know something about the art of the trade."

Hazel crossed her arms, knowing it was a condemnation of her. Her past life as a courtesan, her present life as wife to Sutton. Although she suspected her stepdaughter resented her more for the latter. For daring to take her mother's place.

"Och!" Her father looked as though he were strangling. "Do not say such things. I cannot bear to see you two quarrel."

"You cannot? *You* cannot bear it? Funny, is it not? How you could bear for me to be unhappily married to Dedham all those years. He was horrible to me, Papa. You had to know that."

He knew. Just as Hazel knew. She had said as much to her husband on more than one occasion. They had spent many a holiday, many a dinner together, and Hazel had seen Dedham's subtle and not-so-subtle behavior. Valencia's flinches when he came too close, when he made any sudden move. She recognized such behavior for what it was, and she had done nothing. Nothing more than speak to Sutton about it, hoping he would intervene as Valencia's father.

Valencia was correct. Hazel should have tried harder to help her.

Sutton gave another thump of his cane. "You were at the apex of society as Dedham's wife. Any discomfort you felt as his wife was certainly worth that."

"He was a cruel man," Valencia rebutted. "And you did nothing."

Hazel made a move to approach, to lend comfort—she knew something of cruel men, after all, and what Valencia had endured—but Valencia sent her a withering look, stopping her cold.

"Don't," her stepdaughter commanded. "Do *not*."

Hazel nodded in acknowledgment.

A heavy silence fell.

Sutton sighed and reached for another scone. Biting into it, he chewed, considering his daughter as crumbs fell from his very thin lips. "Very well. You can move in with us."

Valencia flinched.

Hazel blinked.

Sutton fluttered his fingers. "Call for your maid. Let her know to begin packing your things."

Valencia laughed, shaking her head. "Oh, no. That is not an

option. As enticing as the offer is, I will be staying here." She rose slowly to her feet. "Now, if you will excuse me, I have much to do. As you can imagine, it is not a simple feat readying six girls for the season."

Sutton made a sound of disgust and struggled to his feet. His movements were more labored these days. Hazel stepped forward to take his elbow and offer assistance. "That sounds wretched," he muttered with a grimace.

Valencia smiled tightly. "Well, let us face it. That was never your forte. You did not even oversee my first season. You left that to Great-Aunt Helena. Other than signing the bridal contract, you did very little."

Valencia turned then and very properly walked them to the foyer.

"Good-bye, m'dear." Sutton pressed a kiss to her cheek.

"Good-bye, Papa," she replied in a stilted manner.

Hazel paused, sending her an encouraging look. "Best of luck to you, Valencia."

Valencia stared back mutely. For a moment, Hazel thought her expression softened, but then no. Nothing was there. Impassivity once again.

They took their leave.

Once in the comfort of their carriage, Sutton vented his spleen, pointing one gnarled finger to his chest. "It is a tragedy that a daughter of mine should be reduced to a glorified governess."

Hazel nodded in commiseration despite thinking that was perhaps a flawed assessment of the situation. She was a little surprised that her husband would empathize with Valencia's plight. She was, after all, a woman. And he was never particularly sensitive to the injustices dealt to women. Of course, she was his daughter. Of his own blood. That made her different. Special. His ego was affected. His vanity wounded. He viewed this as an attack on him, on his dignity.

"My daughter . . . a duchess cast out with the rubbish because she never gave Dedham an heir. Disgraceful. I expected Dedham to provide better for her."

Hazel blinked. Really? He expected better of Dedham?

The late duke had been frequenting houses of ill repute ever since he was a lad. She would know. Marriage to Valencia had not stopped him from indulging his proclivities. Sutton could not have been blind to all that. The two men had likely run into each other at such unsavory establishments.

Still, rather than argue with him, Hazel nodded. She did, after all, agree with him. Ultimately. It was unjust that after suffering her husband for so many years, Valencia now found herself at the mercy of yet another duke of Dedham.

"If she had given him a son, then she would be quite well situated."

That was the rub of it. Unfortunately, there was nothing to do about it. It was the way of things.

"I dread that for you, my dear. What happens when I am gone?"

She blinked at that and lifted a shoulder in a weak shrug. She was well acquainted with living without. She might have a full belly every day and sleep in silk sheets now, but she had not forgotten what it was like to do without.

"Let us not contemplate that."

She need not contemplate it, because she knew her fate once he was gone. Society would shun her as they had long wanted to do. She was only spared such treatment now, only tolerated and suffered by the *ton* and permitted into their drawing rooms, because her husband still drew breath. Because Sutton lived, and a marquess was not to be denied.

Valencia was the only person who *openly* disliked her. That did not mean everyone else liked her. Indeed not. Everyone else merely hid their contempt behind polite masks. Lied with eyes and words and deeds when they greeted her on the streets and in ballrooms. In that regard, Hazel almost appreciated Valencia. At least there was honesty between them. There was no artifice when it came to how Valencia felt about her.

"I will have my widow's jointure like Valencia." It would be enough. More than she had enjoyed as a child and a young woman making her way in the world. She would not go hungry. She would not be homeless.

"A pittance when you could remain in the house here in Town. And keep the family seat in the country."

She shook her head in confusion. "But I cannot . . . Only your heir can claim that—"

"My cousin's wastrel of a son, Martin." He grunted and shook his head. "That fool boy does not deserve it."

Hazel was not certain anyone deserved a marquessate. It was not a thing to be earned. It was given through a vagary of fate.

"Three young wives and not one could give me a son," he grumbled with an aggrieved sigh.

She resisted pointing out that he might have had something to do with that, also. He certainly played a role in the begetting of children.

He went on, "It is not fair. *You*. You should have had my heir."

She shrugged. "It was not to be."

"No! It should *be*. It should not be Martin." He thumped his cane on the floor of the carriage for emphasis. "You shall have my heir."

She stared, opening and closing her mouth as she sought for speech, wondering if he had lost his mind. Was this finally it? Had he descended into senility? The begetting of any heirs had long since passed for him. That time had come and gone. That much she knew with certainty.

Her husband was impotent.

She kept a cold bed these days. For years now. It was her comfort after making her living as a courtesan. She did not mourn the lack of company of a bedmate. Not in the slightest. She had earned this bit of peace for herself. She reveled in it—that her bedchamber was her own, her bed her own. *My body my own.* Sutton's curse had become her blessing, a true gift.

"My lord," she murmured. They were husband and wife, but she still clung to that formality between them. She knew he liked the deference, and she liked the space, the distance it inserted between them. "You cannot . . . We cannot . . ."

His hand patted her gloved one on the seat between them. "I must look to your future. I must do better for you, better than Dedham did for my own daughter."

"That is commendable, my lord, but . . . how can you . . ." She motioned in his general direction with a vague wave of her hand, treading carefully, having no wish to insult his virility—or rather, lack of virility.

He nodded with surety. "There are ways, m'dear."

Frowning, she stared at him, wondering at his air of confidence, wondering if he knew of some magic potion to cure him of his impotence.

A small shiver coursed through her as she imagined the pale, skeletal frame of her husband's body pressed to hers. She swallowed, fighting against the sudden thickness in her throat, a cold wind skimming over her skin. A tremor of apprehension rippled over her.

"Always a way," Sutton repeated with an enigmatic smile.

Chapter 11

The most cunning of suitors understand that the quickest
way to a debutante's heart is through her father.
—Valencia, the Dowager Duchess of Dedham

Rhain was sitting in his study when he spotted the dowager.
She crossed in front of his open door, passing through the
corridor.

In that brief glimpse, he saw that her head was bent, her pro-
file pensive, the elegant line of her neck stretched in a way that
he ought not find so very enticing. Even in that stolen glance
the dark brown wisps of her hair curling softly at her bare nape
snared his attention and made his heart thump a little faster.

The innocent sight struck him as anything but innocent. He
shifted in his seat, his body suddenly alive, tense . . . aware that
the view should not seem so very erotic. He felt like a green lad
caught up in the fervor of his first infatuation.

She did not even glance in the direction of the study as she passed, and he felt an inexplicable stab of disappointment. He frowned, not understanding himself.

It was not his custom to leave open the door of a room he occupied. With a houseful of women, an open door was an invitation for company. He had learned that from an early age. Even a closed door offered little protection. Most of his sisters were of the knock-once-and-enter-whether-he-bade-them-entry-or-not variety.

And yet he had left his door open. A decided invitation. Clearly not for his sisters or mother though.

It made him wonder if perhaps he wasn't hoping the dowager would be a little like his sisters and curious enough to pay him a visit.

Except she was not anything like them.

She was not like anyone he had ever known. Back home women vied for his attention. She was an entirely different breed of woman. Not curious, unimpressed and disinterested in him. He supposed that was natural given who she was. Why would a man like Rhain impress her? Her father was a marquess. She had been married to a duke. He possessed the hands of a common laborer.

His frown deepened until he was forced to acknowledge that he wanted her to lift her head and look into his study, to look at him. He wanted her to cross the distance and invade his privacy.

Invade me.

He sucked in a deep breath at the sudden and unwanted thought, at the sudden stir of his cock, annoyed with himself.

When he had greeted her haughty father and fully realized who she was, what she was, where she had come from in life, he had felt certain she would pack her things and leave with them that very day.

And why not?

A daughter of a marquess and the widow of a bona fide duke—not a man like him, who wasn't bred for the role—would not want to live beneath the same roof with him.

Certainly Sutton had arrived to help her, to rescue her. Rhain's offer to aid her in exchange for her assistance with his sisters felt rather embarrassing now. Insulting, even.

She did not need him. Her papa could set her up in grand style in Town in a house of her own. He certainly had the resources. She was his dear daughter. *Or* she could simply return home with Sutton. The dower house in Yorkshire was not her only option, as he had foolishly assumed. The marquess doubtlessly had an impressive home in some posh area of Town.

The agents of the estate never mentioned her high-placed papa, but that did not mean anything. They were rather remiss in what information they deemed relevant to impart—and everything concerning her had seemed irrelevant to them. Remarkable, really. How could anyone look at the Dowager Duchess of Dedham, how could anyone *talk* to her, and think she was inconsequential?

He cringed now, thinking of their arrangement. Why had she agreed to it?

He was no expert on the hierarchy of the peerage, but even he knew that a marquess was only one rung beneath a duke. It was a small exaggeration to call her a princess. The bluest of blood flowed through her veins.

Whilst his boyhood consisted of his family of fifteen crammed into a modest house with too few rooms, she had been pampered from birth. Whilst he'd slept on a pallet in the kitchen near the stove to stay warm at night, she'd had her own chamber and servants to wait on her. Wealth and privilege were the only things she had ever known, whereas he had come to such things only later in life.

With a muttered curse, he flung down the latest report on his mines from his chief foreman. The words had been swimming before his eyes ever since he sat at his desk.

He was on his feet and out in the corridor following her, far too agitated.

He had to know if she was leaving.

He had to know why she would have agreed to their *arrangement* in the first place when it obviously failed to benefit her.

He caught up with her before she entered her chamber.

"Your Grace," he began. She turned, and he noted a flush in her cheeks. He hesitated at the sight. "Are you unwell?"

"No," she said hastily but not very convincingly. "I am fine."

"How . . . was your visit? With the marquess and his ladyship?"

"Fine," she repeated quickly.

"Are you . . ." *How to ask this?* "Are you remaining here?"

She frowned. "Why would I not be, Your Grace?" Her chin lifted, and a militant light entered her eyes. "Have you changed your mind and are casting me out?"

"Of course not. It is only that your father and stepmother . . . Well, I thought you might have decided to depart with them."

"Why would I do that? We have an agreement, you and I." Her lovely dark eyes narrowed sharply on him. "Unless *you* have changed your mind?"

"No, no," he assured her. "I thought *you* might have though. I mean—" He expelled a breath and rubbed a hand along the back of his neck. "Your father is the Marquess of Sutton."

She nodded jerkily. "I am aware of who my father is. What does that have to do with our . . ." Comprehension lit her eyes. "Ohhh." She laughed lightly, shaking her head almost ruefully. "That is amusing. And sweet of you."

Sweet?

He could claim categorically that no one had ever accused him of being sweet.

She continued. "You think he might help me? That he might support me in the manner that you have offered, promising me my own house and money to live out my life independently and in relative comfort?"

He winced. "Well. He *is* your father."

She laughed mirthlessly then, her neck arching, exposing the fine line of her throat in a way that captured him, beckoned his fingers to touch, to stroke . . . to taste with lips and tongue. He gave himself a hard mental shake. When had the sight of a lady's neck ever aroused him?

She lowered her face, fastening her bright gaze on him again. "Oh, I see how that might have confused you, Your Grace. Don't tell me. You had one of those incredibly loving and altruistic fathers who put his children ahead of himself?"

"Ah..." He did not quite know how to answer. "My father was a good man," he admitted.

She nodded brusquely, looking every inch the haughty dowager. "Of course he was. Lucky for you and your sisters."

"I . . . Yes." Had he, only moments ago, been marveling over what must have been her silver-spoon upbringing? Now she was telling him that *he* had the enviable upbringing? It was a little jarring and something he would have to think more on later.

"Let me relieve you of your assumptions. My father is not the manner of man to swoop in here and rescue me. He is not like your father." She paused and looked him over carefully. "He is not like you. If he cared about rescuing me, he would have saved me from my husband years ago."

Those final words dropped like rocks, sinking in his stomach, and Rhain flinched. He let that settle over him . . . digesting the implication of her words.

If she needed saving from her husband, then that meant . . .

An awful silence stretched between them. His hands opened and closed into tight fists at his sides. With each passing moment, she looked more and more uncomfortable.

All manner of terrible notions filled his head, the ways in which a woman could be hurt . . . the ways *she* could have been hurt, the *years*, and it filled him with fury. Unfortunately, reprisal could not be inflicted. The bastard was already dead.

"What did he do to you?" he growled, looking her up and down as though he could see evidence of her old injuries.

The blood drained from her face. She shook her head, clearly regretting that she had let such an admission slip. "I . . . Nothing—"

"Tell me. Did he hurt you?" he cut in, already knowing the answer from her sudden pallor. There was nothing noble about his predecessor—his fucking kinsman. Everything in him squeezed tight, and he desperately longed to dig his long-lost relative up from the grave and kill him all over again as he deserved.

She finally found her voice and replied, "He's dead now. It doesn't matter."

He was dead. She was right about that. Except it mattered. It mattered to Rhain. It mattered if someone hurt her. Then or now, it mattered to him.

She mattered.

That was what it amounted to, and he gave himself yet another hard internal shake for his sudden intensity of feeling. He told himself he would feel this protective over any woman he knew, but especially any woman who resided beneath his roof.

"My apologies," he said, because he determined then that he would not be the cause of any more discomfort for her, and she appeared vastly uncomfortable with his interrogation. "I did not mean to pry."

Her lips twisted into a semblance of a smile. "And yet we seem to have become quite adept at prying into each other's lives since we have met."

He shrugged. "I suppose that is to be expected as we live in the same house."

She nodded. "Indeed. We best accustom ourselves to that." Her eyes glinted. "Because I have not changed my mind. I'm holding you to our agreement, Your Grace."

He inclined his head, feeling lighter than he had moments ago now that he knew she was still staying here. "Of course. Our agreement stands then."

He would not have it any other way.

Chapter 12

Widows enjoy many things. But nothing so much as freedom. Even better if there is the money to enjoy it.
—Valencia, the Dowager Duchess of Dedham

A few afternoons following the unwelcome visit of her father and stepmother, Valencia hastened through the upstairs corridor to change for a ride in the park with the girls. She was determined to evaluate the horsemanship of her young charges. They all insisted they were accomplished riders, so she was not too worried on that score. As there was no better place to be seen than Hyde Park, she looked forward to observing them as they showed off their seats to all the eligible gentlemen and, perhaps more importantly, the matchmaking mamas.

Just ahead of her, the door to the duke's study opened and a small group of starch-suited, stuffy gentlemen emerged.

The men paused at the sight of her and offered perfunctory bows.

"Your Grace," the most senior gentleman of the set intoned, his eyes blinking owlishly behind his spectacles. She remembered him well from their previous meetings. He looked searchingly at his companions and then back at her again, his nostrils flaring. "You are still here, then, I see."

Clearly this perplexed the man.

"I am. You see correctly," she agreed, enjoying the befuddled looks they swapped. As far as she was concerned, any aggravation she might suffer was only a good thing. She particularly enjoyed not fitting into the box they wished to forever keep her.

They might bow and scrape and address her as "Your Grace," but it was meaningless. It always had been. They did not respect her. They thought her worthless, her late husband's great failure—a wife who had not given him a child and fulfilled her end of the unspoken and yet understood bargain in a marriage.

"But the new duke has taken residence," the older gentleman added, as though she did not realize this.

"Yes. He has," she agreed once again, her tone admirably unruffled despite her mounting annoyance.

"But you should be at the dower house," one of his associates said, insisted, as though she needed to be enlightened on this point. *Men.* What would women do without being steered and bossed about by them?

She bristled now. "And yet . . . I am somehow here." She did not owe them an explanation, and they certainly were not in any position to interrogate her.

They tsked collectively as though this was an unacceptable response and they wielded authority over her. They were not her father or guardian or husband.

Merely the men to say how much or little money you can have.

She grimaced. Indeed. Only that.

The elder bespectacled gentleman looked her up and down with nothing short of exasperation. "Your Grace, this is simply not done." He pushed his spectacles up the bridge of his nose and gestured around them. "Your time here has come to an end, and you must retire to the dower house. Have some dignity. Do not make this more uncomfortable than it needs to be."

Uncomfortable? For whom? She blinked, her face overly warm.

She inhaled a seething breath, quite finished being shoved about in life. No husband or father controlled her. Not any longer. Nor did these bloody men.

She had thought to never endure this again. She had thought widows enjoyed a unique kind of freedom. That was the lie fed to her as an unhappily married lady, a carrot dangled just out of her reach for so many years.

But she supposed that was simply a dream beyond reach. Even a widow was a woman, after all, and what woman enjoyed any true power in this life ruled by men? Even the bright future looming ahead of her now could be snatched away in an instant if the new duke changed his mind.

"Do you understand what I'm telling you, Your Grace?"

She opened her mouth, uncertain how to reply when nothing she said ever seemed to matter to these gentlemen. They expected only one thing from her and that was submission.

The door to the study opened again, and the duke himself stepped out, looking tall and imposing as ever. The sunlight from the window at the end of the corridor landed on him, catching and turning his hair a burnished brown.

His gaze swept over all of them. "Gentlemen, you still linger here." It was a statement, but there was an inquiry in his voice, mingling alongside a bored idleness. The word *why* hung unspoken. He didn't understand *why* they still lingered.

"Ah, yes. Apologies, Your Grace. We just happened upon the dowager here and were explaining to her that she need not remain here any longer, that she should retire to the dower house posthaste . . ."

The duke's expression turned frosty. "Why would her comings and goings be any of your concern?"

The gentlemen blinked in clear astonishment at the blunt question, then looked at one another uncertainly.

The older man cleared his throat and pushed the spectacles up his nose again. "As agents of the estate—"

"You manage the estate," the duke cut in. "You do not manage *her*." He nodded in her direction. "The dowager is not under your purview."

The old man's face reddened. He blustered, but no intelligible words surfaced.

The duke continued in the suddenly fraught space. "You need not concern yourself with the lady, Hollinger. I assume her stipend has been released to her. Unless you have anything to impart regarding the dower house, which remains available to her in any way she sees fit . . . as a permanent residence or a country house, you have no cause to speak to her."

"Of course, Your Grace." He nodded with hauteur. "And as for her stipend, we see that the funds from it are released in a timely order."

The duke frowned. "I don't understand. Does she or does she not have full possession of her stipend?"

"Well. Every fortnight we portion out a sum from her stipend as an allowance—"

"No," he pronounced flatly.

No?

As Valencia could attest, that was precisely what they had done over the past year. Once a fortnight, every Monday morning, an envelope was delivered with the funds *they* deemed sufficient for her needs. There was no negotiation. No petitioning for more than they considered acceptable.

"I beg your pardon, Your Grace, but it is the truth." The older man huffed. "We most certainly do. You can see our account ledgers if you don't believe me."

"Oh. I believe you have been doing that, but it shall cease at once." He looked at Valencia then, his deep gaze holding hers. "The entirety of her stipend shall be released to her for her keeping, posthaste."

She played back his words in her mind, certain that she had misunderstood. Had he really used the word *entirety*?

After a beat of stunned silence, all three agents blustered in fierce protest.

"Your Grace!"

"Absurd! What nonsense!"

"A woman cannot manage funds! It is not done!"

"Females haven't the mind for it!"

"Enough," his voice boomed over the offensive remarks. His eyes turned to flint as he addressed the gentlemen, and in this he was more a king than a duke. "There is nothing that stipulates her stipend be given out in dribs and drabs. That is what you decided to do, no?"

After a long moment Hollinger nodded. "Yes. 'Tis for her own good though, Your Grace. We simply wished to protect her. Financial matters are too much for a lady's delicate sensibilities."

My own good . . .

His words disgusted her but served as no surprise. No, the surprise came from the duke, who disagreed with this philosophy.

"Such a decision does not belong to you," he continued. "Release her funds to her in full sum. See it is done."

Her surprise only mounted. She gaped at him. What was he doing? What was he saying?

"Your Grace," one of the younger men in the group began, with a conciliatory smile that was the height of insult, "you are new here, new to the title. You do not yet understand—"

"I know you are not questioning me," he growled. "That much I *understand*."

The conciliatory smile vanished. The agent shot a worried glance at his colleagues, grasping that he had overstepped.

"Of course, Your Grace." Hollinger put a hand on the younger man's arm, silencing him from spouting further nonsense. "It shall be done." He looked at Valencia then with a cool gaze. "I will settle the matter at once for you, Your Grace." After a final quelling look at his young companion, he nodded deferentially to the duke.

The duke nodded in approval and gestured in clear dismissal. "You may be on your way now, gentlemen. I will send for you if I have need."

If I have need.

Valencia fought back a smile. As soon as the trio was out of sight, she addressed him. "You seem rather adept in your new role, Your Grace."

"Do I?"

"Yes. I quite enjoyed watching them depart with their tails tucked. I do believe you have mastered the domineering qualities required of a duke."

He shrugged. "It must come naturally. I confess, I have received no formal training."

She studied him closely, catching the wicked gleam in his brown eyes. He was jesting with her.

"How convenient for you," she tossed back.

They stood there then, each smiling, the air swelling with something between them that felt *good.*

Dangerously good.

She moistened her lips, and his gaze dropped, following the motion. Her stomach fluttered as though holding a thousand butterflies.

After a few moments, she sobered and inhaled, struggling against the sudden thought, the sudden rise of troubling feelings swirling around inside her. It should not be that a mere word from him could save her. It was not fair. A simple decision that cost him nothing . . . ought not affect her so greatly.

She knew she sounded like a petulant child, but it was not *bloody* fair.

Resentment bubbled up inside her that one word from him should result in so much positive change in her life—that he could do for her what she could not do for herself. It was galling. She acknowledged that her resentment was bubbling up from another place, too. Another deep well of emotions.

He *knew.*

He knew more than her own friends did about her, about what she had lived through, about her past. He knew what manner of man and husband Dedham had been.

He knew the dark things she hid. Not the details, but he knew enough. That she had been hurt. That his own bastard kinsman had not provided for her beyond his death other than what the dukedom demanded as a basic entitlement to the dowager duchess.

It was enough to make her feel seen straight down to the bone. Exposed. Vulnerable. It was a wholly uncomfortable sensation, and she did not know what that made him to her exactly, but it made him something.

It made him someone suddenly significant in her life.

"I suppose I should thank you." Not that she wished to, but she knew she ought to say the words. She owed him that . . . and that was the bloody crux of it all. Despite the words of gratitude she expressed, her tone was not appreciative.

He considered her with a touch of bewilderment. "For what?"

"For doing what they never would have done on their own." She gestured to where the agents once stood with a motion that conveyed all her disgust. "I would have continued receiving my stipend in small amounts every fortnight well into my old age."

"You owe me no gratitude. The money is yours. Not theirs. Not mine. It should not have been withheld."

And yet it had been. Because of him she would now have access to all of it.

Perhaps she could invest some of it. She would have to be smart about it. A modest venture, but a way in which to grow her income even if only moderately.

Her chest swelled a little at the prospect, at the knowledge that she now had some control. At long last. She could truly be her own woman, and a woman of enterprise at that.

"Just the same, it would not have happened without you." She stared at him, beginning to see him . . . and beginning to realize that she, too, was not being very fair. Her resentment was misplaced.

It was not fair to blame him for *helping her* and being an honorable man. He did not create this world, but through helping her he was taking a stand against it.

It was also not right to fault him for knowing who she was . . . for knowing her secrets. She should not punish him with a surly attitude. He was not like the men she had been exposed to all her life. Not her father or Dedham. Or those three men who had just departed who thought her too incapable, too dim, too fragile to manage her own money. "I am certain to you it does not seem a great deal of money—"

"Because it is not."

She flinched, shamed in a way she should not have been. It was not her fault that her husband had left her so little, that he'd left her with just enough to live out her days in humble gentility.

Before she could add anything more, he continued. "I will increase your stipend to something more respectable."

She blinked. "You cannot mean—"

"I decided on this before we even met, when I first learned the amount left to you."

Shaming heat crept up her neck and face. *The paltry amount.* The words weren't spoken, but she heard them nonetheless. "Oh, no. You needn't do—"

"Accept it. It is not a gift. It was your husband's money, left to me, a stranger. You should have it, by rights. It is only fair. It is your due."

And there she heard it in his voice again. The censure. The disdain for a dead man. *More* than disdain. He thought her husband had failed her.

He thought him a right bastard, and her heart swelled within her chest, feeling as though this man were on her side—an ally to help her even though her husband was dead now and could harm her no more.

The truth was glaring. This duke taking her husband's place was a decent man. Good and decent in a way her Dedham had not been. Decent in a way she had never known men could be.

She stood there in the corridor struggling with that realization, struggling against her softening feelings for him. It was not something she would have thought when she first met him on the barge. Or even the next afternoon when he showed up and ordered her gone from the house.

And yet it was becoming irrefutably evident now.

"When you are finished ushering my sisters through Society, you can choose where to go. You shall have income enough to continue on to the dower house if that is your wish or to remain in London in a house of your own."

You can choose. Choices. Thanks to him she had those now.

She stared up at him, a lump forming in her throat as she became lost in the depths of his gaze. Her gentling feelings became too much then.

Unthinkingly, she stretched out a hand to touch him, yearning to do so. She could hear her heart beating in her ears as they stared into each other's eyes.

At the last moment she caught herself, stopping and pulling her hand back, remembering herself and what was proper in this moment. Then that word jarred her.

Proper.

What did she care about what was proper?

She was a widow now. She could do what she wanted to do, touch whom she wanted to touch . . . within reason, of course.

Within reason.

That was the sticking point. Reasonable would not be dallying with the *new* Duke of Dedham. Reasonable would not be harboring feelings for her late husband's kinsman. The man with whom she presently shared a house.

That would be decidedly complicated *and* unreasonable, to be certain. And yet she could perhaps explore that side of herself—that *im*proper side of herself. She could satisfy her needs. Just not with this man. She could find some other man, discreetly, to feed the fire within her. He could not be the only one out there who stirred her.

With her hand pressed firmly to her side again, her fingers curling inward, nails digging into her tender palm, she said instead, in a properly neutral voice, "You are too kind . . . Your Grace."

He was looking down to where her hand buried into her skirts. Clearly he had noticed her movement. He'd marked it and knew she had almost touched him.

He looked up at her face again. His jaw seemed to tighten, a muscle feathering beneath the taut skin that only—unfairly—made him more attractive. How was that right? A scowl did not make her prettier. It should not make him more handsome.

"I am not a kind man. Not soft or easy or *kind*. Never make that mistake, Valencia."

Valencia.

He said her name and in such a way, with that burr in his voice. She ceased to breathe, holding his stare, marveling at his hard words combined with the intimate use of her name that sent ripples over her skin. It was all dreadfully confusing.

With a single nod, he turned and disappeared back inside his study, closing the door behind him with a click.

She remained there, staring at his door in deep contemplation.

Why did it matter to him that she *not* think him good and decent? It was almost as though he wanted her to dislike him. She had a flash of that grumpy, taciturn man on the boat, and the rude man in the drawing room. She had not liked him upon either of those occasions, but the more time she spent around him, she was beginning to see there was more to him than what he had revealed in those moments.

"Your Grace?" a soft voice behind her inquired, jarring her from her thoughts and reminding her she was not in a position to expect privacy in the middle of the day in the corridor of a bustling house—only further validation that putting her hands on the duke would have been a bad idea.

She turned to find a familiar kitchen maid there. "Yes, Jenny?"

"You told me to let you know when my father has arrived. He is downstairs in the kitchen now."

She stared at the girl for a few moments before remembering. "Oh, yes." She had almost forgotten she asked Jenny to send for him. "That is brilliant, Jenny. Thank you. Let us not keep your father waiting. I appreciate him coming so quickly. He has brought them with him, then?"

"Yes." The maid grinned. "A fine selection. You will be most pleased."

Valencia nodded and started for the kitchen, eager to see for herself.

Chapter 13

A duke is very nice, but the heir to a dukedom? Even better.
—Mrs. Maeve Bernard-Hill

Valencia's skirts swished swiftly at her ankles as she strode hurriedly through the house. She had much to do. She'd been up since dawn, preparing for this important night for the Lloyd sisters. It would be a busy day for them all.

She had already breakfasted with three of the sisters. Isolde, Bronwen, and Nesta were the early risers of the family. The others, including Mrs. Lloyd, preferred to sleep late. They even sometimes took a tray in their beds.

The dancing instructor would be arriving in an hour along with the musicians Valencia had scheduled so that the girls might have a proper practice before their first soirée. Additionally, in the afternoon, the girls had voice lessons with Mrs. Singh. Valencia had decided the girls did not have time enough to learn the pianoforte, but they could hone their singing voices at least with the talented Mrs. Singh. And following all of that, tonight they would be putting an appearance in at the opera. The girls' first official outing. It would be significant. A vital moment in their coming out.

They would not be required to do much more than watch the performance and look lovely for gawking eyes. Not too much pressure. No dancing or, God forbid, dining. If anything, they would appear elusive and intriguing. It would, indeed, be quite the busy day.

She peeked inside the ballroom to make certain the staff had arranged some chairs and a dais for the musicians. Following that, she turned, intent on making certain the other girls were awake and readying themselves for the day.

She marched down the corridor determinedly. A soft giggle made her stop and glance around. She was alone in the stretch of hallway. All the nearby doors were closed. Pausing, she listened until she heard it again. Whispers. Giggles.

She inched toward each door, listening at them until she concluded the voices came from one particular room—the billiards room.

Pressing her ear to that door, she confirmed it was occupied. She placed her hand on the latch, ready to interrupt what she assumed would be two members of the staff trysting. She wasn't so naive to think that never happened. There was a time and place for that, however, and it was not in the middle of the day in the billiards room.

Suddenly the door swung open, nearly bumping her nose. She jumped back.

"Oh!" Tildie emerged, cheeks flushed prettily. Her eyes widened when she spotted Valencia. "Your Grace," she breathed, sending an alarmed glance over her shoulder.

"Tildie," she said rather lamely, surprised to find her maid emerging from the room. Tildie was always so circumspect. She would not have thought her the type to engage in a dalliance in her place of service.

Valencia followed her gaze, expecting to see one of the handsome grooms appear behind her.

She felt her eyes widen in her face. It was not a groom, however. Indeed not. It was not *any* member of the household staff.

Valencia's breath caught, the air freezing in her lungs at the sight of the duke's very dapper and charming cousin from the barge, the affable Dewey. He smiled warmly at her as though he had not just been caught alone in a room with her lady's maid . . . up to what was undoubtedly unsuitable behavior. The gall of the man!

It was not the first time she had seen him since the barge, although she had not come directly face-to-face with him beneath this roof. Truthfully, she had avoided him, too embarrassed over the spectacle she had made of herself en route to Vauxhall. She supposed it was inevitable they meet again, however.

He had been a frequent visitor over the past couple of weeks, calling upon his cousin. She was aware of that, of him, as she was aware of everything that happened in this house. It was her role to know. That much had not changed. It never would as long as she lived and breathed under this roof.

This *dalliance*, however, had somehow slipped beneath her notice, and she could not say she approved of it. Questions whirled in her mind. When had Dewey even met Tildie? How long had this *relationship* been taking place? It could not have been very long . . . The duke had been in residence only a fortnight now. Dewey had no opportunity to meet and interact with Tildie before then.

She was not comfortable with any gentleman toying with Tildie's affections, but this gentleman smiled too much. He was always flashing those teeth of his like some kind of devouring wolf. Even though he had been the one to dive into the Thames and rescue her, there was something about him that made her slightly ill at ease. He would have been precisely the type of man to charm her at eighteen, but she was a different person now—a woman who learned discernment when it came to men.

"Well, good day, Your Grace! Good day to you!" He wore a green morning jacket that appeared slightly rumpled, and she could only guess it was from Tildie's roaming hands. His brown eyes reminded her slightly of the new duke's. For all their warmth, they were a little flat and a fraction smaller, but a similar brown. But not the same fathomless, gleaming wells that inspired a riot of butterflies in the pit of her belly.

"Er. Hello, again, sir," she returned stiffly, her gaze seeking Tildie, who seemed far too interested in the shape of her shoes in that moment.

He stepped forward and bowed very handsomely over her hand. "It is a pleasure to formally meet you. I am Dewey Pugh, your Dedham's cousin."

She flinched at that, his use of *your* chafing her. The new duke ... Rhain ... was not *hers* in any way.

He continued. "Such a small world, is it not? To meet again after our earlier meeting en route to Vauxhall. And then to learn of your connection to Rhain. Why, you're practically kin!" He leaned in slightly. "Shall I call you cousin, too?"

She flushed, thinking it generous of him to not directly detail the indignity of that first encounter. And yet kin they were not. He was no more kin to her than Rhain was.

"If you like ..." She supposed it would have been rude of her to deny him.

There was nothing about him that struck her as familial. Not in his flirtatious manner or the fact that she had just caught him in a compromising situation with her lady's maid. The man had cheek, to be sure.

He seized her by the fingertips, bending over her hand to press a fervent kiss to the back of her bare fingers in a rather unnerving display of familiarity. Her questioning gaze sought Tildie again.

The woman's face was stained scarlet now, but she said not a word.

Valencia cleared her throat. "And you know Tildie, I see."

You more than know her. The beastly man was making free with her lady's maid. *Unacceptable.*

As much as Valencia had been led about and controlled and

hurt by men throughout her life, she knew it was worse for women without the privilege of wealth or rank. Someone like Tildie, without a father or brother or deep pockets, was especially vulnerable. She felt a responsibility to Tildie, to make certain she was not being taken advantage of—even by flashy gentlemen with pretty manners. *Especially* by such men.

"Ah, yes." He turned then to acknowledge the woman he had been cloistered away with inside the billiards room. "The lovely Tildie."

Lovely indeed.

"And please," he insisted, looking back at Valencia, "you must call me cousin, too."

Must she? Valencia nodded even though that was the last thing she would ever do. She would sooner stick a fork in her eye.

"Dewey," a hard voice declared.

They all three turned at the arrival of the duke. He strode across the foyer toward them, his boots thudding over the carpet.

"You are early. I thought you were not coming until this afternoon." Even as the duke spoke to his cousin, his gaze remained fixed on Valencia with an intensity that was becoming far too familiar.

"I am early," Dewey Pugh confirmed unhelpfully. "I woke hungry, famished, really. Then I realized you must have an impressive breakfast buffet here daily, with your houseful of people and, well, you are a right proper duke now . . ." His voice faded suggestively.

And she supposed he thought to help himself to her maid alongside his eggs and toast? She looked him over distrustfully.

The pause held, stretched, and Valencia realized that the duke was not going to pick up on his cousin's unsubtle hint for food.

"Mr. Pugh," she began.

"Ah-ah." He wagged a finger. "Call me cousin."

Ah. No.

Wincing a little, she continued. "Would you care for breakfast?"

"Cousin?" The duke frowned. "Why should she call you that?"

"I invited the dowager to call me cousin," he said, as though it were perfectly logical. "As we are all practically related now, and it only seemed—"

"We are not *all* practically related here," the duke cut in, with a look of exasperation. He gestured to Valencia. "In fact, we are not related to the dowager in any fashion."

She held back her glare. As much as she agreed with him, clearly the notion of her as a kinswoman to him was unpalatable. His reaction was mildly insulting. The man had approximately five hundred sisters. What was one more female in his family tree?

"Well, I disagree. She is the late duke's wife." Dewey Pugh shot Valencia a properly sympathetic look at this rather insensitive mention. "Rest his soul." He looked back to his cousin. "You are the new duke. And I'm your cousin. Clearly that connects us in some way."

"Connects, yes," the duke agreed, looking at Valencia in an assessing manner. "But makes us family? No."

Valencia decided it was time to put an end to this. "Mr. Pugh, may I escort you to the dining room?" She really had no wish to be in his company, but she would not leave the task to Tildie. He might compromise her softhearted maid along the way. It would also present her with the opportunity to warn him off Tildie. She would not blindly turn an eye from his behavior. If he was respectfully and properly interested in Tildie he could formerly court her. No more having his way with her behind closed doors or in darkened corners. She would let him know that in no mincing terms.

Together, she and Dewey Pugh turned to proceed down the corridor, when a small ball of fur erupted around the corner.

"*What* is that?" the duke demanded.

"Why, it's a dog," she replied evenly, as though it was the most obvious thing in the world. Or a puppy, rather.

The brown-and-white spaniel reached them and spun in ecstatic circles around their legs. He was blindingly fast, his plump little body wriggling with joy.

"I can see it's a dog." The duke frowned, looking back and forth between her and the animal. "What is it doing *here*?"

Mr. Pugh reached down to pet him with an exclamation of delight. "What a handsome pup!"

"Well." She paused a beat. "*He* lives here now."

The duke blinked, watching as the dog chose that moment to squat and relieve himself before them, leaving a bright puddle on the runner.

Tildie gasped, her hands flying to her mouth.

Mr. Pugh chuckled.

The duke swore. "Why was I not consulted about this?" he demanded.

The little beast then decided to direct his attention to the duke. Perhaps the puppy detected his less-than-happy tone. He growled and jumped up on one of the duke's legs, leaving wet paw prints on his trousers as he let loose a frenzy of aggressive yips.

She closed her eyes in a miserable blink. It was not the introduction she had imagined between these two.

The duke glared at her in accusation. "What made you think bringing a puppy into our household amid the mayhem of my sisters was a good idea? Do you not have enough to do managing the six of them?"

She bristled at his tone, disliking being taken to task—especially in front of his cousin and her maid. A flush of embarrassment heated her face.

"Tildie," she said tightly. "Please escort Mr. Pugh to the dining room for breakfast." She sent Dewey Pugh a sharp look, aware that she was tossing the woman to the wolves. Or wolf, rather. "I trust that you will both reach there with no detours, Mr. Pugh."

His smile faded.

"It should take no longer than two minutes," she pressed, not caring that she fully conveyed her displeasure with him. "I will know if you tarry longer than that." He needed to know she did not approve of him toying with the woman. She sent a warning look to Tildie for good measure.

The young woman ducked her head in agreement. "Of course, Your Grace. And I will send someone to clean the carpet."

"Thank you, Tildie."

They strolled away. Valencia waited until they were out of sight and then bent down to scoop up the puppy into her arms. She stroked him between the ears where his fur was the softest. "Have no fear. I am attending to your sisters as we agreed, Your Grace." She hefted the dog a bit higher in her arms as though to demonstrate. "That is precisely what I am doing with this little darling."

"Little darling?" He glanced to the wet puddle on the once fine carpet with an arched eyebrow. "I do not see how adding an undisciplined puppy to our lives is helpful . . ." His voice faded then as Isolde rounded the corner, breathing heavily. Valencia deliberately discounted his use of *our*. She would not allow herself to feel any warmth at his clearly unintentional blunder.

"Ah, there he is!" Isolde rushed forward to embrace the wiggling puppy, lifting his plump little body from Valencia's arms with a clucking tongue, then bestowing a kiss on his sweet nose. "I've been looking everywhere for him. He snuck away."

"Isolde," Rhain said in greeting, frowning down at his sister.

She cooed at the squirming animal. "Come now, Caesar, time for your walk. Perhaps you can make some other puppy friends whilst we're out." The young woman grasped his paw and forced him to wave good-bye to Valencia and the duke.

They watched her skip away with her new pet.

After a moment, Valencia asked, "Notice anything different about your sister, Your Grace?"

He angled his head thoughtfully before comprehension lit his eyes. "She was not holding Poppet."

As had been Valencia's plan when she asked Jenny if her father could bring his recent litter of puppies to the house.

"Precisely." She let that settle for a moment and then continued. "Caesar was the cutest one in the litter, and your sister forgot all about Poppet the moment she clapped eyes on him. As I said, I am holding up my end of our agreement."

Still annoyed with him and satisfied her point had been made, she turned to go. He stopped her with a hand on her arm. "What did you mean when you told Dewey to take no detours?"

"Ah. Yes. That. I found your cousin alone with my lady's maid in the billiards room."

"I see. And am I to assume they were not playing billiards?"

She snorted. "No. They were not. Your cousin is a bit of a philanderer, I fear."

He settled back on his heels, his grasp loosening on her arm. "Indeed? I will speak with him, rest assured. It will not happen again. I am certain he will not—"

"You are so certain of his character, then? You would vouch for him?"

A determined look came across his face. "He will stay away from her. You have my word on that. He can be trusted."

"Oh?" She arched a skeptical eyebrow. "Can he?" Life had taught her that few men could be trusted . . . especially when it came to how they treated the women in their orbit.

"Yes. He can . . . which is why I've asked him to manage my affairs here once I am gone."

She frowned. "Gone?"

"Aye. Once I have returned to Wales."

She shook her head in confusion. "Return to Wales? But you are the Duke of Dedham."

"Dewey is a bookkeeper by trade. He is competent. A clever man. A kinsman I can trust. He can manage matters here in my stead."

"I do not understand." He was needed here. A dukedom was not something one turned over to someone else's care, kinsman or no. She knew blood ties did not always translate to loyalty and devotion. She need only think of her father to confirm that in her mind.

"He is not the duke," she explained. "You are."

"I did not ask to be."

"And yet you are. All this"—she motioned around her—"is your responsibility."

He inhaled thinly. "It's just a house."

"What of the staff?" she pressed. "The tenants in the country? You'll leave them to someone else? These are lives, people. You would trust them to someone else?"

He stared at her for a long moment. She started to hope she had reached him, that she had persuaded him. Then he shook his head once, hard and decisive, his features like granite, resembling so little of that decent man she had decided him to be.

"You need only concern yourself with our agreement. Anything else is none of your affair."

She felt his words like a slap to the face.

Refusing to be cowed, she pressed on. "And what of your sisters?"

They were her concern. Most definitely. He had made them so. He had brought his sisters here to find husbands, to tackle London Society, and he had enlisted her to help them. Would he simply abandon them right here alongside his dukedom?

"They are not children anymore. If they wish to stay here and marry Englishmen, then so be it. The choice is theirs."

Valencia blinked at that, unaccustomed to the notion of autonomy given so readily to young ladies. It was very forward-thinking of him. And yet she was still appalled at his rejection of the dukedom and all its obligations. He thought he could simply hand off his responsibilities to some underling . . . to Dewey Pugh's dubious care?

She shook her head, grappling with her frustration and disappointment in him. It wasn't her place to have any expectations of him.

And yet . . .

"And that's it?" she demanded, searching his face. "You'll leave them and go and that's it?"

"I have a life waiting for me. Responsibilities. I don't know what you want from me."

I want you to say you will stay.

The words welled up in her chest, pressing behind her teeth. Stupid, foolish, ridiculous words. She swallowed them down with great effort and nodded. "Nothing. I don't want anything from you, Your Grace."

Something flickered in his eyes. It was just a flash of emotion.

Impossible to decipher, and then it was gone, the deep impenetrable brown back again.

His hand dropped from her arm. He gave a curt nod and turned away without another word, leaving her standing there seething in frustration and disappointment and determined to feel differently—to find some way, something, *someone* . . . to make her feel differently, even if only for a night. Someone who did not hide himself from her.

It reminded her that before the new duke arrived, she had been on the cusp of something. On the verge of claiming her independence, seizing enjoyment for herself, discovering adventure . . . playing within the *ton* as only a young widow could do.

Perhaps it was time to get back to doing that.

Chapter 14

The last thing you want is to be noticed by the ton.
The thing you most want? To be noticed by the ton.
—Valencia, the Dowager Duchess of Dedham

The Duke of Dedham's opera box offered one of the best vantages in the theater. Valencia was well familiar with the box and its view. From its perch, the occupants could watch and be watched perfectly by members of the audience as well as by occupants in other nearby boxes. Oh, and the stage was nicely visible, too, but that was the lesser consideration, of course.

As delightful as the evening's entertainment was slated to be, no one came to the opera to watch the performance. That would be a naive assumption. They came to see and be seen. The performance most anticipated was not up on the stage but all around them. It was in the real-life drama happening . . . everywhere.

"This is all terribly exciting." Isolde peered through her opera glasses, staring more at the assembling audience than the curtained stage or the orchestra warming up in the pit. Naturally.

"Everyone is so beautiful," Elin murmured nervously, her face a little wan as she looked down. Her fine throat worked as she swallowed.

Valencia reached out and covered her gloved hand with her own, giving it a squeeze. "And you are, too, my dear. So lovely. All of you are." She swept her gaze over the gathered group—all nine of them—properly pleased with herself and all she had wrought in so short a time. Not that it had been difficult to improve upon their appearance.

There was no doubt about it. The Lloyd family was passing fair, and they were on full display this evening. And not only the women of the family sparkled.

Her gaze drifted to the one gentleman in their midst, the only man in their family, impressive and stalwart, sitting so tall and erect in his seat, shoulders broad in his evening jacket. He drew his fair share of attention, too.

Her attention, for instance. Her gaze never strayed far from him, but she was not the only woman looking at him. Indeed not. The duke was striking. He would be striking standing on a street corner, an anonymous gentleman without the title of duke hanging over his head. The title was only an added inducement.

Valencia forced her gaze off him and surveyed the opera house in a quick glance, noting the dewy-eyed debutantes craning their necks to gawk at him in the box, *and* the bent heads of conniving mamas dipped together in earnest conversation. About him. About his sisters.

Valencia knew *she* was not a point of interest. She was just another dowager of the *ton*. One of many. Too many to count. Another dowager with nothing to offer. She had no dowry as she had at the tender age of nineteen. She was no longer a blushing virgin. She could not even tempt a man with the promise of progeny. They would merely look at her many fruitless years with Dedham as proof that she was barren. In the eyes of Society, she was the equivalent of the impoverished silver-haired widows to populate the *ton*.

And perhaps she was the same as them, without the silver hair. It did not matter anymore. At least not to her. She had ceased to harbor aspirations of motherhood. She never intended to remarry and rekindle that long-ago dream.

Now she had new dreams.

The duke and his sisters represented a windfall of riches to several as-yet-unknown members of the *ton*. As gazes locked on him and his, she read the speculation, the hunger, the matrimonial hope in their eyes, and recognized what she was seeing. They longed to be the lucky recipients of those riches.

The Duke of Dedham had landed on London, and they were ready to devour him. It was hard to envision him as prey when he was sitting beside her as such a larger-than-life presence. Confident and casual, one hand resting idly on the arm of his chair, he more resembled the wolf than the lamb.

Dressed darkly head to foot, with a crimson cravat knotted impeccably at his neck, he was a feast for the eyes and doubtlessly triggering all manner of machinations in the marriage-minded mamas and papas in attendance.

Valencia knew at once. They would soon be besieged with invitations, which, of course, was the objective of this night's foray.

Elin smiled shakily and sent Valencia an appreciative glance for her kind words. "Thank you."

She had not been effusive in her praise. They were truly lovely. All six of them. *Seven*. Even Mrs. Lloyd glittered brightly in her gown of amber muslin, like a shining topaz in their midst. It would not surprise Valencia if she attracted a suitor, as well, for she was a handsome woman *and* the mother of a duke, after all. A connection not to be dismissed lightly.

She felt a swell of pride as she looked over her charges. All of her efforts had come to fruition. No box could boast six young ladies so well appointed. Their gowns, their elegantly coiffed hair, the jewels adorning their throats and earlobes, wrists and fingers—all of it was flawlessly orchestrated.

They were a remarkable tableau, and she had no doubt that every gentleman and mama in attendance had learned their identities. Tomorrow they would wake to a flood of invitations. Everyone was busy settling into their seats, but that did not stop the whispering or the rapt faces from looking upward and pointing at the Dedham box.

Valencia continued, saying meaningfully, "And I am not the only one admiring your loveliness."

The sisters tittered and actually appeared bashful—something she would not have thought possible upon first meeting the conquering viragos.

Mrs. Lloyd slapped her ornate jade fan on the air, her expression one of supreme satisfaction as she fanned herself.

The duke, seated beside her, rolled his eyes.

Valencia leaned into him. "I should think you would be pleased at your sisters' success. Is that not the point of all this?" She motioned around them. The point of their arrangement. She would not be here otherwise.

After some moments, he replied, "It is what they want, yes."

She considered that. "And that is what matters to you."

"Precisely," he agreed. "Would I be happier if they remained in Wales like our other sisters?" He shrugged in acknowledgment that he would very much prefer that. "It is their choice."

Wales. Where he would return once he was satisfied his sisters were properly settled, leaving the dukedom in the hands of someone else.

Resentment that she ought not to feel stirred in her heart. It was none of her concern what the new duke did (or did not do) with his dukedom and where he chose to reside. It should not affect her in any way. She would be happily ensconced in her new home in London by then with a stipend that would comfortably support her. What did it matter if he was somewhere else? If he was somewhere she was not?

"It is their choice. I see. And yet you will grumble and roll your eyes through all of it. How very fatherly of you," she teased. Except not like any father she had known.

Her papa had never been so indulgent. Most Society papas were not. Nor did they give their daughters something so democratic as a choice.

Valencia's papa had scarcely been around in her youth, too busy chasing women other than her mother. When she had come out in Society, he had paid attention only when Dedham showed up to ask for her hand.

"I'm not their father," he said.

"You're acting in his place though."

"Of course. I'm their brother." He declared this as though that were explanation enough. Again, she knew what he meant only in theory. Protective papas or brothers were not something she had ever experienced firsthand.

"Valencia! I had no idea you were going to be here!"

Valencia shot to her feet at the new arrival to their box.

"Delia!" She greeted her warmly, hugging her young friend, a glittering jewel in a gown of shimmering blue. She looked so much like her mother, and that was no insignificant thing.

Tru was admired throughout London, and not only for her beauty. She was a doyen of *ton*, leading the way in fashion, Society, and everything else.

Valencia peered over her shoulder. "Is your mother here?"

"No, she and Jasper had other plans this evening."

It came as no surprise to anyone that the Dowager Countess of

Chatham was already betrothed a mere year after the passing of her husband. Like Valencia, Tru had been married to a wretched man, but *unlike* Valencia she chose to risk it all again, to cast aside her newfound independence and enter into the state of matrimony for a second time. As much as her betrothed appeared to be the complete antithesis of Tru's late husband, Valencia could not fathom taking such a risk.

Even Tru's and Delia's mannerisms were similar. Delia's gloved hand pushed back an errant curl from her forehead in a gesture that echoed her mother. The resemblance between them was uncanny. Even without her rank and connections, Delia was an enticement for any gentleman. Her beauty would not fade. One need only look at her mother to confirm that.

Delia was in the midst of her second season. She had been hailed as the darling of the season last year. She would have received countless offers and been wed by now if not for her father's sudden death. Now that she had completed her necessary year of mourning, she was once again out and about Town, diving into the choppy waters of the Marriage Mart.

The duke had lifted up from his chair beside her in a very gentlemanly manner. Even without looking at him, Valencia was as aware of him standing close. She felt him beside her.

She made short work of introducing Delia to everyone in the box—first to Mrs. Lloyd and her daughters, all of whom eyed Lady Delia with a healthy dose of awe, and then to the duke.

"Oh." Delia's eyes rounded as she looked him up and down.

"Your Grace." She dipped in a flawless curtsey. "I heard you arrived in Town. A delight to meet you."

He took her gloved hand and bowed over it in a demonstration of gallantry that Valencia had not witnessed from him before. "My lady."

A charming pink stained Delia's cheeks. "Welcome to London, Your Grace. I hope you are enjoying your new city . . . and home."

Home?

He had been very clear. He did not consider London his home—nor did he ever wish it to be. Valencia watched him closely, expecting him to flinch or his lip to curl, but his features remained coolly polite as he said, "I am. Very much. Thank you, my lady."

She was hard-pressed not to react. A small sound of derision escaped her, and he glanced her way. She arched an eyebrow at him.

Was he so dazzled by Lady Delia that he thought to feign enthusiasm for his current surroundings in order to charm her? A hot stab of jealousy came swift and fierce. He had never charmed Valencia. *Her* first encounter with him had none of this good cheer. He had not spoken kindly or looked at her the way he was looking at Delia. He had scarcely been civil.

Delia continued, with a gesture to Valencia, saying, "There is no better hostess to introduce you to the delights of Town. And *La donna del lago* is wonderful. I've seen it twice. Our dear friend is performing: Miss Fatima Chaves. She has a glorious voice."

His smile was temptation incarnate, and Valencia's heart gave a treacherous little flip. "I am looking forward to it."

That smile is not for me.

Delia continued. "Perhaps you and your sisters would like to meet her after the show?"

"Oh, yes!" Isolde clapped her hands together excitedly at the prospect of meeting Fatima. Her sisters nodded eagerly, all of them murmuring in agreement.

"That is very kind of you, my lady."

"My pleasure," Delia returned, looking fairly besotted now as she stared up at the duke.

Valencia studied his face in irritation, quite certain she read admiration in his gaze as he looked down at her young friend. She inhaled a stinging, seething breath. Delia may not yet be twenty years old, but plenty of girls Delia's age married men much older than the duke. She knew that very well. She need only look to her own father for evidence of that.

Not that the duke could be mistaken for old or frail. He must be close to Valencia's age. Anyone would judge him to be in the prime of his life. And he was undeniably virile.

Suddenly it dawned on her that his sisters may not be the only ones amenable to marriage. Just because he did not wish to remain in London did not mean he would not marry someone he met here and take her home to Wales with him. And just because he did not relish the role of duke did not mean he was opposed to marriage with an eligible young lady like Delia. Any number of ladies would follow him to the very edge of the earth. Delia was an accommodating girl. She would likely be up for the challenge.

Valencia shifted, clenching her hands into the folds of her silk skirts, grappling with the ugly feelings swirling through her.

The musicians stirred in the pit, instruments rousing, indicating they would soon begin.

"Oh, I best return to my seat. I am here with the Richardsons." Delia indicated a box across the way where a young gentleman sat, leaning forward in his seat and tracking her anxiously with his gaze. He sent a rather worried glance the duke's way, no doubt marking him as a rival for Lady Delia's affections. Earlier Valencia would have thought his worries misplaced. Now she was not so convinced. Now she could appreciate his feelings.

"Delighted to see you, my dear." Valencia pressed a parting kiss to Delia's cheek.

"Likewise. Let's to tea soon." Delia gave the duke a final look that could only be described as flirtatious and inviting. The duke could have no doubts of her interest if he should wish to court her.

Valencia inhaled, cautioning herself that she best grow accustomed to such occurrences and not permit them to affect her. Delia would not be the only beautiful woman to set her cap for him this season.

With farewells exchanged all around and a promise to meet up again after the performance so that they could all venture together to meet Fatima, Delia took her leave.

Valencia lowered back into her chair, facing forward until the theater fell to shadow, the attendants snuffing out the lamps almost simultaneously. Only then did she risk a glance to her right at the duke.

Their box was crowded to fit the nine of them, and her shoulder was practically brushing his. She thought she was being surreptitious, but she turned her head slightly only to discover that he was looking directly at her.

Almost as though he were waiting for her to turn and look at him.

And now she was.

In the gloom of the box, surrounded by his suddenly oblivious family, their gazes locked and held as the opening chords of the opera filled the theater. Whilst Mrs. Lloyd and the Misses Lloyd leaned forward in their seats, breathlessly transfixed as the mesmerizing Miss Fatima Chaves emerged onto the stage, Valencia and the duke stared hard at each other, cloaked in air the color of a deep purple bruise.

It was strange to be sitting among so many people and yet feel as though they were alone, as though it were just the two of them trapped in a little bubble.

He shifted, and she felt the press of his thigh alongside hers, the fabric of his trousers and her gown the only thing separating them, and it did little good to prevent the heat of his body from searing into hers.

She moistened her lips. "Delia is the daughter of my dear friend the Dowager Countess of Chatham," she whispered.

Valencia did not know why she felt compelled to speak at all.

The opera had begun. She should simply ignore him and lose herself in the performance.

Except how can you do that when you're lost in his melting gaze?

He inclined his head slightly. "She is a lovely girl. Her mother must be proud."

Valencia blinked. *Lovely girl. Her mother must be proud.*

That did not sound like the words of someone with very real, very carnal interest in Delia. They were the words of a man praising a girl. A young girl and not a prospective wife.

He shifted again, leaning in even closer to her in the crowded box, and suddenly she felt as though she were suffocated by the clean scent of him, a heady and intoxicating thing. Not to mention the breadth of him so close, the pressure of his thigh solid and burning against hers . . . It was all quite exhilarating.

Her mouth went dry, and she worked to swallow.

Before she could help herself, she murmured, "You do not think her a lovely woman?"

Certainly every other male with a pulse would consider Delia a woman full-grown. Even—as troubling and disturbing the thought—her own ancient father.

One corner of his lips curled. "I see only a young girl when I look at her."

"Oh," she breathed, her heart hammering wildly in her chest.

His eyes gleamed in the near dark, his head angling closer to hers as he rasped huskily, "Unlike you."

Her lips twitched and she attempted to jest, "Unlike me, a mature dowager."

"Unlike you," he corrected, "a thoroughly ripe and beddable woman."

"Oh," she breathed yet again, her voice different this time, even to her own ears. The single word escaped her as a choked, strangled sound.

"Oh," he echoed without the faintest hint of a smile. If anything, he was grimly serious. His eyes dark and pervasive in the gloom of the theater.

After a long beat he turned his attention back to the stage, removing his gaze from her, but keeping his thigh aligned with hers, the heat of him continuing to penetrate her through her gown amid the entire performance. A definite distraction. She could not be counted upon to recount what she saw or heard on the stage below. She was too busy thinking about the man beside her.

Chapter 15

In a world where gossip is the main form of social currency, a discreet friend is worth her weight in rubies.
—The Right Honorable Lady Rosalind Shawley

Valencia sent a missive to Ros as soon as she returned home from the theater, inquiring if she was available to join her the following night.

If it weren't already so late upon returning home, Valencia would have ventured out right then, such was the fever pumping through her veins. It was overwhelming and bewildering how sitting in that darkened box with Rhain pressed beside her had fired her person to such a degree . . . reigniting her resolve and determination. She would do something about that. Clearly she was ready for passion. She would find a more suitable candidate with whom to swim those waters than the man who presently occupied the bedchamber adjoining hers. Her breath caught as her gaze floated to that closed door. No matter how convenient, he was wholly forbidden.

As it turned out, she might as well have gone out. She spent a restless night, tossing and turning, thinking about the duke—Rhain—her hand reaching down to stroke the side of her thigh where she still felt him. Her fingers drifting to her tingling lips as she recalled his gaze on her face.

Ros was the ideal partner to accompany her for a night of clandestine activity. Aside from being a loyal friend, she was unwed and happy with that status and always up for adventure. She had no husband to inhibit her actions, expecting her to be home in bed at a certain time. And as a spinster, her parents did not closely monitor her comings and goings.

Tru and Maeve would not be interested in going where Valencia planned to go. They were ladies well contented and settled with their lives, specifically their love lives, and they had no yearning to visit someplace where the seeking and fulfillment of liaisons was the objective. Maeve would be scandalized at the very notion. It would not matter to her that dominoes were encouraged for the sake of anonymity. The mask would not make Maeve feel any better about being in a house with so much vice and licentiousness.

No, The Palace was for those with hearts unfettered.

It was for those who burned . . . who felt the imprint of a man's thigh singeing through her skirts hours after such contact had occurred.

Valencia's venture to Vauxhall had not turned out the way she wanted, but she vowed that this night out with Ros would go better.

The Palace was known by all, even if not discussed in polite circles. The pleasure house was a place where one might engage in peccadilloes with like-minded individuals. There was entertainment, gaming, food, drink . . . and assignations. It was a place where she could act out all her most lurid passions and fantasies, should she wish it.

Ros was all about experiencing new things. Valencia knew she could be counted upon to join her. She might have no interest in dalliances, but she was voraciously curious and would not resist exploring a place where dalliances were on full display. She might not partake in the drama, but she was a happy observer.

And who knew? Perhaps Ros would have a change of heart once she was there and get caught up in the spirits of things. Perhaps she would jump into some handsome masked gentleman's lap. Perhaps then she would forget her stalwart inhibitions. It was not impossible.

That morning, the suitors arrived early for the girls, just as Valencia predicted they would. It was a long day. Dozens of swains filled the drawing room to capacity, flowers and boxes of candy in their hands as they vied for the attention of the Duke of Dedham's sisters. It was a rather cutthroat affair, young gentlemen—and not-so-young gentlemen—all trying to outdo themselves for the six young women.

The girls were exhausted as the dinner hour approached, their cheeks hurting from smiling. Never had they been so courted. Everyone agreed that a quiet evening at home would be ideal.

Mrs. Lloyd, quite spent, announced she would be taking dinner in her bedchamber.

"What an eventful day! Curling up with a book in my dressing gown sounds just the thing," she had declared.

Valencia seized the opportunity to echo the woman's sentiments. "Indeed," she agreed. "I believe I shall do the same. Tomorrow will be another busy day, after all." She looked to each of her charges. The girls nodded in happy agreement.

Once in her bedchamber Valencia began readying herself for the evening out. Tildie informed the kitchen staff that she would be dining in her chamber for the night and required a dinner tray sent up.

Valencia felt a buzzing anticipation as she took a leisurely bath in steaming rose water, washing her hair and scrubbing her skin until it was sweet-smelling and gleamed pink and new.

Tonight would keep her going.

It would feed her spirit and give her something that was hers alone, and it would make her stop longing for what could not be—for *him*.

It was vastly unfair that the first man to turn her head in a decade was her husband's replacement. It was some bitter irony.

She was finished with her bath and nibbling on some food, browsing through her armoire, when Tildie brought a missive from Ros.

Her lady's maid eyed her expectantly as she opened it and read her friend's words. Of course Tildie knew of her plans. There was nothing about her life that she did not know. She winced as she thought of Rhain. She reached down and rubbed a palm over the sudden warmth that radiated along her thigh. Well. Almost nothing. Some things need never be spoken.

Valencia smiled in satisfaction. "I will be collecting her at half past nine."

Tildie nodded perfunctorily. "Very good. I am glad you will not be venturing out alone to such a place." *Such a place.* As though Valencia were braving Hades's den. "Now . . . what do you think of that amethyst gown with the velvet rope trim?" her maid asked. "With a matching velvet domino?"

Together they turned their attention to her wardrobe, fully aware that her dress would be an important choice, a critical decision when it came to the evening.

It would have to be one she had been saving for just such an occasion. She did not wish for it to be immediately recognizable when she went out and about in Good Society.

She had met with her dressmaker a few months ago, preparing for this very night, knowing it would eventually come and knowing she would need gowns that could be worn only once.

Although she was a widow and Society was tolerant to a degree when it came to indiscretions, a certain amount of caution was expected. She could not be too flagrant and disregard all propriety. Common sense was needed. She could not wear a daring gown out one evening, domino only partially obscuring her face, and then be seen wearing it again on another occasion as her true dowager self. That would not be well done of her. Not well done at all.

Tildie helped her into the gown. She turned and twisted before the mirror, evaluating herself from every angle. The low-cut bodice with velvet trim was precisely the dramatic statement she was hoping to make.

"I knew that was the perfect choice." Tildie smiled in approval. "This color is stunning against your skin."

"Thank you." Valencia nodded and lowered herself down to her dressing table so that Tildie could arrange her hair.

The house was dark and silent when she left her bedchamber, and only a few wall sconces were lit as she hurried down the corridors, her cloak flowing soundlessly behind her. No one noticed her slipping out into the night, and she wondered if everyone had retired to their chambers.

She collected Ros along the way as planned. The carriage barely slowed before the Shawley town house and her friend was rushing out the door and down the front steps.

A groom helped her up and inside.

"You look beautiful," Ros declared as she settled back on the squabs, getting her first sight of Valencia.

"You're lovely, as well. Red suits you."

"My mother declared me scandalous, so I know I'm dressed appropriately."

"Oh, dear." Valencia giggled. "You did not tell her where we are going, did you?"

"And watch her succumb to apoplexy?" Ros released a single

bark of laughter. "Certainly not. I'm not that foolish. She thinks I'm attending a poetry reading."

Valencia laughed. "Wearing that?"

Ros nodded merrily. "She thinks I've quite lost my head."

"I imagine so."

Ros chattered excitedly on the drive across Town, which spared Valencia from having to take on too much of the conversation herself. A good thing. The pulse at her throat hammered wildly against her skin and she couldn't still her hands. She alternated between folding them in her lap, tucking them under her thighs, crossing them over her chest. She was a big ball of overworked nerves.

"We're here!" Ros announced unnecessarily when the carriage rolled to a stop.

Upon knocking, they were admitted inside with ease. Ros had made the necessary arrangements long ago when they first talked about visiting The Palace. She'd secured a membership in preparation for when they finally got up the nerve to venture forth. The fee was no hardship. Ros's parents were quite wealthy (they had supported their wastrel son-in-law, the Earl of Chatham, for years) and gave her more than enough pin money, most of which she scarcely used. She was a woman of modest habits. She was not an enthusiast of gowns or hats or jewelry. She was happy to invest in a membership to a pleasure house.

Clasping hands, the two of them stepped inside, prepared to face the debauchery together.

Chapter 16

*The eyes of the ton are everywhere. To assume
otherwise would be a grave mistake.*
—Valencia, the Dowager Duchess of Dedham

Once again Rhain found himself at the mercy of Dewey.

Granted, it was his choice, but he was already aware
that Dewey's leisure activities did not precisely align with his
own interests.

And yet when his cousin suggested an evening out, he readily agreed and put himself again in Dewey's eager hands. Anything to get himself out of the house and away from the barrage
of women under his roof. Away, especially, from one woman in
particular.

The days since he had moved into Dedham House had been
trying, but not in the manner anticipated. He had expected living as the duke to be a chore. An unwelcome chore, yes. He had

expected the mantle of a dukedom to be a suffocating weight. He had expected his family's excitement over London High Society to be distasteful and trying. He had expected living yet again in close proximity to his mother and sisters to be a difficult adjustment. He had expected handing off his sisters to this gilded life and inevitably to Englishmen to be challenging.

All of that had proven true.

He believed bringing the dowager into the fray would not only help his sisters but help *him*. It would spare him from the worst of this unwanted development in his life.

As it turned out, that was partly true.

His sisters might be getting the assistance they needed, but it seemed he was not spared, after all. Quite the opposite.

He was in torment.

"I did not think you would join me," Dewey proclaimed as he relaxed back on the squabs of the carriage on the way to some destination yet to be revealed. Rhain did not ask where they were going. It did not matter. He simply needed to escape the house. Today had been a particular ordeal.

The dowager had been true to her word and effectively taken charge of his sisters. It was a process, he had since discovered. Strategy he cared not to consider. And none of it was happening quickly or quietly enough for him. Indeed not. The house was in an uproar, and today was the most awful yet. His house had been bursting at the seams with refined Englishmen. He could still smell their cologne. It was forever singed inside his nostrils.

"I needed a night away."

Even working in his study—

His. He winced. That still did not feel correct in his mind. And yet the study was his. The house was his. He'd inherited it all.

Not the wife though.

He did not get to have her, and he needed to do well to remember that when he found himself gazing at their adjoining door.

Even working in his study, he could hear the chaos outside his door at all times. His sisters and tradespeople and the various instructors and now the army of suitors coming in and out of the house all day long did not seem capable of operating at any level other than glass-shattering volume.

And the dog.

The bloody dog was a yappy little beast and had taken a dislike to Rhain. The pup appeared fond of everyone in the house except for him. The mongrel pissed on his slippers. He was not certain how or when Caesar had invaded his bedchamber, but he had done so. Rhain felt singularly targeted, which he knew sounded unreasonable, so he kept that opinion to himself.

And yet he understood why the duchess had acquired the dog. He could not fault her logic. His sister had entirely forgotten about Poppet, and that was something that had needed to happen. Now it was a real dog in her arms. A dog that growled and nipped at him, but he supposed it was an improvement.

His mother and sisters were thrilled. They now raved about the cleverness of the woman. The duchess had even won over his more difficult sisters.

"She gave Isolde a dog. I would not call that genius," he'd grumbled on one occasion when they had been singing her praises.

"No one else thought to do so. *You* did not," Elin countered, blinking her eyes in false innocence.

Even if he could not admit it, he knew the woman was clever. She was clever and resourceful and so pretty it made his teeth ache to taste her. To kiss her.

None of this was improved by the knowledge that the dowager slept one room over from him. A mere door separated them. It was agony.

He bloody well *liked* her.

She was not what he had envisioned a blue-blooded lady to be. She tantalized the hell out of him. It did not bode well. He did not need her liking him back, and he was quite concerned that he had earned her admiration when he had wrested control of her money from those high-handed agents, forcing them to relinquish the funds to her.

You are too kind. To bloody hell with that.

He was not a kind man. A kind man would not long to fuck her.

He could not have her looking up at him with her big doe eyes, thinking him *kind* and filling him with all manner of improper thoughts.

"New dukedom a bit much for you, eh?" Dewey grinned.

"I'm becoming acclimated well enough. It's the women in the house that are setting my teeth on edge."

"Not *all* the women in your house though." His cousin winked suggestively.

And *that* put Rhain's teeth on edge even more. Was he that transparent? Did Dewey sense that he wanted her? Did he guess that Rhain lay awake fantasizing about all the improper things he would like to do with the proper duchess?

Seeking a change in topic, he growled, "You need to keep your hands off the dowager's lady's maid."

Dewey looked at him blankly for a moment and then said, "Oh, Tildie? Nothing happened."

"Leave her be, Dewey . . . and any other woman beneath my roof."

Dewey held up both hands in contrition. "I meant no offense, coz. The lass put herself forward. She's a pretty girl. I did not see the harm, but it will not happen again."

Rhain grunted in acknowledgment of his apology. He told himself that Dewey had realized his mistake and would not repeat it. He told himself Dewey was merely young and jovial and carefree. Still, a decent man. Still, the right person to act as a steward and manage the dukedom in his stead.

His cousin continued. "I must say though. If there is one woman under your roof to tempt me, it is that delectable duchess of yours . . ." His voice faded, and he blew out a breath and waved his hands through the air in what was an imitation of a voluptuous female form.

His meaning was unmistakable, and Rhain did not like it.

Dewey watched him closely, and for some reason, he felt as though his cousin knew his words rubbed him ill. Rhain felt as though he were being tested, poked and prodded for a reaction. As though his cousin wanted to see just how deep his feelings ran for the dowager.

Determined to reveal none of his inner thoughts, he responded as he ought to, saying, "She is not mine, as you say, and she is every bit as bothersome as my sisters."

"That lady could bother me anytime."

"You'll do well to behave yourself. She is under my protection as long as she is beneath my roof. That means hands off her."

Dewey leaned forward. "Come. You can tell me, coz. Have you not considered dipping your cock in that? That would be damned convenient . . . a bit of muslin like that within arm's reach."

Rhain grunted, knotting his hands into fists at his sides, unwilling to reveal that his cousin's crude words stirred something primal inside him, something dark and possessive. This would not be the moment to reveal an adjoining door separated their rooms. Presumably, Dewey did not know that particular detail. Unless Tildie had spoken out of turn in their earlier dalliance. He could only imagine what Dewey would say to *that*.

"Dewey, need I remind you again to watch your tongue? The lady is a guest in my house."

Of a sort. She was certainly . . . something to him.

Someone he needed to keep out of his thoughts . . . and certainly out of his hands.

"Ah. So when she leaves the shelter of your house, may I then cease to tread so carefully with her? She is a widow, after all. A mature woman." His fingers flickered mildly in the air. "Interesting. Let me ask you one question . . . What will become of her when you depart?"

Meaning, would she remain in the house when he left Dewey in charge?

Rhain grimaced at the thought of leaving the flirtatious Dewey in proximity to her. Leaving his duchess—who was not *his* duchess— at his cousin's mercy struck him as altogether unpalatable.

The notion of Dewey at the helm whilst he returned to Wales was indeed starting to sour his stomach. Rhain curled the hand resting upon his knee into a tight ball to stop himself from planting it in Dewey's face.

His cousin held up both hands. "I jest! Wipe that thunderous scowl off your face, coz. I am only jesting."

Rhain forced out a breath, reprimanding himself for showing any outward reaction. He glanced out the window into the night rather than say anything else.

The man was jesting. Still . . . Dewey's remarks made his jaw clench until it ached. He did not like the idea of his cousin making advances on Valencia.

Valencia.

For some reason, her name had insinuated itself into his mind. Suddenly it was the only way he could think of her. He told himself it was because he was not a man to frequent with titled nobility and did not think of people in such exalted terms. Ironic, considering he was now one of those exalted personages himself. Ironic and distasteful.

The carriage began to slow. "You are in for a delight tonight. I can assure you there is nothing like . . . er, the place we're going back home in Bryn Bychan," Dewey said, a welcome change of subject.

Of course, his cousin had said that about everything he had shown to Rhain so far, and it was becoming a bit tedious as a refrain.

"That is not so difficult to imagine." Bryn Bychan was not precisely a bustling metropolis.

When the carriage stopped, they stepped down, and Rhain found himself staring up at an ordinary-looking house in what appeared to be a modest neighborhood.

"This is the place?" He was thinking they were going somewhere more public, like Vauxhall or a theater house, where he would not be required to converse with strangers. He was not keen on the idea of an intimate gathering where he would have to converse at length.

"Untold delights await us within." Dewey grinned and rubbed his palms together in an exaggerated display of anticipation.

He digested that slowly, hoping he was not about to enter a brothel. He'd warned his cousin he did not relish such places. Such establishments had never been to his tastes. They always reeked faintly of desperate men and sad women.

At the door, a gentleman who more resembled a veteran pugilist than a butler greeted them. He was dressed in livery, but his hands were like hams and his shoulders stretched the seams of his jacket. His nose took a sharp turn at the center, a clear testament that it had been broken several times. He looked Dewey up and down dispassionately, not uttering a sound.

"Hallo there, my good fellow," Dewey said cheerfully, undeterred, flattening a hand against his chest. "I am Dewey Pugh."

A blank stare and silence met the introduction. Clearly the doorman was not impressed.

From deep within the house a sudden burst of feminine laughter rang out.

"Ah. It sounds like a right cheery party in there." Dewey rose up on his booted toes and strained for a glimpse inside, clearly eager to gain admittance.

The man at the door did not budge. Moments passed. Still no movement from the giant. Apparently Dewey's name was not significant enough to gain entry, and Rhain felt an impatient sigh welling up inside him.

Dewey gestured to Rhain. "And this is my cousin, the Duke of Dedham."

At that, the doorman blinked.

He did in fact budge then, shifting his substantial weight upon his feet. He gave Rhain a quick once-over. "Duke of Dedham?" he echoed.

Rhain gazed coolly back at him, not inclined to argue his identity or to beg entry anywhere. Such things did not matter to him. If his presence wasn't desired here, so be it. He could find someplace else to go.

Apparently Rhain's lack of response validated him in the butler's eyes. Seemingly satisfied, he nodded once and turned to murmur something to another liveried servant standing close behind him.

Stepping back, the doorman held the door wide for them to enter. "You will have to meet with Mrs. Winkler first. She approves all patrons."

Dewey's eyes widened in delight. "The infamous Mrs. Winkler. That would be brilliant."

Dewey smiled smugly back at Rhain as they stepped inside the small foyer. "I've long wished to step inside this house," he murmured with a conspiratorial air.

"You have never been here before?" Rhain asked with some surprise. For everything his cousin had said, he made it sound as though he was a regular patron of the house.

"Well, no, I have . . . not precisely . . ." His cousin floundered a bit. "I've submitted a petition for membership . . . er, twice . . . but they have not gotten back to me yet, and the fee is rather steep."

Membership? His cousin brought him to some place that required a membership and subsequent fee? A membership he did not possess and yet he thought to brave the gates anyway. He thought with Rhain at his side he stood a good chance of gaining entry. Rather manipulative of him, but Rhain supposed he could not fault Dewey for using all means at his disposal to achieve a few perks for himself. He was only human.

Suddenly a woman swept into the room in a flamboyant blue gown festooned with feathers that fluttered and bounced with her actions. She was close to his mother's age. The years and gravity had been exceedingly kind to her. Not a wrinkle marred her plump cheeks. She was very lovely.

"Your Grace," she said in a voice like silk, her painted lips curving in a smile. "Such a pleasure." She offered Rhain her hand.

He marveled that she would know which one of them was the duke. It was as though he were wearing a sign.

He took her hand and bowed over it.

"I'm Mrs. Winkler," she said in greeting, "and this is my establishment."

He shot his cousin a glance, which he hoped conveyed his unhappy thoughts.

Dewey only grinned back, nodding encouragingly.

"I had not heard you arrived in Town," she said. "I was quite saddened, of course, to learn of the late duke's passing. I knew him long ago. Years ago, before his accident, when he was more . . . er, in his vigor. He was a member of The Palace, of course."

He marveled at her for a moment. The lady was certainly well versed in all things *tonish*. She'd known Dedham. Before his accident.

Rhain had heard all about the accident that had almost killed the man. The estate agents had left nothing out when apprising him of his new role. Well, almost nothing. They'd skimmed over Valencia.

He straightened over her hand. "It is my regret that I never met the late duke myself." The words were a lie, of course. Empty words. As empty as he felt when he thought about the man who had been Valencia's husband.

"A handsome man." She winked boldly. "But I must say you have surpassed him in that regard."

His lips twitched. She was quite adept in her role of hostess. "You flatter, madam."

Her gaze landed on Dewey. "And who is this?"

"My cousin, Dewey Pugh. He insisted we visit"—he glanced around the small foyer, still uncertain what this place was—"here."

"Well, I am so delighted he did. Tonight's visit is with our compliments, gentlemen. Hopefully you will both consider becoming members after you see all the many diversions we have to offer."

He blinked, suspecting this place was in fact a brothel. What had his cousin gotten him into?

"Follow me, gentlemen." She waved a feathered arm in a wide gesture before moving to a set of double doors. "Welcome, welcome. Hopefully this place will be your home away from home. The Palace serves as that to many of our patrons."

The Palace? He mouthed the words behind her back to his cousin.

Dewey grinned and nodded like the happiest of fools. "You shall thank me in the morning when we leave this place, coz."

He leaned in closer to whisper, "Just tell me you have not dragged me to a brothel after I expressly told you I do not care for them."

Dewey looked affronted. "'Course not. This is so much better than a brothel."

"What is it?" he hissed. He was still waiting on that explanation.

"It's a pleasure den."

Pleasure den?

He was still at a loss, not certain what that was, but within moments, soon after he walked onto the main floor of The Palace, he understood.

It was a hedonistic playground.

The main floor was a large space full of tables and chairs and chaises. There was an orchestra on a dais. Gentlemen and ladies, many of whom wore masks, mingled among servers and acrobats and fire-eaters. A few gentlemen wore masks, but they seemed to be mostly reserved for the ladies. Scraps of brocade and satin partially obscured the female faces, and Rhain had to confess that it added to the enticement of the women, lending them an air of mystery.

Couples deep into their cups danced with abandon.

An artist on one side of the room painted on the canvas of a naked woman, stroking paint onto the dusky nipple of one large breast and then swirling it around her plump flesh decadently.

Oh, and there were semiprivate alcoves, only partway curtained so that you could see directly inside to unclothed, trysting couples on beds. The lewd sounds from those alcoves carried out into the main room, the lusty moans and smacking sounds of bodies joining mingling with the music. Several of the alcoves boasted chairs where people sat and observed the licentious activities as they drank and nibbled on canapés.

Everything and anything was taking place under one roof in one room. If it was shocking or scandalous, it was happening here. A winding staircase led upstairs, and he could not even imagine what was occurring in other rooms of the house.

His cousin elbowed him. "See? Not a brothel."

He nodded even as he tried to decide if this was equally distasteful.

Dewey added, "Nothing like this in Bryn Bychan, eh?"

"Indeed no," he agreed dryly.

A liveried waiter passed them carrying a tray, and Rhain snatched a drink from it, downing the liquor in one swig. He lowered the glass and swept his gaze around the room, taking it all in and still not seeing everything. There was simply too much to digest.

"Come. I must investigate one of these alcoves," Dewey said, nodding eagerly toward the nearest one.

Rhain followed, stepping inside the shadowy nook behind his cousin. Flames flickered within the red-stained glass of two wall sconces, casting a fiery red glow into the space.

A total of six velvet-cushioned seats were positioned before a narrow bed where a man was tied down, spread-eagle, with silken restraints at the ankles and wrists. One woman rode his cock whilst his mouth feasted on another woman who hovered over his face. The three naked bodies glowed like they were aflame, entities born of a forge. The woman he devoured clung to the headboard, working her hips as he mouthed her cunny.

"Now that is worth the price of admission," Dewey murmured.

Rhain did not bother reminding him that he had not spent a penny of his money on admission.

His gaze slid around the small space. The audience was enthralled. One woman reached into the gentleman's lap beside her to fondle his manhood through his breeches as they avidly watched the spectacle on the bed. It was as though all modesty, all inhibitions ceased to exist inside the walls of this house.

His casual study of the audience came to an abrupt halt. His attention locked on one face. A single woman. A woman wearing a silvery beaded mask. The covering did little to shield her face from him. Nor did the flickering shadows of the alcove.

He knew her at once.

He would know her anywhere.

Over the moans and cries of the trio on the bed, his gaze captured and held hers.

Her brown eyes flared wide and stared back at him in recognition through the mask's eyeholes. Her mouth parted on either a gasp or a sigh.

Valencia.

Chapter 17

A debutante is looking for a satisfactory marriage.
A widow . . . is looking for satisfaction.
—Valencia, the Dowager Duchess of Dedham

God or fate or the devil himself was conspiring against her.

Valencia had left the house tonight to find adventure, to take a much-needed reprieve from the Lloyd family, to escape *him*. The duke. *Rhain*.

It was the bitterest of ironies, of course, to find him here, at the apex of all that was wanton and debauched and uninhibited. Yes, there was freedom in this. A freedom that was frightening in its absoluteness. Here nothing was forbidden.

He knew her.

He recognized her, and she felt the full heat of his stare, from her toes to her face—and everything in between. Her breasts felt heavier, achy and swollen in her suddenly too-tight bodice.

She tugged desperately on Ros's sleeve. "We have to go. Now."

Ros did not spare her a glance. The scene on the bed transfixed her. She gawked open-mouthed. "Already? So soon?" She shook her head as though leaving were not an option.

"Yes. Now. He is here."

"He?" Ros asked distractedly.

"Yes. He." Valencia tugged harder on her sleeve. "*Him.*"

Ros frowned and dragged her attention away from the enthusiastic bedplay. "Who?"

"The duke . . ."

It took Ros a moment to understand. Then she blinked and whipped her head to gape at Valencia. "You mean . . . Dedham?"

Valencia winced and nodded.

Ros glanced around the little red-tinged alcove, searching, her gaze arresting on the one man *not* staring at the scene on the bed but at Valencia—as though she were the most fascinating thing in the room. Or perhaps he was just astonished at her presence. That was understandable. He had just caught the genteel lady he had tasked with steering his sisters through the *ton* in the most sordid of surroundings.

"Oh. My," Ros breathed. "This is . . . awkward."

"We must leave," she insisted.

Ros considered her. And him. Then she surveyed the room again. "Must we? He's already seen you are here . . . and he is not your guardian. Not your father or husband." She shrugged. "You are an adult. You can do as you like."

And what I would like is to leave.

Ros's sound logic did not matter to her. Locking eyes with him amid this wild scene, with the scent of desire thick as vapor in the air . . . it was all too much for her. Her very skin itched and felt too tight. She sucked in a breath. And then another. There was not enough oxygen in the room.

The sounds emanating from the bed intensified. Gasps. Moans. The headboard knocking persistently against the wall. Valencia did not look in that direction. She looked only at him . . . at Rhain.

He only looked at her.

Her face burned hot beneath the scrap of her domino. All the good that stupid thing did. He still recognized her, and she realized anyone who knew her as more than a passing acquaintance would.

She throbbed, aching in places that had been long neglected by anything save the attention of her own hands. She shifted where she sat, as though that would assuage the torment. Somehow it only made it worse. His eyes on her . . . only made it worse.

"Ros," she whispered hoarsely, "I am leaving. With or without you."

Ros glanced around and released a regretful sigh. Clearly she wanted to explore the establishment a bit more. "Oh, very well. Of course." She nodded. "We will go."

Valencia held his gaze for a moment longer and then turned away, diving back out onto the main floor. She felt his stare on her back as she wove through the press of bodies. She presumed

Ros was following, too, but she felt him there, the heat-radiating length of him at her back, following her.

And then she felt his hand clamping down on her, a manacle around her wrist.

She spun around in alarm, glancing at those fingers circling her before looking back at the implacable set of his features.

"Valencia," he growled, using her name as though it were his right to do so. "What can you be thinking to be at a place like this?"

"Me?" she choked out. "What of you?" If she was a degenerate, then so was he.

Suddenly Ros was there, chiming in, too, with a belligerent thrust of her chin. "And who are you to care, Your Grace?"

Rhain looked down at her as though she were a pesky gnat he wished to flick away.

"Rosalind," Valencia said very correctly in an admirably even voice. "Do not fret yourself. Give us a moment, please."

Ros considered this, appearing close to disagreeing, before she relented and nodded. "Very well." She glanced around searchingly. A painter worked nearby, creating a detailed country landscape along a woman's rib cage. Ros inched that way, and Valencia realized her friend did not mind the delay.

"I will wait for you over here," she called without a backward glance.

Still holding on to her wrist, Rhain pulled Valencia through the press of bodies into another chamber. The space was darkened and littered with couches occupied by trysting couples—or trios. Enough light trickled in from the main room behind them to allow her to make out general shapes. He led her deeper into the room and out onto an open balcony. She breathed in the fresh air, glad to taste it.

He released her wrist, and she spun around, rubbing the skin, still feeling the imprint of his hand there. She backed away until the stone railing dug at her hips, the cold penetrating the fabric of her dress.

"Now," she declared, thrusting out her chin. "Say what you will."

"What are you doing here?"

"My friend said it best: Why should you care?"

"I care because you reside under my roof." He flung it at her like an accusation, and she flinched.

A fortnight ago it had been *her* roof. At least it had felt like her roof. She supposed it never had been. She supposed no roof had ever been hers.

"I care because you have charge of my sisters and you—"

"And now you deem me unsuitable?" she snapped, her temper flaring. It was just as she guessed. He now thought her unfit to shepherd his sisters. One glimpse of her in this place and his opinion of her had soured.

He shook his head. "That is not—"

"Am I somehow besmirched now?" she seethed.

He stepped closer. "No—"

"Am I a bad influence? Is that it?"

Another step. "I did not—"

"Are you worried I might corrupt them with my wicked, *wicked* ways?"

Another step. His eyes flashed in the night. "It is not—"

"Come now. Say it. Is our agreement void?" She swiped a hand through the air in a cutting motion. "Shall I pack my bags and leave in the morning?"

He stopped before her, his chest heaving as though he were out of breath from a sprint. "Good God, woman. Do you never shut up?"

She opened her mouth again, ready to flay him for daring to speak to her in such a manner, for daring to judge her, for daring to criticize her for choosing to finally live after years of existing in shadow.

He grabbed her face and kissed her.

It took her only a moment to grasp that this was really happening. That his hands were on her face. That his mouth was on hers.

She sagged against him. The solid length of him kept her from falling—as did those broad palms cupping her face and his long fingers sliding into her hair, loosening the pins.

The kiss went on forever. His lips moved, opening, his tongue seeking. He made love with his mouth. She did not remember a kiss ever being so consuming, so devouring. Not her first. Not any of the ones that came after.

Just this one.

She remembered enjoying sex. In the beginning. Or at least not hating it. Even then, Before Dedham had never devoted such attention to a kiss—to her mouth. It made her wonder how much attention Rhain would devote to . . . other things, other parts of her body. She clung to his wrists, leaning into him, giving as much as she took.

They broke away, breathing raggedly. Staring at each other. This was what she had been looking for, what she wanted. *God*.

But not with this man. Not her husband's replacement.

"I'm sorry," he rasped, his forehead pressing into hers, his warm hands still holding her face, fingers buried in her hair, rubbing the silken strands. His touch felt so good. Delicious and comforting and tempting.

With a choked breath, she tore herself free from his hands and fled the balcony, darting through the darkened chamber and out onto the main floor. She snatched Ros away from the artist, who was in the midst of explaining his work to her with a great deal of animation.

"Are you unwell?" Ros frowned, struggling to keep up with her. "He did not insult you, did he?" She peered over Valencia's shoulder as though she would tear him apart if he had dared.

"No. I am fine. Let us just go."

Once in the foyer, Ros left her to speak with one of the grooms about bringing their carriage around to the front.

Valencia caught sight of her reflection in a gilt mirror hanging from gold chains against the rose-papered foyer wall. Her eyes gleamed like gems through the slits of her domino. Pink stained her cheeks. Her hair was mussed and wild around her head. She looked as though she were afflicted with a fever.

That was where Lord Burton found her.

He entered with a boisterous group of gentlemen, parting from them when he spotted her. He recognized her instantly—unsurprisingly. A wide grin came over his features. Those handsome features appeared rather bloated. Likely all the drink and the excesses of his lifestyle were catching up with him.

He had been in her sphere for many years now. Lord Burton and Dedham had once been inseparable, running together in the same set. That is, until his accident. Following that he had not been up to such activity. She could not count the number of times Lord Burton had sat across from her at a dining table. Of course he would see through the disguise of her domino.

He seized her gloved hand and pressed a lingering kiss to the back of it. "Your Grace, I would know you anywhere. That lush hair and glowing skin . . ." His gaze slid from her ink-dark hair and her face . . . roving all over her body. "You're such a refreshing change from all the milksop ladies of the *ton*. Those ladies look as though they might break if they sneeze too hard."

His licentious manner was nothing new. He had propositioned her over the years. Following Dedham's accident, he was one of the most persistent. Memories of him at the Chatham house party a year ago still haunted her, pulled at her in the darkness of night, in the solitude of her bedroom, in the privacy of her dreams.

The way he had cornered her, his refusal to accept her rebuffs . . . and that moment she had thought she killed him.

She shivered at the memory of that terrible night and tugged her hand back, pressing it into her side.

"Lord Burton. I'd like to say it is lovely to see you again." They were past pretense. She had ceased to be polite to him after that night.

He grinned. "Your constancy is a comfort, Your Grace." He motioned around them. "Am I to take your presence here as a sign that you are finished mourning and ready to play?"

"I assure you, my presence here has nothing to do with you. Please do not take it as a sign of anything."

"Perhaps not. But it can give one hope. Give *me* . . . hope. You're a widow now. Free and ready to explore, eh?" He nodded as though she had agreed with him. "It's taken you long enough. I thought you would never come around."

"Do not harbor any hope for you and me," she said harshly. "There is no us."

He smiled widely then. "I still think of that night at the house party." His eyes flashed with something.

Something knowing and cruel and terrifying.

She went cold.

Everything inside her seized up. Her lungs ceased to move air, and her heart felt as though a fist squeezed it.

"Valencia." Ros touched her arm lightly as she leveled a cold look at Burton. She, too, was well acquainted with the dreadful man.

She settled her hand into Ros's ready grip and clung tightly, grateful for her friend. Ros gave her fingers a comforting squeeze.

Burton nodded farewell. "I am looking forward to seeing more of you here, Your Grace."

She shook her head, bleak frustration rising up inside her. She would not be coming back here. The prospect of seeing him, mingling with him, stayed the impulse in her to ever come back.

Ros shot him a withering glare and pulled her along.

Valencia sent a final glance back, but this time it was not Burton who snared her attention. It was Rhain.

He had left the alcove. He had followed her, ambling forward with deceptive leisure like a predator closing in, stalking through tall grasses. His gaze fastened on her where she stood in the foyer, unblinking, unwavering.

The sight of him gave her pause. Her feet stalled.

He didn't look at anyone else. Not Ros. Not Lord Burton. Only her.

Ros tugged. "Come on. Let's go."

Valencia stumbled into motion, hastening away, presenting him with her back, which, yes, she knew one should never offer to a predator, but there was little choice.

She had to get away.

Chapter 18

*New dukes are like new shoes. They must
be broken in until comfortable.*
—The Right Honorable Lady Rosalind Shawley

The house was silent and sleeping when Valencia returned. Even the groom sitting duty in the front foyer gently snored in his chair. Her hand glided soundlessly along the banister as she advanced up the steps.

"Your Grace," Tildie greeted rather groggily when Valencia entered her chamber. She, too, had been dozing on the settee in her chamber, waiting for her. Yawning, she stretched and began helping Valencia with the tiny buttons at the back of her gown. "How was your evening with your friend?"

"I had a lovely time. Thank you, Tildie." Not precisely a lie. Not precisely a truth.

"I am so happy to hear that." Tildie gave her shoulder a lingering pat. "You deserve only good things, Your Grace."

"Thank you, Tildie. I can tend to the rest by myself. Good night."

"If you are certain. Good night, Your Grace." The door snicked shut after her.

Valencia sank down at her dressing table. One by one, she removed the pins from her already loosened hair. Rhain had ruined the coiffure Tildie had so beautifully wrought earlier.

She brushed the heavy mass until it crackled. Studying her reflection in the mirror, she noted that she no longer looked like a dewy-eyed maid. She looked older. Tiny lines that had not existed before webbed around her eyes. When had those appeared?

So much of her life had been lost, years wasted in an unhappy marriage. For a year, she had waited, stuck in mourning, and now she was still waiting, caught in this strange state of idleness, ushering a flock of young women into the *ton*. She was a glorified governess. Tonight was supposed to have been for her, and it had not lived up to her dreams.

Well. Not exactly. There had been that one moment. That moment when Rhain had kissed her. It had been the stuff of dreams.

A sound drifted from the other side of the adjoining door.

Turning, she stared at the length of wood, trying not to envision Rhain on the other side of that door. Undressing. Climbing into that big bed. What did he wear to sleep? She frowned, struggling to decide whether he was in a nightshirt or naked.

She failed. It was the only thing she could think about, the only thing she could see in her mind. *Him*. Naked.

She decided he would not bother with a nightshirt. He did not seem the manner of man to fuss with a thing like that. He would slide that big body of his beneath the crisp sheets—

She veered her thoughts away and sucked in a deep breath. Climbing into bed with angry movements, she yanked the counterpane up over her.

He had kissed her. Not any kiss. Not any kiss she had ever experienced, at least. Perhaps all kisses were like that for him. Decadent. Consuming. Devastating. Perhaps he was that skilled, that good. She swallowed thickly.

A man who could kiss like that . . .

She flipped onto her side, pulling her knees up to her chest with an anguished exhale. He was in the room next to hers.

So close.

He would be leaving soon. She did not know precisely when. At least not until his sisters were settled satisfactorily, and that did not mean they all six needed to be married . . . but as long as they were smoothly integrated into *ton* life. Based on the number of suitors beating down their door, it could be said they were well on their way to becoming assimilated into Good Society.

She flipped onto her back, lacing her fingers over her stomach, tapping each digit anxiously.

He had kissed her. She absorbed that. He. Kissed. Her. That meant he was not immune to her. He wanted her. At least for a small moment tonight, he had wanted her.

She frowned, trying to consider if he had ended that kiss ... Or had it been her? Would he have kept kissing her? Could they still be on that balcony now, living in that endless kiss?

She stood abruptly from the bed and glared at his door through the gloom of her chamber, her hands knotting into fists at her sides. She took a step forward, and then stopped, whirling back around for her bed with a groan. The bed she had slept in for a dozen plus years. Alone mostly. Alone for so long that tonight's kiss felt like her first kiss.

With a determined growl, she spun around again and marched for his door.

She had decided to end her long stretch of abstinence before he even arrived. If he had not arrived, she would probably be happily involved with a lover by now. But he had arrived. And since his arrival he was the only man she could think about.

The only man she wanted in her bed.

It was only right that he become her lover. At least only right that she extend the invitation. The logic felt appropriate. She wanted him, and she did not want to lose this chance to be with him.

She closed her hand around the latch.

Taking a big breath, she pushed open the door.

RHAIN LEFT THE Palace soon after Valencia had.

He found Dewey to let him know he was leaving. His cousin tore himself away from the arms of an eager companion he had found in the first alcove they entered. The room where Rhain had first spotted Valencia.

"You're leaving? So soon?" he asked, lifting up from the bench he shared with a masked lady who had been busy nibbling on his neck.

He nodded. "Yes. I have a busy day tomorrow."

Dewey frowned. "You used to be a great deal more fun than this."

"When I was a lad of four and ten?" he countered. That was the last time he and Dewey had been together, before his cousin moved to London.

Dewey ignored the question, saying, "This is because you saw her, isn't it? The dowager."

No surprise that his cousin recognized her, too. Her hair, her body. That mouth of hers alone was memorable. It would be permanently etched in his mind. Wide and full, the edges upturned as though stung from eating something spiced . . .

It was the kind of mouth fantasies revolved around, the kind of mouth you wanted on your skin.

Rhain did not acknowledge Dewey's statement, and it had been a statement. An observation. Not a question.

His cousin continued. "You fancy her." Another statement.

"Nonsense," he said in denial.

Dewey smiled grimly. "You do," he insisted. "She left and now you want to leave as well."

He shook his head. "It's not like that."

"It is. You're chasing after her. Panting after her like a lusty schoolboy."

Any further denial would only seem to prove his cousin's point.

"This place . . ." Rhain lifted a hand, gesturing around them. "It does not appeal to me."

"Right," Dewey said, the single word laced with skepticism.

"I'll see you soon." They had a trip planned later in the week to travel to the Dedham family seat in the country and meet with the land steward and several of the tenants.

Dewey nodded. "Of course." His cousin clapped him on the shoulder, his customary levity returning.

Rhain pointed a warning finger at him as he backed out of the alcove. "Do not get yourself into trouble tonight, cousin."

Dewey settled back down on the bench. His lady companion sidled close to his side again. "I never do."

Rhain left then. He was not a prig. His sensibilities had not been offended. When he spotted the dowager in that room, an excited thrill had zipped through him. To find her in a setting so charged, the air like that right before a storm, arousal thick as a vapor, he'd gone cock-hard, watching her watch him in a room dedicated to tupping.

He did not care about the naked women populating the house. He did not ogle them as everyone else did. He wanted only Valencia. To ogle *her*. To have *her*.

And he had kissed her at the first opportunity like the randy school lad his cousin just accused him of being.

The thrill, however, had abandoned him when she did. When she left the house, he longed to leave, too. He told himself it wasn't because he wanted to follow her. There was simply nothing left to intrigue him at Mrs. Winkler's establishment.

Now he was home again. So was she. Asleep on the other side of that door. It was an untenable situation. He was not a man to curb his desires. He enjoyed women back home. Lovers. There had not been anyone since he arrived in London. Not in the weeks before he left Wales. The longing was real.

She's not a prig. A prig would not have ventured to The Palace. She was curious at the least. Perhaps even more than curious. And the curious were always the adventurous type.

Thoughts whispered across his mind, tempting him, beckoning him to cross his room and knock on that door and see if she was as keen as he was to explore this heat between them. His lips twitched, thinking about what he might say.

Hello, there. Are you interested in using me for your pleasure?

He dragged a pillow over his face to smother his groan. He should never have kissed her. Now he could not stop thinking about that. And doing more. More kissing.

More *than* kissing . . .

He would not be that man to take advantage of a woman, a lady, under his care. He was not that. He was brought up with a mother and too many sisters to disrespect a woman that way.

He'd hold his ground. Keep his distance. Keep things proper and circumspect. He would not kiss her again. Not cross the room and open that door. Not ever.

That was his last thought as he finally drifted off to sleep.

Chapter 19

*What happens at the country house party stays
at the country house party. Well. It should.*
—Valencia, the Dowager Duchess of Dedham

The door opened with nary a creak. His room was murky.
Moonlight filtered through the cracked damask drapes, but
it was enough. No, it was perfect. Any more light, and Valencia
would have lost her nerve.

She walked on silent feet to his bed and stared down at him.
His eyes were closed, his lashes casting ridiculously dark cres-
cents on his cheekbones.

He looked younger in his sleep. Vulnerable in a way that he
never was when awake, and it only added to her sense of power
in that moment.

So much of her life, she had felt powerless. Because she had
been powerless.

Except not right now.

Right now, standing over him, the thin fabric of her robe a sheer layer over her naked curves, she felt alive and pulsing and powerful.

He must have sensed something. Or she made a sound.

His eyes fluttered open. They widened a fraction at the sight of her, but he uttered not a word and she liked that. Liked rendering him speechless for a change. Liked that there were no words between them because this was enough. They did not need words.

She reached a surprisingly steady hand for the edge of the counterpane and slid it down his chest, revealing him.

And then she knew. She had an answer to her earlier musings. He did indeed sleep naked.

Inch by inch she exposed him, laying on his back. He was all hard lines and shadows. Taut flesh and rounded muscle, testament that his was not a life spent floating through ballrooms. This man was no foppish duke, and her breath expelled in a relieved rush. He was not Dedham. Not him. Nothing like him. Her heart swelled, expanded as though cut free from a vise.

She lowered a hand to his chest, marveling at its strength. This man knew labor. Hard work. Her mouth dried and salivated alternately. Her pulse quickened, blood rushing between her legs, her core clenching, throbbing as though a heart beat and pulsed there between her legs, hungry and demanding.

Equal parts desire and trepidation pumped through her veins as his manhood grew before her eyes. Her previous long-ago couplings had been in the dark. Not like this in a moon-soaked room.

Not with him.

Everything about this was different. His body was different. Bigger. Harder. That cock rising up was definitely larger.

Still, she wanted this. She wet her lips. Needed this with an ache that went deep into her marrow. She needed this to wipe free the past, to start anew. Officially. Finally. The sight of him, of his male member, spiked some deep, resounding toll within her.

She reached for the edges of her robe and parted the fabric, letting it slide from her shoulders and drop to the floor in a whisper. She stood there without a scrap of clothing on her body, her robe pooling around her bare feet. Chin lifted. Shoulders squared. The cool air of the room glided over her, turning her skin to gooseflesh, pebbling her nipples, but she did not shrink. Did not cower.

He still did not speak. Only stared, unblinking, his eyes wide and intent, sweeping over her with a devouring look, turning her face to fire.

She acted then, afraid if she hesitated one moment longer she might lose her nerve entirely and stop.

Climbing up on the bed, she straddled him, the slight scratch of hair on his legs abrading the tender insides of her thighs in the most delicious way.

He did not move, not a finger, not a muscle. Not even when she lowered her hands and braced herself on him, her fingers digging deeply into his firm chest.

He continued to watch her in hungry fascination, wonder and awe reflected in those brown depths.

She reveled in that. Emboldened, she hovered over his hips, not sinking down yet, her thighs quivering, more from the thrill, from the excitement and anticipation than the actual strain of holding herself aloft.

Her fingers circled him. His cock pulsed, jumped, thickened in her grasp, silk on steel. She brought him to her, placed the plump head of him directly against her opening, and then sank down, deep . . . seating herself on him. Gasping. Head tossed back.

Her fingers flexed and kneaded into his chest as her long-neglected inner muscles wrapped around his length, learning his shape, molding, hugging him.

It had been so long.

Tears pricked her eyes as she settled over him, wiggling slightly, adjusting her weight, each movement sparking sensation through her body. She panted, swallowing back a sob.

His brown eyes glittered up at her. Tension locked his jaw, the tendons in his neck stretched taut, but still he did not move. Did not touch her. He simply sprawled beneath her, letting her have her way with him.

She was doing it. Taking him. Seizing her pleasure. Claiming her power.

The past was past. There was just this. This moment now.

She gave a little roll of her hips, and he hissed. Sensation shot through her, centered around the throbbing cock buried deep inside her.

She lifted her hands up from his chest, seizing his hands and bringing them to her breasts. He eagerly cupped the full mounds, and the action sent another tug low in her belly. She rocked on him again, and the motion sent heat and friction flaring at the juncture of her thighs. She leaned forward, putting pressure on that sweet spot, grinding deep on the sensitive button.

"Oh, God," she choked out, and squeezed him, tightening her channel around his length.

He cursed, and his throat arched as he surged deeper inside her, thrusting and forcefully bumping her up with the thrust of his hips.

She did not think. She reacted, lifting her pelvis and coming back down on his cock with force of her own. From there she could not stop. She pumped, working over him until her gasps turned to labored sobs.

His hands tightened where they clutched her breasts, his thumbs rolling across her stiff nipples, abrading them and sending shards of pleasure through her shaking body, and she begged, "God, yes. Please, yes. More. Do not stop."

Do not ever stop.

He obliged, rolling his fingers more firmly, pinching the erect peaks, and she bit her lip to cut off her scream. Moisture rushed between her quivering thighs, soaking him, and she erupted, crying out, moving wildly over him, clumsily, losing all rhythm as she weakly worked her hips atop him.

He choked out a groan as he reached his own climax, releasing inside her, and then he could hold still no more. He sat up, pulling her close, flush against him, his arms sliding around her back, hugging her to him, her sweat-slicked breasts crushing into his chest as his fingers tangled in her hair.

Altogether it happened in a fevered blur. It could have only been minutes, but she was shattered.

She dropped her palms onto his shoulders and allowed herself his embrace for a few moments, until her breathing evened, until she felt composed enough to move. Then she pushed back. His arms loosened around her and he let her go. She swung one leg around and climbed off him.

She dropped down and gathered up her robe from the floor, sliding it back on and tightening the belt around her waist. Her thighs were slippery wet from both of them and it should have shamed or appalled her. It did not, and she did not know what that said of her. That she was shameless, she supposed.

She shifted on her feet, savoring the sensation, the reminder, the proof of what she had done. It was wickedly titillating, prolonging her own pleasure even now, the aftershocks of which eddied through her.

Clutching the lapels of her dressing gown closed, she stared down at him without a sound. Without a word.

He looked up at her with brown eyes gone glassy, almost as though he had overindulged in spirits. Except she knew that was not the situation. He was sober. He had only indulged in her. Feasted on her and she on him. The smell of what they had done suffused the air like the headiest of perfume, the fragrance filling her nose and her with longing for a repeat performance. She wasn't only shameless. She was insatiable, too.

His chest rose and fell as though he were trying to catch his breath. He looked . . . altered. Not himself. Not the composed gentleman to pick up the mantle of duke. His hair was mussed, wild and in disarray. His features were lax, no longer the impassive mask, but open, vulnerable, revealing that he was equally shattered. Her chest pinched at the sight.

Without a word between them, she turned and padded across his chamber on her bare feet, slipping back through the door that served to connect their rooms. She shut the door almost carefully, reverently, with both her hands, and then collapsed against it, her hand clutching the front of her robe shut at her throat.

Now that the barrier of the door was between them she exhaled, breathing hard, raggedly, struggling for air. It did not seem enough. She could not draw enough air through her lips.

That happened. I did it.

The experience felt surreal. Dreamlike already. As though someone else had walked into the Duke of Dedham's room, dropped her robe, straddled him, and took her pleasure from him.

Over the past year she had thought often about taking a lover. And yet a part of her had doubted it even of herself. There were things you thought about, wild and bold and forbidden things you wished for. Things you told yourself you wanted. Things you told to your friends that you wanted to do. But never did. That line was always there. Permanent. An invisible line you never crossed. Convention and a lifetime of propriety and behaving demurely were hard things to forget.

Tonight though she had crossed that line.

She had crossed the line, and she did not regret it.

WHEN RHAIN FIRST woke he thought he was dreaming.

Opening his eyes, he found Valencia standing over him in her dressing robe, her midnight hair unbound. And then soon she rid herself of that robe. She'd disrobed and stood over him naked, with her full breasts and hips and sloping belly and cunny on display. All that warm brown hair of hers flowed around her shoulders, one tendril curling over a dusky nipple. He practically spent himself right then. He closed his eyes, recalling the sweet weight of her settling over him, the silken glove of her sex taking him inside her.

His cousin was wrong. He did *not* fancy her. That was too weak a description. If it were only *that* his life would be decidedly less complicated. He ached for her with every fiber of his being. He wished she had not gone. He wished she had stayed. For a little longer at least.

For all of the night.

It was not what he had anticipated when he came to London. This dukedom was a chore. A vast business. Something he had to do for his family. For his mother and sisters. For the tenants and endless dependents.

There was not supposed to be anything in this for me.

He stared at that still door. She was on the other side of it, but he did not wish her to be. He wanted her with him. In this room. In this bed. He wanted her with him every night for as long as he was here.

And suddenly he could not think of a reason why she should not be.

Chapter 20

*Never underestimate the actions of a
desperate man hungry for position.*
—Valencia, the Dowager Duchess of Dedham

Valencia woke up the following morning deliciously sore. She
stretched and remained in bed for a moment, flexing her
thighs and feeling the faint stirrings of arousal as the memory of
last night flooded her. She smiled softly to herself, still unable to
summon any regret or shame.

After a few moments, her smile slipped. The muted light of
dawn crept in around the edges of her drapes. Daylight brought
with it reality. Consequences.

There were always consequences.

She better than anyone knew that. A reaction to every action. A result to every decision made. Even if she felt no shame
or regret . . . cruel daylight was coming.

As much as she did not regret going to his room, to his bed, it would not happen again. It would be a mistake to make this into something more than a single night's indiscretion.

She dressed for the day, trying not to stare at that adjoining door, the portal to temptation . . . trying *not* to think how easy it would be to slip in there again tonight and crawl up alongside Rhain in bed. Perhaps this time she would even speak. Perhaps this time she would manage words and do more than take her pleasure of him and flee.

Pushing those thoughts aside, she emerged to take breakfast with the family. Rhain was absent—both a relief and a disappointment. She really was going to have to make up her mind on what it was she wanted.

Following breakfast, she and the Lloyd sisters relocated to the ballroom to meet with the dancing instructor.

Fortunately, six pupils meant an equal number of dancing partners, but the lesson ran long. The quadrille was difficult to conquer for beginners, involving many intricate steps, especially for the uncoordinated Glynnis and Del. These were the least graceful of the Lloyd sisters.

Vincenzo, their dancing master, was patient. The silver-haired gentleman was the same man her own mother had engaged to teach Valencia years ago. He was Spanish, like Mama had been, which meant an immediate connection. He and Mama would speak in their native tongue and swap stories of home.

"Ah, now there was a lady born to dance," he reminisced about

Valencia's mother. "So graceful. She loved it all and looked beautiful doing it."

Smiling in memory, Valencia nodded. "Yes. She did."

Her mother danced and painted and made music. She had brought beauty into this world. She was skilled at so many things, and embraced it all before she fell ill.

After the lesson ended, Vincenzo departed, and they all moved toward the dining room for luncheon. The girls chatted animatedly about their upcoming engagements. The opera had only whetted their appetite, and they were excited for the next affair. Valencia had settled on a musicale hosted by Maeve. A good entry point for the girls to spread their wings and interact with more people beyond the suitors who called upon them. Indeed, the musicale would be a good outing to follow the opera, a place where the sisters had been seen—as the sudden influx of invitations and barrage of suitors could attest.

The Bernard-Hills were very well-connected, and, perhaps most importantly, the musicale was on friendly ground. Maeve would be only kindly welcoming and would endeavor to cast the Lloyd sisters in the best possible light, for Valencia's sake if nothing else.

"Oh, Your Grace." Wilkes stopped before her bearing a tray with a single envelope at its center. "This just arrived for you."

She plucked the letter off the tray, hanging back and allowing the other ladies to precede her into the dining room. She ducked into the study, fetching the letter opener so that she did not savagely tear into the missive.

She expected it to be from one of her friends inviting her to tea or for ices, but as her gaze scanned the scrawl, her heart stopped. Her stomach roiled, rebelling, and she forced back a sudden surge of bile in her throat.

Dear God. She was going to be sick.

The words swam before her eyes. She reread them as though she had been mistaken.

Her heart gradually resumed beating; only instead of blood swimming in her veins it was terror.

I know it wasn't an accident.

The missive fluttered from her hands to the carpet, where it sat for a moment like a broken little bird before she bent and snatched it up with a furtive look around, as though she were being watched.

Of course, no one was in the room with her, but she felt as though she were not alone, as though eyes were on her. She felt . . . violated. Invaded.

Desperation rose up inside her chest, making it difficult to breathe. Stuffing the letter into her pocket, she fled upstairs, forgetting about luncheon. She could not sit down at the table with others and act merry as though nothing were amiss.

Once in her chamber, she locked the door behind her, for all the good that would do. Whoever was out there, whoever was writing her letters did not need to break down her door to get to her.

They were already here.

They already knew how to reach her, how to get to her and affect her.

She moved to the drapes, peering out at the street that overlooked a courtyard and beyond that the busy Mayfair lane.

Was he out there among the casual passersby, watching the house, staring up at her window even now?

Who was he and what did he *think* he knew?

On impulse she pulled the servants' rope. Within moments, Tildie arrived, knocking on the locked door and then trying the latch with no success.

Valencia opened the door and demanded she fetch whoever it was who accepted the letter this morning. With a curious look, Tildie obliged. In moments, one of the housemaids was before her—one of the maids who arrived with Rhain and his family. And just her luck . . . the girl did not speak English.

She waved the letter in front of the nervous girl, speaking slowly and overly loud as though that would somehow aid in comprehension. "Who gave this to you?"

A shadow suddenly fell over the threshold.

"Is something amiss?"

Valencia's head whipped up at the sound of the duke's deep voice. Rhain stepped inside her chamber, looking between her and the maid.

"Megha?" He looked to the maid and then said something Valencia did not understand.

The girl replied, her words a feverish rush.

His gaze returned to Valencia. "She thinks she is in trouble. She does not know what she has done to offend you."

She shook her head in exasperation. "No. Please tell her she has done nothing wrong. I merely want to know who delivered this letter." She waved the dreaded missive. "She accepted it earlier today. I want a description of the person." She smiled as though there was nothing distressing afoot and her interrogation was totally normal.

He studied her for a long, measuring moment before returning his attention to Megha and asking, presumably, Valencia's questions.

The maid replied, looking only somewhat more at ease. Then, facing Valencia again, Rhain said, "She says it was a boy. No more than ten."

"A boy?" she echoed, frowning. "Was he wearing any kind of livery?" She motioned vaguely to her body. Perhaps he worked for a notable family, and his livery would give her a clue.

He asked Valencia's question, and Megha answered, shaking her head.

Valencia nodded, her despair returning, thick in her throat, choking her. Of course it could not have been that simple.

Rhain dismissed the girl, and then he was alone with Valencia. He stepped close, looking down at her. "What is this all about?"

She shook her head. "Nothing." She pressed her lips into a mutinous line. She could not say.

He gestured to the letter in her hand. "What is in the letter?"

She bristled, and folded her fingers more tightly about the crackling parchment. "Nothing," she insisted.

He frowned. "You seem quite distraught over a great deal of . . . nothing."

"It is a . . . personal matter."

His hand lifted to brush her arm, and the kindness of the gesture nearly undid her. She longed for nothing more than to lean into him, to feel his arms around her and accept his comfort. "Clearly it has upset you—"

"It is none of your concern," she snapped, pulling away.

Something tightened in his expression.

His hand dropped away, and he sank back on his heels, nodding curtly. "I see. Of course."

He saw nothing, but she could not argue the point. She could not let him in. She could not let him see. Not without explaining the letter to him . . . not without explaining everything, all the things she could never talk about.

She swallowed and agreed. "No. It is not." Motioning to the door, she suggested, "If you would not mind taking your leave, I am suddenly very weary. I would like to rest before the musicale this evening."

His eyes sparked with anger, but his words were only polite. "Of course. I did not mean to inflict myself upon you . . . Your Grace."

She inclined her head, trying not to feel the biggest fraud, trying to pretend they were never intimates—never lovers. That she had not climbed aboard him in his bed a short time ago. She winced. One time did not a lover make. One time was . . . one time. No more than that.

"Have a nice rest." Instead of striding out into the corridor, he crossed her chamber and departed through the door joining their rooms, reminding her in that moment that they were not strangers no matter how she pretended they might be. Her cheeks warmed just thinking about how *very* well they were acquainted.

Once he was gone, she rummaged for a reticule inside her wardrobe. She was stuffing the letter inside the bag, yanking the drawstring tight when Tildie entered her room.

"Your Grace?" Tildie inquired. "Can I help you—"

"Have a carriage brought around, please."

"Oh. Are you going somewhere?"

She had thought about it often over the past year, since the last time she ventured there, but she had lacked the courage to return.

I know it wasn't an accident.

Until now.

Chapter 21

*When one requires answers, it's only common
sense to consult someone all-knowing.*
—Valencia, the Dowager Duchess of Dedham

Following the receipt of the anonymous letter, Valencia felt her burn of panic subside just enough for her to conclude there was only one place left for her to go. One thing to do. One destination ... obvious if not dreaded.

Once she reached the decision, she wasted little time boarding her carriage and making her way across Town, before she could change her mind.

She was soon shown into the well-appointed parlor. The fragrant aroma of incense and lemons and other herbs filled her nose.

"You have returned."

Not a question. A statement of fact, voiced in an accent of ambiguous origin. There were many rumors concerning Madame

Klara. They ran the gamut. Some said she was an impoverished princess from a faraway land. Others said she was a peasant girl from Greece. At any rate, she was a point of interest in the *ton* for the very valued nature of her services.

Valencia tugged off her gloves and passed them to the waiting maid before taking her seat, a table separating her from the young woman.

Madame Klara was seated in a chair that more resembled a throne, and Valencia was fairly certain it was the same ornate chair she had sat in a year ago on that fated night of the séance.

The clairvoyant's popularity had only grown over the past year. She entertained guests from the highest echelons of Society; one of her most frequent patrons, perhaps ironically, was wife to the Bishop of Winchester. The lady sought counsel from a soothsayer rather than her own husband. It was a diverting bit of *on dit* enjoyed by the *ton*.

"I have returned," she agreed. "I suppose you knew I would," Valencia challenged with a lift of her eyebrow.

Madame Klara smiled rather enigmatically, her ink-dark eyes fixing on Valencia intently. "It does not always work that way, Your Grace. It is not a trick to be summoned or controlled at my whim."

"Well, that must be most inconvenient for your business."

The lady's lips twitched. "It certainly can be, Your Grace. But I have been fortunate to have found the loyal patronage of several people in Town who have come to rely on my services." Such as the bishop's wife.

Valencia nodded. At least she was honest. Valencia appreciated that.

Doubtless there were plenty of women (and men) who shared Madame Klara's profession who were far less honorable, preying on the vulnerabilities of those desperate to believe in the skills of a clairvoyant.

Valencia had always believed that there were things that defied explanation. She had been most eager to visit Madame Klara last year. Tru had been less so. Her friend found the art of the occult rather suspect. Upon their visit to Madame Klara a year ago, Tru had been full of doubts and judgments. She had not even wanted to attend the séance. Valencia had been more trusting. She was much more inclined to believe in the existence of the extraordinary, such as . . . spirits.

She recalled her mother telling her stories of ghosts, of the miraculous acts of saints and the Blessed Virgin. She believed supernatural phenomena to be possible.

She might have come here on a whim. She did not think Madame Klara could solve her problems necessarily, but she was desperate enough to give her another try.

With that optimism and hope fueling her, she placed her hand in Madame Klara's waiting palm, letting the woman's cool fingers fold around her.

"The last time you were here—"

"A year ago," Valencia volunteered. "Approximately."

Again with that enigmatic smile. Madame Klara was a beautiful woman and surprisingly young for her accomplished and veteran reputation. "Yes. I remember well."

Valencia pressed her lips closed and nodded, telling herself it might be best to hold silent and not supply any unnecessary information, so that the lady's input would be, in fact, genuine and not affected.

"The last time you were here," the mesmerist continued, "I told you . . . to have a care near the stairs."

"You remember." Valencia nodded grimly.

"Yes. That . . . message came through very strongly."

Valencia might not have remembered . . . if the warning had come to mean nothing.

If the words had remained empty.

As it turned out, the warning was justified.

Two times that caution would have been useful if she had taken the warning seriously. And yet what could she have done other than run away from her life?

Stairs had played a significant part in her life over the past year, to be certain. The first time had been a nasty tumble—or rather a nasty push. Dedham had been in an especially foul mood when she returned home late from a merry outing with her friends. In fact, that night had been the night of the séance. The night she had met Madame Klara for the first time. A prodigious night all around. Her husband had reacted badly, all his vile suspicions and vitriol bubbling over and spilling onto her.

"As I recall, you said—"

Madame Klara cut in, quoting herself from that long-ago

night, "It is quite easy for someone to take a misstep and meet with dire consequences."

"Yes." Valencia blinked at hearing those words again from her. She had committed them to memory, and yet they gave her a little chill, knowing the events that came to be. "That is precisely what you said." Valencia nodded, her throat constricting, thinking of those *dire consequences* and how badly they had hurt.

Despite the warning, Valencia had not been able to help herself then, and she had suffered for it.

Perhaps now, however, she could help herself in a way she had not the night Dedham sent her down the stairs, or even later . . . the other time.

The other time. Could that have been avoided? She had asked herself that countless times over the past year.

The lady tapped her temple with an elegant finger covered in the black lace of her glove. "I never forget a premonition like that."

Valencia slid a piece of paper across the table between them, offering it to the woman, her chest tightening with breathlessness. "Tell me, please. Am I in trouble?" Strained breath. "Am I in trouble . . . again?"

The woman studied the note without expression. Then, after several moments, Madame Klara's beautiful dark eyes lifted to capture Valencia's. "Your trouble has never gone away. The danger is not over. You are not safe." She paused as though choosing her words carefully. "It is still coming for you, Your Grace."

Valencia nodded jerkily, that panic from earlier rising up inside her again. "Can you see what . . . or who? Who sent the letter?"

Could she do something to help herself this time? It would be different this time, she reasoned. This time she would heed the warning.

Madame Klara returned her attention to Valencia's hand, her grip clenching tighter. Closing her eyes, she exhaled and angled her head as though she were listening to something in the distance. Or someone.

After some moments she reopened her eyes.

Valencia inched forward in her seat, anticipation humming through her as she looked into the lady's fathomless stare. "Well? Can you see him?"

"This person clings to shadows. Darkness surrounds them, but they are watching you. They will not stop. They mean you ill."

Valencia's shoulders slumped.

Madame Klara shook her head. "I am sorry I cannot be more specific. Have you any idea who might want to hurt you? Have you any enemies?"

My husband. But unless he'd returned from the dead, it was not him.

"No. There is no one."

"Oh." She nodded, smiling sadly. "There is someone, Your Grace."

Valencia fell back in her chair, dejected. "You've been helpful." Not as helpful as she had hoped, but good manners always prevailed, even in such circumstances.

"Is there somewhere you can go? Can you leave Town?"

Valencia stifled a snort and bit back an immediate denial. Leaving Town had been the very thing she had hoped to avoid. And now . . .

Yes. She had a place to go. Perhaps she should. Perhaps she would be safe there, but she didn't want to be safe if it meant she would never see Rhain again.

What good was safety if you felt dead inside?

The notion of leaving London loomed as unbearable as ever. It would be all the more bittersweet because of Rhain. He was here, placed conveniently close in the chamber next door to hers, one door between them, within arm's reach. She didn't want what she had found with him to end. It had just begun.

They had just begun.

For however long he was here, she wanted to be here, too. In London. With him. She wanted to spend more nights—every night—in bed with him.

"Your Grace?" Madame Klara gently prompted.

She shook her head, suddenly calm with resolve. "I cannot leave."

The woman frowned. "I fear for you . . ."

Valencia feared, too, but she had lived so much of her life in trepidation, in fear of her next move. She would not permit fear to keep her a prisoner any longer.

She lifted her chin, saying slowly, "I am not without friends." She knew the danger was real. She knew someone was out there, watching her, stalking her . . . but she was not alone. She had never been alone.

Her friends were the most loyal of comrades. As fierce as any warrior. They would help. Perhaps they could put their heads together and work out who might want to harm her. Again.

The House Party

One year ago

No matter how many times Valencia's husband had put hands on her—*hurt her*—and it had been a number of times over the years, she never accustomed herself to the pain of it. The suddenness. The shock. Pain was always an astonishment to the body, no matter how familiar.

As a little girl, she had been warm and loved and cosseted by her mother. It was hard to reconcile the woman she was with that child she had been. She supposed no one ever imagined their future becoming one of fear and pain. No one ever imagined becoming a victim.

No one ever imagined a fate like this.

She went down on her knees. There she stayed, crawling, scampering to escape him. They had almost reached the end of the corridor. The only way left to go was down. Down the stairs.

She started to rise, ready to take flight, when she felt the sharp smack of his cane against her back. White-hot agony seared through her.

She fell back down again, palms burning as they ground into the runner. With a furious whimper, she turned, flipped over and faced him, kicking his cane out from under him so that he came crashing down in the corridor beside her.

"Valencia! Are you hurt? What is happening?" Ros and Delia appeared like a pair of angels with their nightgowns floating around them like billowing wings. Their bare feet padded over the runner in their haste to reach her, and hot shame rose up in her throat, choking her. *No.* This was not something she had ever wanted her friends to see.

"N-nothing."

The girls seized her hands, helping her up.

Dedham managed to get to his feet without help, leaning heavily on his cane. None of the rage had left his eyes. He waved a wild hand at them. "This is none of your concern. Return to your beds."

"This is not your house," Ros rebutted, her nostrils flared.

"Valencia?" Now Maeve arrived, slipping on her dressing robe and tightening the belt as she advanced on them.

"Oh. It's a party now," Dedham declared. "All your friends are here. Splendid."

Maeve looked from him to Valencia in consternation. "Are you in trouble, Valencia? Can we ... help?" she asked in that ever-reasonable voice.

"Everyone, it's fine," she assured, fighting the sting of tears and managing not to suffocate on that obvious lie. Her friends weren't supposed to see this. They weren't supposed to ever know. "Just go back to bed. I'm sorry we disturbed—"

"Oh, shut your bloody mouth, you stupid bitch. Do you think they believe that?" Dedham growled, and she could not help herself. She reacted.

Perhaps it was the presence of her friends, surrounding her, giving her courage. Her hand lashed out, cracking him solidly across the face. It felt so good. So satisfying.

He froze for a long moment, and then his eyes turned on her, shocked and glittering with hate.

Needles of cold prickled through her. She knew what was coming.

More fear. More pain.

He lifted his cane and brought it down toward her face. She flung an arm out, bracing herself for the attack.

It never came.

The pain never landed.

Her friends charged forward. Almost as one, they barreled into him. She caught a flash of his face, the bulging eyes, the stunned expression the moment before he toppled over and plummeted down the stairs, his mouth wide on a silent scream.

They all stood at the top of the stairs, gasping, sobbing, clinging to one another, gazing down at the broken, lifeless body of her husband.

Chapter 22

*In the jungle the lion is the greatest predator. In the ton
it is the rake. I am not certain which is more dangerous.*
—Valencia, the Dowager Duchess of Dedham

No one spoke as the note was passed from Ros to Maeve to
Delia, and then it went another round among them.

Valencia watched the color drain from her friends' faces.

Delia offered her the letter, and she declined it. She did not
need to see it again. She could see the words perfectly in her mind.

When she left her house, she fetched Delia and Ros and went
directly to Maeve's house. The four of them sat in the garden, as
the staff was busy readying for tonight's musicale, but that wasn't
the only reason. There was less chance of being overheard out of
doors in the garden.

Finally, Maeve spoke, her eyes brimming with hope. "Perhaps
it's not about that night."

Ros snorted. "What else could it be about?"

Maeve shook her head and looked beseechingly at Valencia. "Could it refer to anything else, Valencia?"

"I cannot think what else it could be . . ."

"It is rather vague," Delia provided, as desperately hopeful as Maeve.

"I am sorry, but this is a threat." Ros waved the parchment in the air, crinkling it with her fist.

"It was an accident!" Delia's lip trembled. "We did not mean to kill him."

"Of course we did not," Maeve agreed in that calm and reasonable voice of hers. Nothing rattled her. "We were defending Valencia."

"Oh, we're murderers." Ros shrugged as though it did not matter in the least to her. "But he deserved it. Let's not pretend otherwise."

Maeve gasped, and then whispered hoarsely, "We're not *murderers*."

Ros shrugged. "Well. None of us will rot in hell for what we did. I think we can all agree on that."

"What should we do?" Delia asked. "Should we tell my mother? Jasper?"

Valencia shook her head. "No. The fewer involved, the better." She did not wish to implicate Tru in this. The house party had been at her country home, after all. If the truth of that night came to light, they could at least spare her any other involvement. She was on the verge of marrying the love of her life. At long last, she had found happiness. Valencia would not cast a shadow over that. "No. We should keep this between us."

That had been the original agreement. Tell no one. They would keep to the pact.

At least, she thought they had all kept to the pact. Except someone outside their group knew. Had someone talked?

Clearly Valencia was not the only one speculating in such a manner. Ros sharpened her gaze on her niece. "Delia . . . did you tell anyone?"

Hot color splashed across the girl's face. "No! Never. We agreed."

Maeve patted her hand. "Of course you did not." Maeve sent a reproving look at Ros. "We made a pact."

Valencia sighed. "Well. Someone knows. Someone who was there, presumably. One of the other guests . . ."

Maeve chewed her lip, fretting. They all exchanged grim looks.

"Who would even do such a thing?" Delia shook her head in perplexity.

Silence fell as they considered this, thinking of that long-ago night in the Lake District at Chatham House. She cataloged all the guests in her head, their faces shuffling through her mind one after the other.

"Lord Burton," Valencia whispered, the man's dreadful visage rising above all others. He had been awake at that late hour— assaulting her shortly before Dedham showed up to heap his abuses upon her. It had to be him.

"Ohhh." Delia nodded in commiseration. "Yesss. He is a

wretched man." As a longtime friend of her late father, she was well aware of Lord Burton's profligate ways.

"Or Ashbourne," Ros chimed in.

"Lord or lady?" Maeve queried.

Valencia winced. "Either one."

Ros nodded with a sniff. "Both are despicable people."

"So, in truth . . . quite a few suspects," Valencia grumbled, continuing to consider the others.

Ros tsked with a shake of her head. "Except Burton and the Ashbournes . . . why would they have waited a year? That seems unlikely. If they wanted to blackmail you, would they not have done so sooner?"

Valencia nodded. And Burton would have certainly used this against her. It would have been an effective way to manipulate her into doing whatever he wanted.

"Well. Who, then?" Delia demanded, her pretty features twisted with anxiety.

Who indeed?

And then suddenly Valencia did know.

She knew *precisely* who would send such a threatening letter to her.

Chapter 23

The only thing more important than a nobleman is his heir.
—Hazel, the Marchioness of Sutton

Hazel's husband found her wrist-deep in the garden, pulling weeds and setting them aside in a pile. Sutton did not often brave the out-of-doors. He complained the sun was too bright (yes, even in London) and the garden too far a walk from the house. It was just a few paces from the back door, but for him it might as well have been a league's distance.

He still refused to be pushed about in a wheelchair, although she thought it might be time for that. At this rate, he was destined for a fall.

She dreaded that, and admittedly it was not for entirely altruistic reasons. A broken leg or hip would not be fun for anyone in their household. It would be a misery for him, the staff, and

Hazel especially. His demands on her would only increase in that unfortunate event.

"There you are." He brandished a sheet of parchment in his free hand that was not clutching the head of his cane for support. "I've been looking for you, m'dear." His upper lip curled as he assessed her labors. "Should have surmised you would be out here. You know we have servants to do this. Gardeners for this very purpose."

She sat back on her heels, dusting the loose soil from her gloved hands, and blew at the fiery strand of hair that fell loose before her eyes. "You know I prefer tending the garden myself." She had grown up in the city, in narrow tenements. Never a room to herself, never a scrap of green, never earth under her feet. Nothing grew or flourished. There was only ever gray. She loved this.

She nodded to the parchment in his hand, then bent back over her flowers. "What have you there?"

"'Tis a list. I've been working on it ever since our conversation."

She stilled, her hands pausing on her tulip bulbs. "What conversation was that?" she asked with deliberate vagueness.

She feigned ignorance, but she knew. Oh, how she knew.

That dreadful conversation they had after visiting Valencia had stayed with her, playing in her mind in an awful loop for days now.

You shall have my heir . . . There are ways, m'dear.

What could Sutton have meant? She had been too afraid to demand clarification. She had lived braced tight as a coil ever since his declaration, half in terror that he would show up in her chamber in the middle of the night intent on ravishment, and half in disbelief, because the man could not get his trousers on without assistance. Surely he was not capable of begetting an heir on anyone.

"You goose, have you forgotten? We must get you with child, with an heir, so that you shall be properly protected in the future and not fall to a fate similar to our own dear Valencia."

"That was not a jest?" she asked weakly. Or a nightmare?

"Indeed not. It is a brilliant plan. Do you know who my heir is? My cousin's son, Martin. That fop fancies himself a poet, an *artist*, and he holds these ridiculous salons."

She was aware of the salons. She and Sutton were often invited. Of course, they never attended. It was not her husband's cup of tea, and Hazel was only too happy to stay at home. The only time she went out about Society was when her husband insisted on it. Why should she care to endure the ladies with their false smiles and the gentlemen with their leers?

He shook his head. "And we cannot count upon *his* kindness to see you through. Indeed not."

Indeed not. Poet or not, he fell into the category of leering gentlemen. She had heard that his salons were something that would make Dionysus blush. Sutton must not know that, or he would probably have dragged them to join.

"Ah. This list of yours . . ." she prodded for him to continue, pointing her shears at the parchment.

"Ah. Yes. I've thought long and hard on the matter, and I've come up with four candidates."

"Candidates?" she echoed dumbly.

He looked at her in exasperation. "You are being ever so dim, m'dear. Candidates to father your child, of course."

She blinked. *Of course?*

What was so very *of course* about it? He was shopping for a stud to . . . She glanced down at her garden. To *fertilize* her. He announced this plan of his as though it were a natural conclusion.

"Husband, you cannot mean . . . You are speaking of adultery." Wives were killed for less, and the world looked the other way.

Sutton waved a gnarled hand dismissively. "Oh, 'tis not adultery."

"Er. I believe it is the very definition, my lord."

"Not when I am in support of it," he countered, and shook the parchment in the air.

"I do not think that is how it works," she said wryly. Even if he was agreeable to being cuckolded, it was still infidelity.

"Well, it *should* work that way. I am your husband and I am not complaining and I am saying that you *can* do this. For the greater good, m'dear . . . you must bed one of these men." He gave the paper another shake.

She blinked. It was absurd.

His words were . . . absurd, and they struck a chord of terror deep within her. She did not want to bed anyone. That part of her life was thankfully over.

When she had wed Sutton, she told herself she would never have to let a man into her bed again. That had been the comfort in taking vows with him. She was marrying an old man, but he was an impotent one and her bed would be her own.

He gave another rattle of the parchment. "Come now, I've thought long and hard on who can be relied upon for discretion and who has already proven himself."

"Discretion?" She shook her head.

Proven himself?

"Aye." He nodded and then looked at her crossly. "Really, Hazel. You're usually much brighter than this."

Never had such an outrageous scheme been laid at her feet. How could she be expected to make sense of it?

He continued. "All these gentlemen are married, so you know they will be discreet, and they've all proven their seed and sired multiple sons."

She recoiled. He made it sound all so very sordid. As though she were naught more than a broodmare, which did not seem such an improvement from *whore*, her designation before her marriage. Arguably, she was still *that* in the estimation of many.

"H-how do you know any of these married gentlemen would wish to do such a thing? Break their vows . . . and give away a child of their bloodline?"

Sutton laughed. "You're terribly naive, my dear. These are my peers. I know them because I was one of them."

And he would have agreed to such a thing.

She still had her doubts. "I think you misjudge—"

"A chance to wet their cock with you free of consequences?" He chuckled. "I misjudge nothing. I know men."

She flinched. "I cannot . . ."

Sutton straightened to his not-very-considerable height and

leveled a stern glare at her. "I insist you do this, wife. 'Tis the only way to keep all that I have from the hands of those who do not deserve it."

Anger rose up in her. Here she was yet again, commanded to spread her legs, expected to obey and surrender her body. Things had not changed so very much, after all, it seemed.

Forcing a smile, she reached for the list to see the gentlemen he had decided worthy to stud.

He gladly released it, returning her smile, clearly thinking he had won.

This was what she had learned over time. It was easier to let men believe themselves the victors. Let them think she was beaten. Then she would do as she liked and live as she chose.

Out of curiosity, she scanned the list. All married men, as he had said. Even one of the late king's bastards had made the list.

"Faultless bloodlines all," he added, nodding agreeably. She supposed that was true. Bastard or no, his blood was blue.

Still clinging to her tight little smile, she folded the parchment and tucked it inside her glove. "I shall think on it."

"Please, do so. You should get started on the matter at once. Not that I think I'm about to expire, but what if you have a girl child? You will want to try again for a son."

I do not want to try at all.

Did he not understand that?

Once he was gone, she would take whatever jointure was provided and retire into happy obscurity. She did not care to cling to any of this life and did not require anything to tether herself to this world.

And yet he was set on this course. He had that militant gleam in his eyes—it was the look he always got when he was most implacable.

He went on. "It must be a son. And," he said with emphasis, "you're not getting any younger."

She laughed humorlessly at that. He was calling *her* old?

Sighing, she nodded. She'd let him think he had won for now and stall for time . . .

For how many years though?

Aside from his physical limitations, he was scarcely on his deathbed. What would she do if he did not let the matter rest and lived another decade or more? How could she put him off?

In that scenario, what can I do except give him what he wants? An heir.

"Very good," he crowed. "Now I must go inside for my nap. All this sunlight is making me feverish."

Hazel glanced up at the cloudy sky.

He departed with a steady clacking of his cane. Once he was out of sight, she slipped the list out from her glove, contemplating the names now as one might consider a list of entrées.

"My lady!"

Her head snapped up at the breathless cry.

The Sutton butler huffed, his face pink with exertion as he barreled toward her where she knelt among the flowers. "I told her to wait in the drawing room."

The identity of *her* was soon evident. Her stepdaughter dogged the butler's heels and soon overtook the gentleman on the pebbled path.

"My lady," he rather belatedly intoned as he stopped before Hazel. "The Dowager Duchess of—"

"Oh, be gone," Valencia snapped. "She knows who I am, and I will have a word alone with the marchioness."

To his credit, the butler looked to Hazel for direction.

She nodded. "Leave us, please, Ritter."

With a wary look at Valencia, he took his leave.

Valencia waited until he was gone before charging ahead. "Was it you?"

Hazel angled her head. "Me . . . what?"

The color rode high in Valencia's cheeks. She took a breath as though fighting for composure. "The letter I received this morning . . . was it from you?" she bit out in a hard voice.

She was upset. Hazel studied her intently. More than that, she was . . . scared.

Placing one gloved hand on her bent knee, she rose to her feet. "I did not send you any correspondence."

Valencia peered at her intently, clearly assessing her for the truth. After some moments, she said, "I know we do not get on . . . but I need you to be honest with me."

"Valencia," she said carefully, uncertainly. Her stepdaughter was speaking to her gently, almost kindly, and she did not know what to make of that. "I did not send you anything." Pause. "What was in this letter?"

At that, Valencia's lips compressed. Clearly the contents of that letter were not open for public consumption.

She shook her head. "Do not concern yourself."

Hazel bristled. "Need I remind you that *you* came *here*?"

Valencia exhaled sharply and gave a slight nod of acknowledgment. "Yes."

Hazel knew she was being accused of something ugly, without knowing the particulars. She was the last person in whom her stepdaughter would confide, but the woman looked on the verge of collapse. Her eyes were red-rimmed, and her dark hair was mussed, as though she had run her fingers through it several times.

"Valencia." It was her turn to speak gently. "Are you unwell? Can I help you with something?"

Valencia's liquid-dark eyes locked and held hers. After a long moment she released another breath. She shook her head slowly. "No. No one can help me."

That said, she turned and departed the garden.

"Valencia!" Hazel called, taking a step after her, but she continued on, not stopping, not looking back.

Chapter 24

If you truly wish to know all the happenings of
Good Society, ask the maid. She always knows.
—Valencia, the Dowager Duchess of Dedham

Valencia was already packing by the time Tildie arrived in her chamber.

She'd wasted no time upon her return home. As soon as she entered the room, she pulled out her valises.

After leaving Hazel, she was fairly certain that her stepmother was not the one behind the letter. She did not know who was responsible, and that was perhaps the most frightening thing of all.

The predator in the dark, the shadow at the window, the unknown threat . . . it all felt so much worse.

She could not stay in London. She accepted that now. As much as she wanted to stay, she could not. She could not stay here, constantly afraid, looking over her shoulder. Perhaps it was cowardly, but she was running away. She would feel safer anywhere that wasn't here, where ominous letters were sent.

"Your Grace? Are we . . . leaving?"

Valencia sent the girl the barest glance. "Yes, please help me. I would like to be on our way within the hour."

Tildie's face paled a bit at that. "On our way? Now? Where?"

"Yorkshire, of course. The dower house." She shot the girl another quick glance. "That is, if you still wish to come with me."

There was a long pause before she replied, "Of course. Yes." Despite her agreement, her words did not ring with conviction. With a small shake of her head, she blinked and then took over the packing. They left more than they packed. The rest could be sent for. She had to be on her way posthaste. Even now, she felt as though she were being watched . . .

After a few moments, Tildie stepped out to fetch a footman to help with the luggage, leaving the door open behind her . . . leaving Valencia exposed.

"Valencia?" She froze at the deep voice. "Are you going somewhere?"

She turned slowly to face Rhain. He was not alone. Dewey Pugh was with him. Pugh with his infernal grin, looking vastly amused at the entire situation.

Rhain stepped inside her chamber, approaching. Pugh followed several paces behind as though it were completely acceptable for him to enter her chamber.

"Rhain," she breathed.

He looked from her to her luggage. "Where are you going?"

She paused. "The dower house."

His nostrils flared slightly. "In Yorkshire?" As though there were another one.

"Yes."

"Why? I thought you didn't want to go there. I thought we had an agreement. My sisters have not yet acclimated—"

"Your sisters will be fine," she assured him, returning her attention to the luggage. "I believe there are a score of gentlemen down in the drawing room even now. The girls will have their pick."

His hand was on her arm then, tugging her back around to face him. "What has happened? Why are you leaving? Did someone offend you? One of my sisters? My mother?"

"No. No. Nothing like that." But he knew her well enough by now to know that something *had* happened.

His lovely eyes crawled over her features. He leaned in, his husky voice dragging over her skin. "It is me, then. You are leaving because of me?"

Heat bloomed in her face, and something crumpled inside her at the vulnerability in his voice. She sent a hasty, embarrassed glance Pugh's way. His cousin continued to watch raptly. "N-no."

"Valencia. You agreed to stay."

His earnestness made her chest squeeze. "I must go."

Tildie returned then with a footman. They both stopped abruptly, glancing at everyone in the room. Pugh nodded at them as though welcoming them to the exhibit.

Rhain did not give them a glance. He did not seem to care that they had an audience at all. He fixed his gaze intently on Valencia with the sharp focus of a wolf.

"Don't. Go. Stay." A hush fell over the chamber. And then: "You cannot leave. I do not want you to."

For a moment she, too, forgot the others. She could only look back at Rhain and wish that she could stay. Her heart swelled at his words, to know whether she stayed or left mattered to him—that he gave a bloody damn. That he cared about . . . her. He cared about *her*. Even without his words, she saw that in his gaze, in the intensity of his expression, in the tension tightening his body.

It all gave her pause, weakening her resolve. She moistened her lips. "Rhain," she said softly, pleadingly, "do not do this." Do not make it so hard. Don't make it hurt.

Still staring at her, he commanded the others in the room: "Leave us."

The footman fled at once. Tildie and Pugh hesitated.

Rhain's voice fell harder, louder. "I said leave. And do not disturb us."

Tildie jumped slightly. Pugh obliged, reaching for her arm and leading her from the chamber, closing the door behind them with a soft click.

Once they were alone, Valencia attempted to explain—at least what she could explain. There were secrets, after all, that could never be brought to light. "I know I am reneging on our agreement, but the girls are lovely and they will be fine. Please understand that I really need to leave—"

He cut her off. Stepping forward in one long stride, he took her face in his hands. "*You* understand this," he growled, his thumbs swiping across her cheeks. "You cannot leave me."

She fell into his gaze, drowning in those brown pools. She tried to speak but managed only a choked sound. Had she thought this wouldn't hurt? That she could avoid this pain?

"Tell me you don't want me, and I will let you go."

Oh. God.

She opened her mouth, readying to put voice to that lie, but only a sob escaped.

Then he was kissing her.

Blistering her lips with his. His tongue tasted of brandy and man and *him*, filling her mouth, sweeping across hers, and her knees buckled. She clung to him, her fingers digging into his shoulders.

He gently bit her lip. "Tell me you want me, too."

"I want you, too," she sobbed.

One of his arms wrapped around her waist, hefting her up against him. He carried her the few feet until he dropped her down onto the bed. Then he was over her, between her thighs.

Their hands worked in a fever, tearing at each other's clothes in a frenzy until they were free. Until he was driving into her, his mouth still on hers, swallowing her cries, their hands everywhere, groping, squeezing, holding.

They worked in tandem, desperate for each other, wild as animals.

Her hips lifted, meeting each thrust, as hungry to take him as he was to give, to claim—to become one.

THEY FELL ASLEEP in her bed.

Valencia woke him one more time that night, crawling over him, and they made love slowly, leisurely, with long, forever kisses. Their bodies pushed and strained against each other until they were spent, sated. Until she had filled her memory to the brim of him. Even then she wanted more. It was not enough. It never would be, but it would have to be.

She wanted this every night.

Him, every night.

She wanted to love him. For him to love her. *Dear God.* This hurt.

Just before dawn she crept from bed, lifting one of her valises as quietly as possible. She would worry about the rest of her things later. Send for them when she arrived in Yorkshire.

She crept from her chamber and waited out in the corridor for a few moments to see if he would follow. Satisfied she had not woken him, she continued down the silent hallway.

The staff would rouse soon. Some may very well already be awake. She needed to fetch Tildie.

At least she would have the full day for travel. She would put as much distance as possible between herself and London.

She was almost to the servants' staircase when she was pushed hard and suddenly from behind. She went down on her knees with jarring force, the layers of her dress offering little protection. A sharp cry escaped her at the unexpected pain before she was quickly silenced with a gag. Then a hood came over her head.

She struggled wildly and managed to land a blow somewhere on her attacker's person.

He grunted, clearly unhappy with her efforts. He released an *ooof* and then agony exploded in her face. She went limp and oblivion rolled in like a great fog.

Her head felt woozy. She whimpered, fighting for consciousness, fighting for her life, but it was too hard.

She slipped away as the fog grew thicker, and her world became darker and denser and deeper inside her hood.

Her last fading thought was of Rhain.

VALENCIA FELT AS though she were swimming up from the bottom of a pond, pushing off the marshy bed through the denseness, searching for the surface. She burst free with a gasp, her eyes flying open on a fresh wave of pain.

Wincing, she reached up with her bound hands to feel her face, managing to lightly finger her swollen jaw where she had been struck.

Blinking, she peered around her, assessing her surroundings.

She was in a small room. On a narrow bed. A single lantern burned dully from the bedside table. A window beckoned from the far side of the chamber, and she knew she needed to reach it. To see where she was. And yet her world undulated around her as though she were underwater.

She inhaled through her teeth, drawing in a seething breath, waiting for the world to right itself and for everything to stop rippling and blurring around her.

The gag was still stuffed in her mouth, and that was its own small misery. She shifted, making a move to rise to her feet and realized she could not. Not only were her ankles bound, but they were tethered to the bed. With her hands also restrained, she could not manage to undo the binding no matter how much she tried. She wasn't getting up to inspect that window even though she desperately wanted to. At least her hood had been removed. There was that. She could see whatever horror was coming.

She waited on the bed. She had no choice. She was a prisoner.

Minutes passed. Hours.

It was impossible to know how much time passed. Light filtered in through the cracks in the shutters. Dust motes danced on the narrow ribbons of light. She dozed, coming in and out of awareness, thinking about Rhain, wondering if he realized she was missing yet, if he knew she had been taken.

She desperately needed to relieve herself, and she was beginning to wonder if she was going to have to do that on the bed when she heard a lock lifting on the door.

She held her breath. Lifted her head and looked toward the door, ready, finally, to see who had done this to her.

It was the same person who had sent her the menacing letter. It had to be. How many enemies could one person have? *This* had to do with *that*.

The door opened with a creak, its hinges in need of oil. Her gaze sharpened, searching, seeking the face of the person who had abducted her.

At last, the villain stepped over the threshold, staring coldly at her.

She gasped in bewilderment. "You."

The House Party

One year ago

Tildie eased the door shut behind her, careful not to make a sound. She should not be here. Not this time of night. Not in this part of the house. Not emerging from this chamber.

She knew her mistress would not approve of such behavior from her. It was the kind of thing that could get her sacked.

And yet Ashbourne had charmed her. He was handsome and titled and rich . . . and not a terrible lover. She smiled at that. That might have been enticement alone. But there was even more than that. The sapphire necklace he had gifted her sat heavily in the pocket of her skirts. How could she be expected to resist? She was only human.

Easing back from his bedchamber door, she slid her hand inside her pocket, caressing the jewel's cool, reassuring shape. She had earned it, and there was something about the attention of a nobleman that fed her ego . . . that made her feel beautiful and special. Important.

All day every day she waited on these people. Most of the time they did not even see her. She was invisible. She did not even exist to them. Especially to the ladies. They pranced around in their gowns and jewels, blind to her. So when the men in their lives wanted her, when they coveted her and pursued her over their own exalted wives . . .

Yes. It gratified her. It made her feel whole and decidedly not invisible.

She started toward the servants' stairs with light steps, stopping at the sound of . . . voices. Muffled voices. Multiple voices.

She turned, following the noise, curious as to who was awake at this late hour.

Tildie moved stealthily, nearing the corner. Pausing, she peered around. That was when she saw the duke and duchess arguing. She winced. He was a right proper bastard, always mistreating her ladyship.

Her mistress tried to hide the bruises, but Tildie knew. She knew that he made the duchess's life hell, and she actually pitied the woman—one of the only noblewomen to ever earn, and deserve, her sympathy. And yet Tildie knew better than to intervene. She needed this position. She could not go against a duke of the realm. She had her grandmother and sister relying on her. She could not afford to get sacked and fail them.

Shaking her head, she started to turn, ready to retire to her chambers . . . and then the others appeared. Her mistress's friends: the Lady Cordelia and Mrs. Bernard-Hill and Lady Shawley.

She released a small breath of relief. *Good.* They would help her. They would see that the duchess was unharmed.

Riveted, she watched as things escalated, unable to look away from the terrible scene unfolding.

She watched in mounting horror as the duke lunged for his wife with wild eyes, lifting his cane high to strike her. Tildie gawked . . . right up to the point when the ladies came at him as one, pushing him down the stairs.

Gasping, Tildie turned and fled, hastening away on silent feet until she was safely inside her chamber. There she remained even as shouts of alarm went up in the house, signaling what she already knew.

The Duke of Dedham was dead.

Chapter 25

There is no trouble a new dress and beautiful shoes cannot cure. Well, almost no trouble.
—Valencia, the Dowager Duchess of Dedham

Rhain woke to a cold bed.

It wasn't his bed either, but he'd fallen asleep with Valencia, so it was the bed he wanted to be in. Except now she was gone. He propped himself up on one elbow and peered around the chamber, his disappointment at not finding her acute. Almost as intense as the disappointment he had felt when she announced she was leaving yesterday. He'd persuaded her to stay, and now he knew he had to convince her to stay . . . forever.

Her valises still sat on the floor . . . except perhaps there was one fewer case than before. Sliding on his trousers, he strode across the chamber and opened the door, peering out into the corridor. Frowning, he stepped out, inspecting the valise in the middle of the corridor, as though it had been discarded and forgotten there.

He picked it up, turned it over in his hands.

Footsteps sounded on the runner. He looked up. Valencia's maid Tildie advanced down the corridor. She paused when she saw him, her eyes widening as they traveled from him to the valise he held.

"Your Grace," she murmured, her voice heavy with uncertainty.

"Have you seen the dowager?"

"Um." She bit her lip and looked away, clearly uncomfortable holding his gaze. "She is gone."

"Gone?" She would not have left her bags. Something was not right.

He approached her, still holding the valise in his hands. "Have you seen Valencia?" he pressed, his voice harder. She was acting strangely. He was convinced the maid knew something.

"Um." She continued to stammer, and his stomach churned with unease.

"Answer me, woman," he demanded. "What has happened?"

She looked suddenly ill. "She is gone, and . . . I think . . . she's in trouble."

All of him tensed, ready to battle, except he did not know who or what to fight. He only knew that fight for her he would.

For her he would fight to the death.

"What trouble?" he growled.

She exhaled. "I need to explain."

VALENCIA STARED AT him uncomprehendingly for several long moments. She could not make a sound beyond muffled noises through her gag, but she did not know what she would have said anyway.

It was all so bewildering.

So many things whirled through her mind. Her principal thought seemed to form into one word though. It burned through her like wildfire even as she watched him advance toward the bed. *Why?*

"Good afternoon. I see you're awake."

Pugh stopped beside the bed and tugged her gag free. She recoiled, afraid he might touch her or strike her again.

He continued. "I am very glad to see that my blow did not render you permanently impaired." He angled his head thoughtfully as he considered her. "I've never struck anyone before. You'll have to forgive me for that."

She worked her sore jaw and licked dry lips with an equally dry tongue. "You're admirably skilled at it for all your inexperience." Her voice came out hoarse and strained.

He smiled frostily. "Good to see you still have your wits about you. That will make things easier."

She studied him warily. "What ... *things*?" She glanced around the room. "Where am I? Why am I here, Pugh?"

He tsked. "Call me Dewey. And so many questions, Valencia ... but I suppose that is understandable. I would feel the same way in your position."

She scowled. "Let us put aside the false compassion. You've

abducted me and imprisoned me . . ." Her voice faded, and she looked around again searchingly.

He flicked his fingers in the air. "This is my home. Nothing as grand as what you are accustomed to, but it is only temporary. Soon I'll be living in Mayfair." His chest lifted, puffed up a bit.

"In Mayfair?"

"Indeed. When my cousin returns to Wales and you retire to Yorkshire, someone needs to be lord and master of what was once your home."

Slow understanding began to take hold. "You want me out of the way."

He nodded cheerfully. "I thought that was a given the moment Rhain showed up . . . but then you had to go and seduce him. He is quite enamored of you." He clucked his tongue and sank down onto the edge of the bed beside her. "I tried to show him all the delights London had to offer, but he's only had eyes for you, Duchess." An eye roll at that. "Such a provincial. I blame his upbringing. Bryn Bychan doesn't exactly brim with Society." He looked her over insultingly, and she shrank under his gaze. "You must have some magic cunny, Duchess."

She flinched at that. "I do not understand. What does his relationship with me matter?"

"He's appointed me his steward when he returns to Wales. I will be his representative. It's as though I will be the acting duke. Do you have any idea what a boon that is for me?" His gaze drilled into her.

Apparently enough of a boon for him to abduct her.

He continued. "He cannot stay here because of you."

Ah.

She worked her dry mouth again. "It is not like that between us."

"Of course it is." He scoffed. "You're not that stupid. You have him on the hook. Well done, Duchess. It did not take you long."

He thought she set out to seduce Rhain? To trap him?

"I am aware you never wished to go to the dower house," he added. "You want to stay here, and now he wants you. I can see where this is all headed." He nodded, so very certain of himself.

And now he wants you.

She saw Rhain's face in her mind then . . . heard his voice.

Stay.

How she wished she was with him now.

"So you've abducted me to . . . what? For what purpose?" She swallowed against her impossibly tight throat. He wanted her out of the way, clearly. The fear crept back in, riding higher in her throat . . . It had never completely been at bay, but now it strangled her. What would he do to her?

He laughed then. "Do not look so worried. I'm not going to kill you. I'm not a villain."

She resisted arguing that was precisely what he was.

He continued. "I merely will invoke your promise to leave London . . . and have nothing further to do with my cousin."

She studied him for quite some time. She told herself to merely say the words. She *should* say whatever he wanted in order for him to free her. Lie, if need be. Anything to get away.

Except she knew he would expect her to follow through

and actually leave London, leave Rhain, and suddenly she was quite definite she did not want to do that. She did not want to walk away from Rhain. She could *not* do that. She was in love with him, and she was not giving him up. Not as long he wanted her, too.

She had tried and failed at love before. But this time felt different. It felt different because she was different. Rhain was different.

He was good and decent and beautiful—inside and out—and she knew that to be true in a way she had never known anything before.

She was not a trusting little girl anymore who took everything at face value. She peered closer at people. She listened to *her* mind and heart and gut . . . instead of listening to what everyone else in Society was telling her.

"Of course you could promise me that and be lying." He nodded mildly. "I'm no fool."

No. He was not. He was a blackguard, but not a fool. She narrowed her gaze on him, studying him warily, bracing herself for his next move.

"Which is why I took precautions to compel you to do as I ask," he added.

She shook her head. "I do not understand—"

"Tildie."

"Tildie?" She frowned. "What about her?" Was he threatening to hurt her maid? "If you lay one finger on—"

He laughed. "Oh, I did not hurt her. On the contrary. She

quite enjoyed what I did to her. She likes me." He gave a strangely self-deprecating grin and shrugged. "She trusts me. So much that she confides things in me. Very interesting things."

Things.

"What things?" she asked, the fear twisting anew inside her.

"Things like what happened at a house party one year ago. Things like how you and your friends murdered your husband."

She gasped. He *had* sent the letter.

Because of Tildie.

The pieces all clicked together. Tildie must have seen what happened that night. She knew all this time and never said a word. Except to *him*. She had told Dewey. Now he knew. He knew their secret.

"It wasn't like that," she insisted, thinking of her dear friends. "We did not mean to kill him. We *did not kill* him. It was an accident—"

He waved a hand indifferently. "Oh, I do not really care what happened. I only know that the authorities would be vastly interested in justice for the murder of a duke."

A sob welled up in her chest and sat there, pressing down on her like a pile of bricks. She fought for breath against the crushing weight.

He had her. She could not fight him. Could not risk it. She could not risk her friends.

He tsked and shook his head. "Can't have a group of murderesses mingling about in Society, can we? The *ton* would not tolerate such a thing. I'm assuming that as soon as I release you from this room you will return home, finish your packing, and be on your way to Yorkshire."

She shook her head, unable to speak, trapped, helpless, defeated.

The creak of a floorboard was the first alert that they were not alone.

Dewey spun around.

"You would be assuming wrong, coz."

"Rhain," she choked out.

Tildie hovered behind him for a moment before rushing past and reaching Valencia. She quickly set to work freeing her bindings. "I'm so sorry, Your Grace. Please forgive me. I never meant to hurt you."

She scarcely paid any attention to her lady's maid or the sweet agony of blood rushing life back into her wrists. Her gaze fixed on Rhain. He looked her over thoroughly.

"Are you harmed?" he asked.

She shook her head doggedly, awe and relief tripping through her.

"Good." Then he struck a fist against his cousin's face with a satisfying crunch.

Dewey went down hard with a howl, cupping his nose.

"You think I will ever keep you around now?" Rhain asked in a surprisingly even tone. "Forget about being my steward. Forget about all the many dreams you had of riding upon my coattails."

Dewey shouted through the hand cupped over his nose. "Very

well! Go ahead! You think I will not tell all and sundry about your fine duchess?" he cried out in a garbled voice. "*Everyone* will know that bitch and her friends killed the duke!"

Rhain reached down and grabbed him by the cravat. He twisted the fabric until his cousin was wheezing for breath and clawing at his hands.

"Fine," Rhain said in a calm voice that belied the fury she felt radiating from him. "Tell. Tell the world."

Valencia shook her head, wondering what game Rhain was playing at here. It was not just her life. It was her friends'. Young and lovely Delia with so many years ahead of her. Kind and generous Maeve with a doting husband and children who needed her. Fierce and loyal Ros, who had yet to discover what she wanted out of this world.

Rhain went on. "Just know I will ruin you. Destroy you. You think doors are closed to you now? I will make sure no one receives you *ever*. I will so thoroughly muddy your name, no one in the entirety of this country, from Wales to London, will permit you to keep their books. You'll never find work. Nor friends. Not a hearth will be offered to you. You'll die alone. Friendless. A pauper."

Dewey gaped at him. "But, coz . . . we're blood, family," he pleaded.

"You should have thought of that before you sought to keep the woman I love from me."

Valencia gasped. *He loves me?*

He loves me.

Rhain still held his cousin's woeful gaze. "Just so we are clear. You understand what will happen to you if a single word of that night ever surfaces? You will forget about it. About her." He nodded at Valencia. "About me. And I will, in turn, do my best to forget about you."

Dewey nodded jerkily. "I understand."

Tildie freed Valencia from her last binding, and Valencia swung her legs over the side of the bed, planting her feet solidly on the ground. The blood returned to her limbs in a painful rush of sharp needles. She must have made a sound or altered her expression.

Suddenly Rhain was there, sliding an arm around her waist and helping her to her feet. His expression grew thunderous as he examined her swollen jaw, gingerly touching the tender skin with the tips of his fingers.

"Cousin," he said thickly as he brushed her swollen skin, "the threat of ruining you suddenly does not feel nearly enough. I suggest you remove yourself from my sight lest I put hands to you again."

Dewey hesitated only a moment, his bleak gaze sweeping over them before he darted from the room.

Valencia gave Rhain a wobbly smile, and greeted lamely, "Hallo there." His admission of love still played over and over in her mind.

He smiled softly back. "Hello, my love. Are you ready to go home?"

Home. Her home was with him. She let that sink in and settle.

"You came for me." The words broke a little on her lips. Tears stung her eyes.

"Shhh, sweetheart." He pressed an almost-reverent kiss to her mouth. "I would follow you anywhere. Yorkshire. London. Wherever you go, I want to be with you always."

"I love you," she whispered, and for the first time in her life she meant that.

She knew what it meant to love and be loved, and she meant it.

His smile turned a bit wicked then. "So does this mean you will become the Duchess of Dedham . . . again?"

Epilogue

*Romantic love is ephemeral. It is best to
approach marriage as a transaction.*
—Hazel, the Marchioness of Sutton

One month later...

The wedding was beautiful.

It was a small affair. Family and close friends only. Private and circumspect, but no less grand for all that. The groom was as wealthy as Croesus, after all. Perhaps the wealthiest hotelier in the country.

Following the church ceremony, they all relocated to the Harrowgate for an elaborate bridal breakfast on the hotel rooftop (of course!).

Flowers were in full bloom everywhere, brought in fresh from area hothouses. Fragrant lemon trees with bright, waxy green leaves surrounded the long linen-covered table as the sun emerged to bless the occasion. No expense was spared. Champagne was poured freely into glasses set alongside platters of langoustines and oysters with bowls of caviar and delicate buttery soufflés that melted on the tongue.

Valencia moaned in delight as she tucked into some strawberries and clotted cream sprinkled with shaved hazelnuts. "That settles it," she declared over the lively chatter around her, leaning into Rhain beside her. "We are having our wedding breakfast here."

Rhain dipped his spoon into her bowl and sampled the treat for himself. "Hm. Perhaps we can lure Thorne's cook away for ourselves. Can you imagine eating like this for every meal?"

Valencia scraped the inside of the bowl, desperate to get every last morsel. "I fear Jasper might go to battle over such a transgression." She glanced at the handsome couple sitting at the head of the table in their wedding finery. They glowed, love in their eyes as they gazed at each other.

Rhain shrugged and grinned. "It could be worth it."

Smiling, she gently wiped a bit of cream from the mouth of the man she was scheduled to marry in precisely four months.

Four interminably long months.

She could not wait.

Once they had officially announced their betrothal, Rhain had moved into a town house of his own across the city, at his mother's behest, leaving Valencia in the house with his mother and sisters.

It was the respectable thing to do, especially as Rhain had a houseful of sisters who had every wish (still) to be brought out properly in Society. It would not do for their brother to create a scandal, sleeping in the bedchamber that adjoined with the room of his future wife.

Valencia's happiness was overwhelming . . . and possibly catching.

She and Rhain were not the only ones staring at the prospect of matrimony in the family. Surprisingly, Del—still more sullen than not—was on the verge of accepting a proposal of her own from the second son of a viscount, a very cheerful and garrulous fellow who declared Del a wit and found her prickly nature most beguiling. Valencia would not be surprised if all six Misses Lloyd were married or betrothed by this time next year.

The concern for propriety was valid, but Rhain moving out was a damned nuisance. She had spent enough time living without the love and passion that Rhain was only too thrilled to shower upon her. She loathed every night spent apart from him.

She was no maid, and she considered herself too old for restraint. Rhain felt the same way. Since he had moved into his own residence, they had been sneaking around like a pair of clandestine lovers—except for the fortnight he had ventured home to Wales to oversee his business there.

That fortnight had been a torment. The night of his return she had woken to his feverish kisses. He had stolen into her bedchamber, propriety and his mother's wrath (should she discover them) be damned.

Valencia longed for the day when they could wake up together, when she could be with him . . . in London, Wales, or wherever, so long as they were together and they had their own bedchamber. A space that was theirs and theirs alone.

They had decided to divide their time between London and Bryn Bychan. Since discovering Dewey's perfidy, there had been no discussion of finding another steward to represent Rhain. He had accepted the mantle of dukedom and all its inherent duties and responsibilities with nary a blink. As for Dewey . . . he had left for America at Rhain's *ungentle* suggestion. Valencia was relieved, breathing easier for his absence from their lives.

Rhain captured her hand under the table, lacing their fingers together intimately. He squeezed, and that simple contact sent a spike of heat through her. He must have read something of her reaction in her eyes, for the brown of his eyes deepened, signaling his own swift need.

Without thought or care for the guests surrounding them, he pressed a quick kiss to her lips, muttering, "I can't wait until it is *our* wedding day."

She shared the sentiment, wishing, not for the first time, that they had simply eloped.

Her heart swelled, marveling that she had found this . . . that she had found him—a love that was real. Something that would not fade or retreat at the first hardship. She knew that they had found this together, just as she knew with certainty that it would last.

She blinked her suddenly tearing eyes and looked away, fighting for her composure. In that moment, her gaze landed on the couple seated across the table. Her stepmother and her father.

Papa was busy devouring the food on his plate with complete abandon, grease dribbling down his chin, which he did not bother to wipe clean with a napkin. Hazel had hardly touched her food.

She was looking at Valencia and Rhain with an enigmatic, preoccupied expression. When she realized Valencia had caught her looking, she fixed a quick smile on her face and sent her an overly cheerful nod . . . but not before Valencia read the expression in her eyes for what it was. Sadness.

Sadness?

Valencia had never seen Hazel with such a look before. She always seemed so composed and, if not precisely happy, contented. Well-pleased, even. It was that air of gratification that had often rubbed Valencia the wrong way.

Perhaps I've never looked closely enough at her before?

With that uncomfortable thought stirring in her mind, Valencia looked at Hazel now. She looked past her mother's jewels that Hazel wore around her throat.

Intently, perhaps for the first time, with her heart overflowing and her hand clasped reassuringly with that of a decent man, a man she loved and who loved her, Valencia looked at her stepmother and saw something of her old self in her expression. She saw the familiar sadness that used to reside deep within her.

She recognized in Hazel the shadow of a person she had once been . . . and she did not like it. She did not care for it at all. She wished better for her stepmother. Any woman deserved better. They deserved what Valencia had found. A love she would have for the rest of her life.

ABOUT THE AUTHOR

SOPHIE JORDAN grew up in the Texas Hill Country, where she wove fantasies of dragons, warriors, and princesses. A former high school English teacher, she's the *New York Times*, *USA Today*, and internationally bestselling author of more than fifty novels. She now lives in Houston with her family. When she's not writing, she spends her time overloading on caffeine (lattes preferred), talking plotlines with anyone who will listen (including her kids), and cramming her DVR with anything that has a happily ever after.

MORE FROM
THE SCANDALOUS LADIES OF LONDON
SERIES

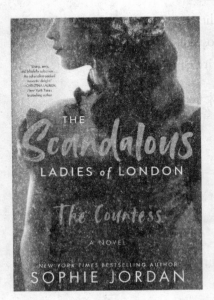

New York Times bestselling author Sophie Jordan kicks off her amazing new high concept series, The Scandalous Ladies of London, which chronicles the lives of a group of affluent ladies reigning over glittering, Regency-era London, vying for position in the hierarchy of the ton. They are the young wives, widows, and daughters of London's wealthiest families. The drama is big, the money runs deep, and the shade is real. Life is different in the ton.

DISCOVER THE IVY CHRONICLES